the fight for
FOREVER

MEGHAN

NEW YORK TIMES BESTSELLING AUTHOR

MARCH

ABOUT THE FIGHT FOR FOREVER

You can only keep what you can protect.
That's all I've ever known. It's the way I've lived my life.
Now, everything I never knew I needed is at risk, and I'm not letting anyone take it from me.
I won't let anyone take *her* from me.
They say love is a battlefield, so I'm ready for war.
This time, it's the fight for forever.

The Fight for Forever is the third and final book of the Legend Trilogy and should be enjoyed following *The Fall of Legend* and *House of Scarlett*.

CONTENTS

THE FIGHT FOR FOREVER

Book Three of the Legend Trilogy

Meghan March

ONE

ifteen years earlier
 I read a sign once that said you were only one decision away from a completely different life.

That hit me hard.

So I made a fucking decision, and now we'd all have a completely different life. Me, Jorie, and Bump. Nothing would ever be the same after today.

As I walked past the barber shop, the duffel bag of cash hanging heavy in my grip, the TV inside blared about the storm closing in. In Biloxi, we didn't get too excited about that shit. I didn't give a fuck that people were saying this one was going to be a big one. If it was up to me, we'd be out of this town before it made landfall. That was, if it even really came our way at all.

Rain beat against my hat, dripping off to slide down the collar of my T-shirt. The T-shirt I'd never wear again, because I'd be dressing in better shit from now on. The cash in the bag was going to make certain of that.

I'd finally be able to get Jorie to LA, so she could cut a single in a real studio and get it to the bigwigs at the record companies. I'd conquer the city and build a club where she could perform while she soared on the charts. That was our plan. That had always been our plan.

She'd been quiet lately, and I knew it was because of how fucking tight money was. It was weighing on her. I'd seen the desperation in her eyes, and that's why I did what I did.

I was done robbing Peter to pay Paul.

No, a voice in my head piped up. *You just robbed Moses to get the fuck out of town and save Jorie before she does something stupid.*

The rumble of a cammed-up ride had me dipping my head and turning the corner to duck into an alley.

Moses couldn't have found out what I did yet. I gotta have at least a day or two to get ahead of this.

I already had a plan. I'd get home, we'd pack our shit, buy a car for cash, and be gone by sunrise without leaving a trail to follow.

The growl of the exhaust quieted as the car drove on down the road, but the custom license plate told me everything I needed to know about the driver.

BOSSMAN.

Moses's personal ride.

No. He's not looking for me. Stop thinking that shit. Still, I put some hustle in my step and bypassed the corner store and the flowers I planned on buying to surprise Jorie with when I shared the good news with her.

Get home and then get the fuck out of town. That was all I needed to do. We'd all be better off as soon as we hit the city limits.

When I made it to our shithole apartment complex, some wannabe gangsters sat outside with guns in their laps, like they were the fucked-up neighborhood watch.

They all lifted their chins in my direction, but thankfully their eyes stayed off the bag.

"What up, Gabe?" a kid from Texas asked. He went by Lonestar, but I didn't know his real name.

"Not shit."

"When you gonna quit playin' at the gym and fight for real? I'll take you on."

I shrugged but kept walking. "Talk to me next week."

His crew of boys hollered and hooted as I jogged up to our apartment on the fourth floor. It was only a one-bedroom, so I wasn't surprised to see Bump on the couch with the TV on when I opened the door.

As much as I wished he'd apprentice to learn a trade or something, I'd rather have him working his eight-hour shift at the hardware store than hanging with those assholes out front. Beggars couldn't be choosy, after all.

"You're back early," Bump said as his gaze dropped to the duffel. "What's in the bag?"

"Where's your sister?"

"Said she had to run a quick errand. Did you see the shit they're saying about the storm? We're gonna have to evacuate and go to a shelter. Hardware store is out of every fucking thing because people are freaking the fuck out. It's like they've never seen a hurricane warning before."

I remembered the last storm that changed my life forever, and how my mother wouldn't budge until I lied to her about there being a hurricane party. I wasn't doing that shit again. We were getting the fuck out of Biloxi.

"Pack everything that matters to you. We're leaving before it hits."

Bump's eyebrows went up. "You really want to go to a shelter? I guess they're saying it's a mean one, so maybe it's a good idea."

I didn't want to tell Bump the news before I told Jorie, so I let him think what he wanted. "Order a pizza, if they're still delivering. Jorie's favorite. We're celebrating tonight."

"Celebrating what?"

The surprised tone of his voice was all the evidence I needed to know that I'd made the right choice. We hadn't had shit to celebrate in months. It was time for a different fucking life.

I shifted the bag to my shoulder. "I'll tell you when your sister gets back. I'm hopping in the shower."

"What about cash for the pizza?"

More than anything, I wanted to reach into the duffel and pull out a fat stack of bills and toss it to him—just to see his jaw drop —but that could wait.

I snagged my wallet instead and peeled off forty bucks. "Here. Make the call. I'm fucking hungry."

As soon as I finished my shower, Jorie's voice filtered in through the closed bathroom door.

"What do you mean, we're celebrating? Gabe? What's going on?"

I opened the door, a towel wrapped around my waist and the bag slung over my shoulder, and I grabbed her hands. "Come on. I gotta show you something."

I pulled her into the bedroom and shut the door behind us. Her beautiful face screwed up in confusion.

"What's going on? I'm not banging you right now. I need a shower too, you know. I hope you didn't use up all the hot water."

I shook my head and tossed the bag on the unmade bed. "I'm not trying to get laid, and you're never gonna have to worry about running out of hot water again. I need to show you this." With her hand tugging away from mine, I released her to unzip the duffel and looked at her.

Jorie's eyes widened as she stared into the bag, and her mouth hung open as if it were on a broken hinge.

"What the fuck did you do, Gabe?" she whispered in horror as she began to tremble. "What the fuck did you do?"

The look of horror on her face was *not* what I expected. "I got us a future. Got us out of this fucking town. Just what you wanted. We're going to LA. You're gonna get your record made. I'm gonna build a club, and we'll have the life you've always wanted."

With her hand covering her mouth, she shook her head back and forth, almost in slow motion. "Gabe . . . what did you do?"

My excitement to tell her the good news drained away, and anger grew in its place. My hands landed on my hips, and I straightened my shoulders.

"I'm making shit happen because that's what I do. I'm the one who takes care of this family, and we're leaving. Before morning. Pack your shit. Everyone will think we're evacuating because of the hurricane."

"Leave? We can't leave. We have a life here. Friends. Jobs."

The panic in her voice didn't make sense to me, so I brushed it aside.

"This isn't the life we want, Jorie. We're starting over. All three of us." I pointed to the stacks of cash. "And this is how I'm making it happen."

She swallowed hard. "You stole it, didn't you?"

My jaw tensed, and my fingers flexed. "I made a smart interception and turned it to our advantage."

Jorie shook her head again before walking to the bed to sit down next to the bag. She reached out to trail a finger along the hundreds before looking up at me again. "What did you intercept? From who?"

My teeth grinding together, I bit out my answer. "Moses."

"Fucking hell." Her entire body stiffened. "You have to take it back. Give it back. You can't cross him, Gabe. You can't."

Didn't she understand? We would be long gone before he even suspected me. "That's why we're leaving tonight."

"I can't leave tonight. That's not happening."

I jerked back to stare at her. "What the fuck do you have to stay for? You and me and Bump are going. There's nothing here for us anymore but fucking death when Moses finds out."

"Baby . . ." Jorie bowed her head. "I . . . I gotta tell you—"

"Holy fuck, you guys. Come see this. This Katrina bitch sounds way fucking bad!" Bump yelled from the living room.

Jorie jumped off the bed. As she strode for the door, she looked over her shoulder at me. "I got shit I have to handle before we leave town. We ride out this storm, and then we'll figure it out. Okay?"

"Jorie, no. We go now." It wasn't debatable. I was doing things my way.

"If you go now, you go without me."

Her words hit me like a two-by-four to the chest, knocking the wind out of me.

"How the fuck can you say that?" I called after her, but she'd already slammed the bedroom door. I dropped my head into my hands. "What the fuck is going on?" I asked the empty room, but no answer came.

I couldn't leave without her and Bump. No fucking way.

The storm hit fucking hard, way worse than any of us expected.

I rode it out with Jorie and Bump in the bathtub of our shit-box bathroom, with me lying on top of the mattress covering them. The wind roared so loud, I felt like I was standing in front of a train. Glass shattered. Shit flew. The entire building vibrated until I was sure it was going to fall apart and leave us in a pile of rubble.

But it didn't. Miraculously, we all survived without injury.

And that's when shit got really, really fucking bad.

"I have to go get us some water. We need water. Why the fuck don't we have water?" Jorie said, slamming the empty cupboard door for the dozenth time.

We hadn't prepared for the hurricane, and we were shit out of luck. Not to mention thirsty and hungry after hours on end hunkered down.

"You two stay here," I told her and Bump as I reached for the doorknob. "I'll get supplies and come right back."

"Gabe, no. What if—"

I shook my head once, and Jorie cut off her sentence before she could say the one thing I didn't need Bump to know yet.

Her younger brother looked between us, his eyes narrowing. "What the fuck is going on? You've both been acting fucking weird."

Jorie glared at him. "We just went through a hurricane. Anyone would act weird." She glanced back at me. "Be careful. Please."

I nodded. "I'll be back. Don't go anywhere."

When I returned to the apartment two hours later, it was eerily quiet.

"Jorie?" I called, but there was no answer.

"Bump?"

Apprehension made my blood run cold. I dropped two gallons of water, a bag of food, and the duffel, which I so far had refused to let out of my sight, on the floor, then ran to the bedroom and checked the bathroom.

Empty.

"Where the fuck did you go?" I asked the empty room before pulling out my prepaid phone. I tried Jorie over and over, but she never picked up.

"Baby, call me. Please. Where the hell did you go?" I said to her voice mail after the seventh call.

I dropped onto the sofa for a second and jammed my hands into my hair.

"Where would they go? Where the fuck would they go?" My stomach twisted because I had no fucking answers.

All the thoughts I'd had yesterday about life never being the same again? I was terrified that I was right, but in a totally different way than I'd anticipated.

We should have been long gone by now.

Moses might not know about the truck yet because of the storm—

My thoughts were cut short by someone screaming outside.

"Holy shit! This motherfucker is bleeding out!" one of the guys in Lonestar's crew yelled loud enough for everyone on the entire fucking block to hear.

I bolted off the couch and ran to the door. I didn't know why, but something in my gut told me to move my ass.

They have to be okay. They have to be okay. They shouldn't have left. Why did they leave? Fuck. We should have been out of here already. This never should have happened.

I charged down the stairs, dodging the shit strewn everywhere from the storm, and stumbled when I hit the mud-covered pavement at street level. I whipped my head from side to side, looking for Bump and Jorie.

But there was no Jorie. Just Bump, covered in blood and sprawled out in the nasty pond that used to be a dirt-packed lawn.

I skidded to a stop in front of Lonestar and his crew, hitting my knees beside the only little brother I'd ever known.

"Bump! What the fuck happened?"

When he turned his head to look up at me, the life was draining out of his eyes. "Jorie . . ."

"Where is she?"

He only got one word out before he lost consciousness.

"Dead."

TWO

Scarlett

resent day

P My heart stutters and my lungs freeze as I stare at the towering man sitting behind Gabriel's desk, *with a gun to Bump's head.*

Gabriel's hand tightens around mine until I can't feel my fingers.

Oh God, no. He can't hurt Bump. No one can hurt Bump.

"I said, get on your motherfucking knees, *Gabe.* Make me repeat myself again, and you'll have a hell of a cleaning bill." He nudges the barrel harder against Bump's head, causing him to screw his eyes shut and flinch.

Beside me, Gabriel squeezes even tighter before he releases me . . . and then he does what the man says and gets on his knees.

"No," I whisper, but it comes out louder than I intend, and the man's attention cuts to me.

His eyes alone are enough to unsettle me—the pale greenish gold seems to glow as if backlit with pure evil. Set against the tawny bronze tone of his skin, his gaze seems even more disturbing.

"You got something to say, girl? Wanna beg for your man's life? Because he knows *exactly* why I'm here."

I swallow what feels like a lump of charcoal in my throat as I bite down on my lip to keep from making another sound. I do not want that man looking at me. I don't want that man to know I exist.

"Let her go, Moses. She's got nothing to do with this." Gabriel's words sound like they'd been dragged down a gravel road before he bit them out.

Moses. *Moses.* Who is Moses? And what is *this*?

"She's nice. You can't hurt her."

Bump's plea brings the burn of tears behind my eyes. *Sweet fucking Bump—except for that one time he kidnapped me.*

If I weren't paralyzed with fear, I'd be tempted to laugh at how much things have changed since the first time I was brought into this office. But, right now, I'm more worried about getting out alive.

"Shut the fuck up." Moses jabs the gun harder against Bump's temple, and the hair stands up on the back of my neck.

"Please, don't hurt him. He's—"

"Scarlett, get out of here," Gabriel says, cutting me off.

"Shut the fucking door, *Scarlett*. You're not going anywhere." A cruel smile bends the man's lips.

"She's got nothing to do with this, Moses. Not a fucking thing. Let her and Bump go. You can do whatever the fuck you want to me. But just let them walk the fuck out of here."

From beside me, I can practically feel the burning rage radiating off Gabriel. It's hot enough to blister my skin. I glance down at him—the top of his slicked-back dark blonde hair—and I hate seeing him on his knees. I don't know who Moses is, but I despise him for that alone.

"She ain't going nowhere until I say so."

"My security will be up here any minute. You're gonna be fucked, Moses. So say what you came to say, and do what you came to do, unless you want to find yourself in a goddamned hostage situation. NYPD ain't the same as the Biloxi PD. They'll take you out in a fucking heartbeat. You got no one on your payroll to save your ass."

I don't know where Gabriel finds the composure to speak so rationally. Thank God one of us can.

But Moses doesn't look concerned by Gabriel's words. He throws back his head and laughs.

"Boy, you don't know shit about shit. You never did. You think I just rolled up in the city today and let myself into your office? Fuck no. I've had my eye on you. For a man with a price on his head, you've done a piss-poor job of staying under the radar. I could've popped you so many fucking times, but what fun would that be? You wouldn't even see it comin'. When I put a bullet between someone's eyes, they always gotta know it was me."

What? Oh. My. God. This crazy man has been watching Gabriel? *Jesus Christ.*

"Then what the fuck do you want?" Gabriel demands, and Moses grins forbiddingly.

"You owe me a hundred grand, plus fifteen years of interest. I'm here to collect."

THREE

The last place I want to be is on my knees, in my office, unarmed, with Scarlett beside me and Moses Buford Gaspard holding a gun to Bump's head.

And yet, here I am.

My brain screams for Scarlett to fucking run, but she's frozen like a statue beside me.

Of course this is how it would happen. I'm not even sure why I'm surprised. I've known for years that every move I make is a risk, but I didn't realize Moses would lie in wait. That doesn't seem like his style.

Then again, fifteen years ago, he was a gangster with a crew that followed his ballsy leadership without question. Why should I be shocked that he's changed? I sure as hell have.

Except there's one thing that's always remained. *I can't outrun my past.*

Now it's time to face it and pay the consequences, but I won't allow this to hurt Scarlett. I'll take every fucking bullet while I stand in front of her like a human shield first.

Moses lifts his chin, and the words he spoke finally penetrate the chaos of my head.

"You owe me a hundred grand, plus fifteen years of interest."

"You got your numbers wrong, Moses. I sold your shit for fifty grand."

Those fucking creepy eyes flash with humor before they narrow on me. "Ain't my fault you were a terrible gangster. The cargo in that truck you jacked was worth a hundred K. You only got fifty? We'll call the other fifty a penalty for taking what wasn't yours. And that interest rate? Yeah, it's gonna be about a hundred percent."

He taps his finger alongside the trigger of the gun resting against the side of Bump's trembling head. "We'll call it a million and a half, because I like round numbers. Now, I want my money, Gabe."

Fucking. Christ.

A lead anchor sinks to the pit of my stomach. "If you've been watching me, then you know I don't have that kind of cash."

Scarlett shifts beside me. "I do. I can get it for you, but it'll take a few days. Just . . . leave us alone, and you'll get your money."

Fuck. I jerk my head up to look at Scarlett, not sure whether I should hug her or shake her right now.

On one hand, I'd do anything to save Bump, but I don't want Scarlett mixed up in this. And letting Moses know she has that kind of cash? *Bad fucking idea.*

Before I can say anything, Moses leers like a fucking coyote smelling fresh blood in the air.

"Oh, Gabe. You really fucking leveled up with this bitch, didn't you? Solid choice."

When he shifts his attention to Scarlett, I want to shove her behind me so he can't look at her.

"Noble shit you're trying to do there, *cher.* But I don't want your money. It ain't no good with Moses. I want this mother-fucker to pay, even if it means I take it out in blood. Did you know he stole from me? He tell you that? Gabriel *Legend*—nice fucking new last name, brother—jacked my truck of electronics, sold the shit, and planned to skip town like a little bitch."

"She doesn't need to know," I manage to get out from between clenched teeth, my jaw aching with tension. "She isn't part of this."

Moses purses his lips. "Oh, she's part of it, all right. Every single person in your life is subject to forfeit until you give me my due."

"I told you—I don't have the fucking money."

"That's why I'm here, Gabe. Because I heard you got yourself one hell of a fine opportunity on the table. You're going back to fighting, aren't you? And ain't that fight against Bodhi Black? They're already talking about the odds."

My brain stutters to a halt. "Wait. You fucking come out of the woodwork *now* because of this fight?"

That grin flashes across Moses's face again. "Yeah. You see, I'm betting a fuck ton on Black, and you're gonna take a dive to make sure I get paid. That is, unless you got that one point five mil handy right now."

Scarlett sucks in a breath beside me, but thankfully, she says nothing.

"No. Gabe is gonna win. Gabe won't lose." Poor Bump looks like he's going to blow a gasket, and I pray that he doesn't move or run his mouth any more.

Moses jabs him with the barrel. "What part of *shut the fuck up* don't you understand, kid? You must have nine fucking lives."

The reminder that Moses's crew is the reason Bump is the way he is ignites an inferno inside me. *Keep it together.* I lock down my rage and stare at Moses, mentally crushing him with my bare hands.

"If I lose that fight, I lose everything."

Moses's grin has caused plenty of men to piss themselves, but I sure as fuck am not one of them.

Not back then. Not now. Not ever.

"You win this fight, boy, and you lose everything anyway. Whatever you *think* you have right now, it's only because *I allow it.* I can take any fucking thing from you anytime I want. That's how it works when you're *me.*"

"How long have you known?" I don't need to voice the rest of the question, because Moses gets what I'm asking.

"I've had my sights set on you for years. Been waiting for you to come back and try to fucking kill me, but you never did. Surprised me with that, Gabe. I thought you loved that bitch. You were willing to risk everything for her. Guess she wasn't really worth that much to you if her dying meant nothing."

His words slice through me, eviscerating me like he's just gone at me with switchblades.

"I was biding my time."

Moses's dark eyebrows shoot up. "The hothead grew up. Who the fuck knew that was possible? Now, we got a deal? Or do I need to remind you what you got to lose if you don't play the fight my way?"

Take a dive. Moses gets paid. I lose everything.

Or . . . win the fight, then prepare to fight for my life—and everyone I care about—against the man who has been hanging over my head like a guillotine for fifteen years.

When I don't answer right away, Moses lifts the pistol away from Bump's head and trains it on Scarlett. I jump to my feet and throw myself in front of her, my arms out.

Moses's fucking grin widens. "That's what I thought. You'll do whatever I say, because you know exactly what I'll take from you if you don't. Shit, maybe I'll even keep this one. See if she's a better fuck than Jorie. Might be tough, because she had a cunt like solid gold. Then again, you know all about that."

Bump lunges at Moses, but Moses is quicker, and presses the pistol right between his eyes.

"One more move and you die. And I mean all-the-way dead

this time. I won't graze you like those motherfuckers who put a bullet in your head in Mississippi."

When Bump raises his hands in the air and drops to his knees again, Moses's gaze lifts to me.

"I'll give you one thing, Gabe. Your taste in women has improved. This bitch looks like she'd rather slit my throat than take my cock down hers. I'd hate to see something bad happen to her."

I reach out to pull Scarlett directly behind me so he can't see her. "She doesn't exist to you. Threaten her again, and I'll skin your ass and use it for a fucking lampshade."

Moses's chest shakes, and booming laughter fills my office. "Nice try, *Legend*. I'll see myself out. You get to training. Get those fucking odds right. If I have to, I'll pay you another visit. Just to remind you what you got on the line."

He backs away from my desk, his gun trained on me now, and a panel in the wall opens behind him.

My fucking hidden entrance. How the hell did he find out about my fucking hidden doors?

Another man pokes his head through, but that's not where my attention is focused. He's got a TEC-9 in either hand. Probably fully auto. He'd kill us all in seconds.

"Now, be good little bitches and don't follow us."

But Bump doesn't listen. He charges.

"No!"

Moses lashes out, catching Bump upside the head with the back of his hand holding the pistol. Bump crumples to the floor.

"Don't do anything stupid, Gabe. That's your last warning."

Moses backs away through the door. It closes slowly, until all I can see are his fucking eyes glinting before he disappears into the darkness.

FOUR

Scarlett

My knees give out. I can't help it. As soon as the door closes, I sink to the floor. My head swims, and everything feels like it's happening in slow motion.

I have to get to Bump. But Gabriel is already ahead of me. He launches himself at Bump, and I crawl to them.

A trickle of blood leaks from Bump's temple where he holds his head. "I'm okay. I'm okay. I'm okay." He repeats it over and over, like he's trying to convince himself.

"You're okay," Gabriel says, agreeing with him. "You're totally fine, bud. You did real good. Real fucking good."

I pull myself together and grab my clutch where I dropped it. Yanking it open, I pull out a small packet of tissues and take them to Bump.

"Here you go. Just a little blood."

"I'm bleeding?" His eyes go wide. "I thought I was okay."

"You're fine, bud. Just fine."

A knock comes at the door, and we all freeze. Gabriel moves toward his desk, and before I have time to comprehend what he's doing, there's a gun in his hand pointed at the door.

"Who the fuck is it?"

"Me and Roux," Q says from outside.

Gabriel's chin drops to his chest, and he lowers the gun. "Get in here."

Q opens the door, and shock rips across his face as he sees Bump on the floor with bloody tissues to his head. Then he sees the gun in Gabriel's hand and stills. Roux barrels toward Gabriel, and he shoves the gun in his pants before giving her a pat to calm her down.

"What the fuck happened? Is he okay?"

"Moses was here. He had Bump at gunpoint. He wants his money."

Q's olive-toned skin goes pale. "What? How? When? Where did he go?" He whips his head from side to side, like he's afraid Moses might still be in the room hiding, and then pulls out his cell. "I'm calling the cops."

"No," Gabriel barks out, shaking his head. "Shut the door and put down your fucking phone. We aren't going to the cops with this. No fucking way."

"What?" Surprise rips the word from between my lips. "What do you mean, we're not going to the cops? We have to. This is literally what they're for."

Bump shakes his head. "Can we go home now, Gabe? I want to go home."

"What a fucking mess," Q says, leaning back against the door. "How the hell did he get in and out?"

Gabriel helps Bump and me to our feet. "Hidden entrance. He must have been watching us for months, or paid someone off to get the access info."

"*Fuck.* What did he say?" Q scans all the faces in the room before locking on Gabriel's again.

"He wants me to lose the fight. Wants me to throw it."

If I thought Q's swarthy skin couldn't get paler, I was wrong. "No fucking way. Fuck me. What the fuck do we do now?"

Gabriel throws his arm around Bump's shoulder and pulls me into his side. "We go home and regroup."

The drive to Jersey is silent. Even Bump seems to realize that now is not the time for chatter. Q called in extra security and promised to come by as soon as the club closed. He tried to send Zoe home with us, but she refused to leave.

I want nothing more than to hold Gabriel's hand, but he's got both of them locked around the Bronco's steering wheel. Hal follows behind us in the SUV. He agreed to work overnight, just in case.

I'm completely out of my depth. I have absolutely no idea how I'm supposed to react to everything I just witnessed. All I want to do is make it go away, which is why I offered up the money. Sure, a million and a half isn't exactly chump change, but to protect Gabriel and Bump? I'd gladly hand it over.

But I can't bring it up now, especially considering the way Gabriel is white-knuckling the steering wheel. He won't be receptive to the idea . . . which is probably fair, because Moses already said he wouldn't take *my* money for the debt.

Still, I'd pay a fortune to find out what's going through Gabriel's head right now.

FIVE

Moses came back.

And in keeping with his style, he didn't do it the way I expected.

No, what I expected was a bullet to the head with no warning. Just like Jorie. But, no, he wants to make me play his game and exact his own special twisted fucking revenge.

He wasn't fucking Jorie. There's no goddamned way. She never would have touched him.

But, still, my brain goes back to fifteen years ago, and how fucking reluctant she was to leave town. How strangely she'd acted for months. How it had been weeks since we'd touched each other before that awful fucking day.

Did I miss it? Was her hesitation because she didn't want to leave Moses behind? And how the fuck could his crew have killed her if she was fucking him? Not a goddamned bit of it makes sense.

I slow for a red light, grateful for the silence in the Bronco. The last thing I want to do right now is talk. Every part of me has drawn inward, until I feel like I'm suffocating on the questions running rampant through my brain.

When I finally pull up in front of the service station, Hal parks across the driveway, sideways, blocking us in. *Good.* If I know him, he's got a shotgun in his SUV, and he's not afraid to use it.

I open my door, climb out, and push the seat back to make room for Bump and Roux. I'm strangely fucking thankful that my dog apparently sneaked out of the office while Bump was watching TV. If she'd seen Moses and gone at him with those big teeth of hers, he would have shot her without blinking.

Scarlett meets me around the front of the Bronco, and I hand her the keys.

"Will you get him settled? I need to talk to Hal before I come up."

Scarlett's pale, drawn face guts me all over again. She shouldn't have experienced what happened tonight. None of this ever should have touched her. I should have killed Moses years ago.

This is all my fucking fault.

I stole that truck. Sold the shit. Got Jorie killed and Bump shot.

I might as well be a fucking wrecking ball, and now Scarlett's life is becoming unrecognizable because of my destruction.

"Of course. Whatever you need, cowboy."

Her nickname for me is a balm. But no matter how much I want to let it soothe me, I can't. There are way too fucking many sins I'm answering for tonight. I've earned the pain clawing me apart, and haven't suffered enough for the chaos I've caused.

"I'll be up soon."

I don't lean in to kiss her, but she presses her lips to mine anyway.

I don't deserve her.

As soon as she's gone, I walk over to the SUV. Hal is at the tailgate, unearthing something from beneath the carpet. As I expected, it's a small arsenal.

"No one will get through me tonight, Legend. You have my word."

"Or me."

The voice comes from the darkness, and both Hal and I tense as footsteps crunch in the gravel.

"Who is that?" Hal asks, reaching for a gun.

I put my hand on his to stop him from grabbing it.

Big Mike steps into the pool of light. "This is my property. My people. And no one, not even some gangster from Mississippi, is going to come up here and cause trouble in *my house.*"

"Big Mike, meet Hal, Scarlett's new full-time security. Hal, this is Big Mike, Q's dad and the craziest Puerto Rican I've ever known."

Big Mike lifts his chin at Hal. "Damn right. I'll pull up a chair and sit here all night if I need to."

"What about Joanie?"

"She's staying with Melanie tonight at Dani and Tony's while they're out on the town. I'm at your disposal."

I walk over to Big Mike. "I appreciate it, but Hal's got it covered. No need for you to sit out here all night."

"Q called and told me everything. I think there's plenty of reason to." He glances at the chairs he and Bump leave out front so they can shoot the shit. "I'll take one of those. No arguing with me, Gabe. You're family. We take care of our own."

A wave of gratitude that again, I do not fucking deserve, washes over me. "Thank you. No arguing tonight."

"Good. Now, you go on about your night. We got this down here."

I reach out to shake his hand, but he wraps his big beefy arms around me instead and claps my back hard.

"Go get some sleep. Q says we're talking shit through in the morning."

It's on the tip of my tongue to tell him that Q isn't calling the shots on this, but I'm too fucking beat.

"I'll see you in the morning. Both of you." I shake Hal's hand, and then I head for the door into the service station and lock the dead bolt behind me.

As I take the stairs, I can't help but replay what the hell happened tonight. Moses at my desk. Bump with a gun to his head. Seeing the barrel pointed at Scarlett.

Fuck. I've dreamed it before. And in my nightmares, it ended in a bloodbath. I should at least be grateful that my worst fears didn't come true.

I stop outside Bump's apartment, but his voice is coming from my place, so I move down the hall. When I open my door, I find both him and Scarlett in the middle of the living room, surrounded by pillows, blankets, and couch cushions.

Bump built a fort out of two cushions and a blanket, and he's tucked inside with his long legs sticking out. He's smiling from ear to ear, and it stops me in my tracks.

"I hope you don't mind," Scarlett says from her position on the floor next to a blanket pile. "I told Bump we could have a sleepover."

"Isn't this awesome, Gabe? I made a cave! I'm gonna sleep in it. And you and Scarlett can have the air mattress. I just don't know where it is. You still have it, right? From that time I slept on your floor?"

I meet Scarlett's warm gray gaze with more fucking gratitude. "Good idea, ladybug. A sleepover is exactly what we need."

She rises and comes to me as Bump lowers the blanket to hide himself in his cave. Scarlett wraps her arms around my sides. "I thought it'd be better if we were all together tonight," she whispers.

The warmth of her body against mine settles some of the chaos in my mind. *I could have lost her tonight.* I breathe in the scent of her skin and hair, and close my eyes. "You were right. Thank you."

She shifts, and my lids lift to see her staring up at me. "We're going to figure this out. We're a team. You're not going to push me away and give me some bullshit excuse that it's to keep me safe. I'm part of this, whether you want me to be or not. Okay?"

I rest my forehead against hers. "I don't know what to say right now. Give me a few hours to process all this shit. We'll sort it out tomorrow." I press a kiss to the tip of her nose, and she nods.

"I can handle that. Now . . . where's that air mattress?"

SIX

Legend

Lying in the dark, even with Scarlett's head against my chest and the sound of Bump's deep breathing coming from across the room, there's no way in hell I can sleep. Not after tonight. Not after everything Moses said.

Fuck. Me.

Him and Jorie? How is that even possible? Every time I've tried to think about it, my brain has thrown up roadblocks. But this time, I push through them. I have to consider what he said. Could he have been lying?

I wouldn't put anything past him, and if he was trying to rile or rattle me, that would do the trick. But . . . before I rule it out as total bullshit, I have to consider that he might have been telling the truth, and the only other person who could corroborate it— that I would believe—is dead.

God, I've carried the guilt of her death on my conscience every day since Bump crawled home to tell me. For me, it's always been as if I pulled the trigger myself, because if I hadn't jacked the truck and sold Moses's shit, he never would have come looking for me and found her and Bump instead.

But in the dark, with the woman I love lying in my arms, I have to consider the alternative.

What if Moses was telling the truth?

Jorie, what did you do? And for fuck's sake . . . why?

No man ever wants to think about the possibility that his woman stepped out on him, but for some reason, this feels even worse.

If—*big if*—Moses is telling the truth, then everything I thought I knew is a fucking lie. Every single thing I've done to build this club and go legit . . . it was all because of a lie.

Moses could be playing me, I remind myself. But part of me, a part I don't want to listen to, is showing me signs I never wanted to see.

Jorie and her hesitation to leave. How she would disappear for hours at a time, and come home with something new that I knew we didn't have the money to buy. Like that Coach purse she swore was a knockoff she picked up on the street for twenty bucks, but I thought was too nice to be fake. And how she'd pick up extra shifts at the bar, but would come home smelling freshly showered with new perfume instead of like greasy fried food and beer.

My gut twists as the things that didn't add up back then come rushing to the surface. There's a damn good chance Moses was fucking my girl, and I didn't want to see it.

So, what the fuck does that mean now?

Scarlett shifts on my chest, her fingers flexing and releasing against my skin like she's dreaming.

She's real. She's here. She's . . . it. The one. Everything I never knew I wanted and needed. Everything I never dreamed of having.

She even offered up a million and a half in cash without a second thought, just to try to save my ass and everything I love.

Part of me is glad that Moses said no. The stupid part that's full of pride, no doubt. But, *Jesus*. I *never* want Scarlett to think I'm with her for the money. That doesn't even register on the scale of attributes that made me fall in love with her. But wealth is part of her, just like coming from nothing is part of me. I may not care either way what her bank balance is, but that doesn't change the facts.

Now . . . I've got to make a fucking impossible decision. I've been approached before about taking a dive and losing fights. There's a shit ton of money in it if the right person comes along with a proposition. I've never been interested. I win or lose by my own merit.

But I've never had this much on the line before.

If I lose the fight, I lose my shot at digging us out of this hole I've put us in. I'll keep having to deal with my investors, and their questions about how I'm running my business, and their threats of shutting me down.

Is that really so bad? a voice in my head asks, and I want to slap that motherfucker upside the head. Losing the fight on purpose isn't an option. I may not be the most upstanding guy around, but my honor isn't for sale.

Even if it saves Scarlett's life? I'm sick as fuck of these devil's advocate questions, because I don't know how to answer, even to myself. Scarlett's life shouldn't be on the line, and neither should the life of anyone else I care about.

Moses's threats can't be ignored. He made the call that ended Jorie's life and almost killed Bump.

But why the fuck would he kill Jorie if he was fucking her? That's the part that still doesn't make sense to me. I don't know what to believe anymore.

I lie there as the mattress slowly leaks air, and I sink closer to the floor with each passing hour. It doesn't matter how many times I rack my brain for solutions, nothing new emerges. I finally fall asleep as the morning light seeps in through the windows, but there's nothing peaceful about my rest.

A nightmare ravages my dreams.

Jorie crawls toward me on her knees, reaching up to grab my

hands. Black tears streak her blotchy face as she begs me to forgive her for what she did.

"I'm so sorry. I didn't mean for this to happen. You have to forgive me. I love you. I never loved him; I only loved what he could give me. He made our life easier. For all of us. You know it's true, Gabe."

With horror, I watch as my dream-hand pulls out a gun and presses it to her forehead like Moses did to Bump tonight.

"You lied to me. You never loved me. You couldn't do this if you loved me. Now look what you've caused. Look what you've made me do. Look at what it's done."

Her tears come faster and harder . . . until my finger squeezes the trigger.

I jerk awake before the blast, my nightmare dissipating as soon as I open my eyes to the early morning light. My sudden movement should have woken Scarlett, but she's still asleep beside me.

Sweat beads on my forehead, and I have to get out of the room. It feels like the walls are closing in. I need more air.

Carefully, I roll off the mattress, slowly letting Scarlett's weight dip the surface deeper, and hope she doesn't wake up.

When she doesn't move, I rush to the door and unbolt it before getting the fuck out of the building as fast as humanly possible. I hit the pavement out front, and Big Mike swings around with a shotgun pointed in my direction.

"Whoa, kid. Some warning would be nice. You almost got some double-aught buckshot to your damn face."

I pant for fresh air, my heart pounding. "Sorry, man. Didn't mean to startle you."

The driver's door to the SUV opens, and Hal hops out.

"Quiet night, thankfully," Big Mike says before nodding to Hal. "Neither of us have seen a damned thing."

I scan the street and the fenced parking lot across the way before looking back to the older men. "Thank you both for sitting out here all night. I should have been the one to do it."

"Nah, you needed to be there for your woman and Bump," Big Mike replies. "We held down the fort just fine."

Throaty exhaust rumbles from the end of the block, and both Hal and Mike instantly look tense and on edge. At least until Big Mike sees the make and model of the muscle car rolling toward us.

Q parks on the side of the road and climbs out with a box of doughnuts and a cardboard tray filled with coffees. "I figured Hal might need provisions."

"Bring that coffee over here, kid. I've needed a refill since about four," Big Mike says, waving Q in his direction. "You look like you've been up all night too."

Q's normally slicked-back hair is messed up like he's been running his hands through it over and over. Knowing my friend like I do, his dad must be right.

I meet him as he walks up the driveway. "What happened?"

He shakes his head. "Nothing else like you're thinking. No sign of Moses. Locksmith just finished up. I paid him triple to get his ass there and change every lock in the place, and add new dead bolts to the tunnel doors. I don't know how Moses got inside, but he shouldn't be able to get in again unless he's fucking Houdini."

"Thanks, man. You went above and beyond."

He holds out the doughnuts. "Nah, that was what needed to happen. Above and beyond is the doughnuts. I got three with pink frosting and sprinkles for Bump. Thought it might help him forget what happened last night."

I take the box of doughnuts and pass them to Big Mike before giving Q a back-slapping hug. "Thank you. Seriously. Fucking thank you."

"You'd do the same for me," Q says with a shrug.

"Absolutely, brother."

"We gotta talk this out. Break it down. Come up with a plan," Big Mike says.

I scan the neighborhood again, but I don't see any unusual vehicles, even though I'm suspicious as hell this morning.

With my hands shoved in the pockets of my sweats, I turn to face him. "I'll give you the short version, because we're too exposed to spend hours talking about this here."

"Short and sweet is all I need," Big Mike replies.

"Moses wants me to throw the fight."

"The fuck you will," Big Mike says, jumping out of his chair. He's already turning red in the face. "What the hell is he going to do if you don't?"

"If he doesn't get his money, which, by the way, he's jacked up to one point five mil . . . he says he'll take everything from me."

A vein throbs in Big Mike's forehead, and Hal just shakes his head. "That's a shit deal."

"I know."

"Let's think it through." Q crosses his arms over his chest. "Moses wants this fight to happen without any problem, so that means he's not planning to touch you before it."

"He also said that he could've popped me plenty of times," I add, "but he wants his money first."

"So you're safe until the fight," Q says. "And hopefully Bump and Scarlett are too."

"I'm not taking chances with them." I look to Hal. "You're staying with her everywhere she goes. If she's in her building, you're out front where you have a view of the entrance and the side door. Got it?"

Hal nods. "Abso-fucking-lutely, boss. I won't let anything happen to her."

"What about Bump?" Q glances toward the service station.

"Bump stays with us," Big Mike says. "He can come to work with me, and he'll be happy as a pig in shit to watch football all the time and eat Joanie's cooking. He'll be safe."

I think about the suggestion for a few minutes and then agree. "Yeah, I like that. Keeps Bump busy, which is for the best. I don't want him thinking about what happened last night. Being at the club might freak him out for a while."

Hal shuffles his feet. "Then we got the kid and the girl covered, but what about you?"

I shake my head. "We just said Moses wouldn't come after me. I believe that."

"That's not what I mean. You need to start training. This fight is supposed to happen in a month. That's not a lot of time to get back in shape to go three rounds."

Hal is right. I've kept up training, but not at the level I should have in order to be ready to step into the cage.

"The fight's not even a sure thing yet," Q says. "We haven't heard from the guys. No contracts have been signed. What if . . . it doesn't happen?"

"It has to happen," Big Mike whispers, and I nod, thinking about what Jimmy Jones, Harlow's husband, told me.

"Last night, a high-profile sports agent told me it's happening. He heard through the grapevine that they chose us for the venue too. I'm just waiting for the final word and the paperwork."

"And Bodhi Black?" Q asks. "Are we sure he's going to take it?"

Hal jumps in to answer that question. "Black would never walk away from this opportunity. He wants your head, man."

"Dangerous to fight a man who's got nothing to lose and has been training hard for months," Big Mike says quietly as he meets my gaze. "You sure this is a good idea? You could pull the plug on it before the thing is even on the books. Tell them the venue won't work."

Q glares at his dad. "You're trying to talk him out of it? Really?"

Big Mike's expression hardens, and the crease between his bushy brows deepens. "This isn't a walk in the fucking park, son, and you're not the one getting in that ring—"

"I would."

"I'm doing it," I say to stop them from getting into the argument that's coming. "I have no choice."

Big Mike winces at me. "But you can't win."

"I have to win."

"And what are we going to do about Moses?" Q asks.

I meet my best friend's gaze. "I've gotta take him out before he has a chance to hurt another goddamn person I love."

SEVEN

Scarlett

I wake up with my shoulder blades pressing into the hard floor beneath the air mattress. A wet nose nudges my arm. I open my eyes and smile at a waiting Roux.

"You need to go out, girl?"

She nudges me again. Scanning the room, I spot Bump's feet sticking out of his couch-cushion cave. Soft snores tell me he's still out, but there's no sign of Gabriel.

Roux whines, so I roll off the air mattress, glad I borrowed one of Gabriel's T-shirts and a pair of sweats last night, and yawn as I pad toward the door and down the stairs. A minute later, she's bounding outside, across the driveway, to her dad.

As soon as Roux nudges his hand, Gabriel whips around to see me.

"Hey, I'm sorry. I was coming back up."

Q stands near a man who I assume is Big Mike, his father, because he looks like Q's clone, only about twenty-five years older and barrel-chested. Hal leans against the SUV blocking the driveway. The grave expressions on the men's faces tell me that they've been discussing what happened last night. I have some things to say about it too, so I move to Gabriel.

"What'd you decide?"

He takes my hand and pulls me into his side. "Nothing much. Just getting everyone up to speed and making sure you and Bump are safe."

I study his stubbled jaw and shadowed eyes, knowing I have to speak up now. "What about keeping *you* safe? Because that's also a major priority."

"I'll be fine. I promise."

I nod. "Yes, because you're moving in with me, and Hal can babysit us both. You'll be closer to the club, there are great gyms in the city, and we'll be easier to protect."

Big Mike wipes powdered sugar off his chin as his eyebrows rise to his hairline. Apparently, people aren't used to Gabriel being bossed around. Good thing I don't care.

"That's not a bad idea," Q says, one brow quirked. "Actually, it's a damn good one."

Gabriel's grip tightens on me. "I don't want this to touch you. Me staying with you means—"

"That I'll be able to sleep at night knowing you're safe. Besides, Ryan and Christine have been after me for months to increase my security measures around the building. Now I have an even better reason. It's the right move, Gabe. I already told you last night that I'm not letting you push me away. We're a team. Now, pack your bags, because you're moving to the city."

Big Mike bursts into laughter. "Damn, I like this one. She knows exactly what she's about." He slaps Q in the stomach with the back of his hand. "You need to find yourself a CEO to date next time."

Q glares but ignores his dad. "I agree with Scarlett. It's the smartest move we've got. Now, let's get the fuck out of this driveway because it's making me nervous as hell to stand out in the open like this."

Gabriel and I climb the stairs back up to his apartment, with Roux snaking between us to reach the entryway first.

Before he opens it, he pauses. "Are you sure you want to bring this right to your door? You know I wouldn't blame you if you packed up and left town until this all blows over."

I reach out and lay my palm against his chest. "I may not have dealt with anything like this before, but I'm not a coward. I stand and fight. We're a team, and we'll get through this together or not at all. Understand me, Gabe? I'm in this with you. Whatever happens, happens to both of us. I love you."

He bows his head, and his voice turns hoarse. "I'm not proud of what I've done, Scarlett. You should want to throw me out of your life, not pull me closer."

"Listen to me, Gabriel Legend." I poke him in the chest. "Everyone has a past. What you did isn't who you are. You have to let it go eventually."

He lifts his gaze and snags my fingers. "I'm fucking ashamed. I did this. I brought this to us. You shouldn't be mixed up in it, shouldn't even know shit like this exists. I hate that it's touched you, even a little."

My spine straightens as regret and guilt roll off him in waves. "Listen up, because you need to hear me and hear me well. I love you for who you are. Past mistakes, flaws, and all. I wouldn't change you or trade you for anything. You are *it* for me, Gabriel. So we fight this. We fight for *us*. And you know what? I don't lose."

His arms shoot out and yank me against his chest until I'm plastered against the hard heat of his body. "You're it for me too. I'll find a way out of this. I promise you that."

His lips press against the crown of my head, and I lean into his warmth.

"Good. Now, let's pack your stuff, stud."

"I like that one," he says with a wink, and I can't help but laugh.

"Of course you do."

EIGHT

Legend

Bump was so excited to go with Big Mike that he didn't put up a single word of protest as I helped him pack clothes and toiletries. The only thing he said to me before he waved good-bye was, "Make sure you give Roux extra treats! I slip them to her when you aren't watching. That's why she loves me best."

As soon as I promised him I would, he strode off with Big Mike.

Hal followed Scarlett and me to Curated, and I parked my Bronco on the street out front. Maybe it's not the smartest thing to do—advertising to Moses exactly where I am—but I'm also not naive enough to think he wouldn't find out anyway. If he's been watching me close enough to find the tunnel entrance to Legend, then there's a damn good chance he knows many of my secrets by now. And by bringing the Bronco, I have transportation if I need it, and I don't like being without a vehicle.

Hal also set up shop out front, where he has a view to the side door and the main entrance. I'm going to owe him a shit ton of money, but that's something I'll worry about later. One thing at a time.

Right now, I'm worrying about my old coach getting back to me. My text to him was short and to the point.

LEGEND: I've got a fight in a month. Time to get to work. Let me know when we can meet to discuss a training plan.

It's been three hours since I sent it. My clothes are now in Scarlett's closet and drawers, and I still don't have an answer.

Scarlett is in the shower, where I plan to join her, when my phone buzzes.

I whip it out of my pocket, expecting to see Johnson's name on the screen. But I don't. It's Silas Bohannon. *What the hell does he want?*

After I unlock the screen, I read his message.

BOHANNON: Just came from the gym and heard that Black's training with the coach you used to use. He's spreading the word that he's getting ready to crush you.

I scan the words again to make sure I'm reading it right. *What in the actual fuck?*

Shock and betrayal tear through me. If what Bohannon is saying is true, I want to reach through the phone to strangle Johnson myself.

I type out a quick message to Bohannon.

LEGEND: Are you sure they said it's Ron Johnson training him?

. . .

Then I send another one to Johnson. My blood is boiling as I pace and peck at the screen.

LEGEND: *If you're training Bodhi Black for this fight, you need to tell me right the fuck now.*

Bohannon's response comes first.

BOHANNON: *I know what I heard and the source is reliable. I figured that means you're going to need a new coach. I just wrapped up two weeks early on this MMA project, and my guys said they could take you on. They're top level talent, and not to be a dick, but that's what you need to win this thing.*
LEGEND: *What's the catch? How much?*
BOHANNON: *They've already been paid for the two weeks. The rest, they'll do as a favor for me.*
LEGEND: *Why are you helping me?*
BOHANNON: *Because you need it and I can.*

His answer tells me nothing. Normally, I wouldn't accept help without understanding motives, but I don't have a lot of options right now. I'd be a fucking idiot not to take Bohannon's offer.

LEGEND: *Thank you. Tell me when and where to meet your guys, and we'll get started.*
BOHANNON: *Smart man. I'll text you details.*

The shower is still going, so I leave my phone on the dresser and head for the bathroom. I'm not wasting this opportunity either.

I strip as fast as I possibly can. When I climb into the steamy glass-walled enclosure, Scarlett smiles.

"And here I thought you'd decided you were going to shower alone."

"When I could shower with you instead? I might fuck up some things, but I'm not an idiot."

Her smile could light up the city. "Did you know I've never lived with a guy before?"

My head jerks back and spray bounces off my body. "You're kidding."

"Nope. You're my first."

My palms slide against slippery skin as I curve them around her hips. "Your first? I like the sound of that."

I take her lips in a slow, measured kiss as the hot water beats down on both of us. Even though I've been second-guessing every move we're making, I don't second-guess this. Scarlett in my arms is the one thing that makes total and complete sense.

God, she's incredible.

The words that have been on my mind slip out in the steam. "I love you, Scarlett."

Her entire body stills for a heartbeat. Then another. And another.

Finally, I examine her expression, not sure how she's reacting. But it's fucking better than I could have ever imagined.

This time, the smile on her face could illuminate the entire world. "I know you do. Because there's no way I could feel like this if you didn't feel it too."

"I have no damn clue what I did to deserve you, but I promise, we're going to get through this. Our future is fucking bright, ladybug." Maybe it's a promise I shouldn't be making, but I have to believe it. The more I buy into it, the more likely it is to come true. I just hope she believes it too.

"I know," she whispers. "Because we're just getting started. The best is yet to come."

Her lips skim down my stubbled jaw, and my fingers curve into the slick, firm muscles of her ass.

"I need you. Now," I tell her, the words sounding more guttural than I expected.

Scarlett lifts a knee and hooks her leg around my hip. "Then you'd better take me, chief."

This time, I don't say shit about the nickname. She could call me anything at this point, and I'd still be putty in her hands.

Dragging the fingertips of one hand up her back, I bury them in her mass of wet golden hair, using them to tilt her head sideways and give me better access.

I take the kiss deeper, pouring every ounce of what I feel for her into it, hoping she understands. I love her. It's one of the few things I know without a doubt right now. I'd bet everything on it. Bet everything on us.

Her hips lift as she seeks friction against my cock. When I push into her, she moans into my mouth, and I nip at her lip.

Scarlett pulls back, her gray eyes shining. "I never knew it could be like this, wanting someone all the time. I thought I was broken. You showed me I'm not. I just needed you."

I move both hands to the sides of her face and brush the wet strands of hair away until I'm cupping her cheeks.

"You aren't broken. You never were. You don't need me, Scarlett. But it's the greatest privilege of my life to be with you."

I don't know if it's the water dripping down her face, or tears, but her smile wobbles.

"You slay me when you say things like that."

I lean in to steal another taste of her. "I'm just getting started, ladybug. But don't worry, I've got you. When your knees go weak. When your load is too heavy. When it's all too much. *I've got you.*"

"Then take me."

She jerks forward this time, plastering our mouths together, and I readjust my grip to lift her ass. Her other leg wraps around my waist, and I fit her right where we both need it. My cock nudges against her entrance, and inch by inch, I lower her until she's full of me.

Scarlett's head drops back as her inner muscles flex and clench.

I spin around and press her against the tile, and slowly, lift her off my cock and then power back inside her. Stroke after stroke, our bodies come together, until I lose track of everything, except how tight her cunt grips me and the feel of her skin sliding against mine.

It's like coming home.

This is where I belong. In this moment. With this woman.

There's nothing I won't do to protect her and what we have.

When I can't hold back any longer, I roar her name loud enough for all of Manhattan to hear, and her scream echoes as we both explode.

NINE

Scarlett

Almost every time we have sex, I think there's no way it could possibly get any better. Any hotter. Any more intense. And then Gabriel goes and proves me wrong.

We wrap ourselves in fluffy towels, and I head to the closet to grab my robe. *I'm going to have to get one for Gabriel too.* Because, seriously, the only thing I want to do right now is lounge in bed and listen to the sound of his heart beat.

I know. I have it bad. But I don't care.

Maybe I should, given the gravity of the situation outside these four walls, but I'm not willing to sacrifice my happiness in this moment to the anxiety of worrying about what could happen in an hour or a week or a month. I'm going to be present.

With a smile on my face, I head back to the bathroom to replace my towel on the bar. Legend is in front of the mirror, lathering up his neck to shave, and he shoots me a wink.

"I'll be done in a few."

"Take your time," I say with a smile, knotting my robe and checking to see that Roux is still curled up in her dog bed in the corner of my bedroom, taking a nap.

We both freeze when the intercom sounds at the same time as Gabriel's phone buzzes.

He moves first. "I'll get it."

I hold up a palm. "Let me check the intercom. Then we can decide if you need to go out there in a towel and scare someone away."

His gaze narrows, but he nods. "Deal."

With goose bumps rising on my lower legs, despite the plush robe, I pad to the back door and press the button.

"Who is it?"

"It's me. I need to talk to you. I'm freaking out, and I don't know what to do." It's Monroe's voice, and she sounds like she's about to lose her shit.

"Come on up, babe." I press the button to unlock the door. "It's open."

"Thank you, Scarlett."

"Who is it?"

I whip around to find a shaving-creamed Gabriel standing behind me.

"Monroe. Something's wrong."

Gabriel's brow furrows. "You sure you can trust her?"

My head tilts sideways. "Yes. Of course. Why?"

He reaches out to tug me closer by the belt of my robe. "Because I'm not taking any chances with you."

I press a quick kiss to his lips, dodging the white foam. "It's fine. I promise."

He nods but doesn't return to the bathroom.

"Are you waiting for something?"

He stands his ground, totally buck naked except for a towel. All six-foot-something of him. And he's all mine.

"I'll leave you two alone after she comes in."

It occurs to me that Gabriel must be afraid that someone is using Monroe to gain entrance, and part of me wants to ask if he's got a gun stuffed in the back of the towel wrapped around his waist. But I decide I don't want an answer to that particular question.

A knock comes on the door a few moments later, and Gabriel steps in front of me to open it.

So this is what it's like to live with a super-protective man. I'm not mad at it.

My budding grin blooms when I see Monroe's eyes go as wide as saucers and her lower lip falls to the floor.

"What . . . Wait. What the fuck is happening right now?" Her gaze darts from me to Gabriel and then back to me. "Did I interrupt something? If so, I'm really fucking sorry, but I didn't know where else to go."

"You alone?" Gabriel steps out of the way for her to enter and sticks his head out into the hallway.

"Yeah. Of course."

He shuts the door and gives me a nod. "I'll leave you two to it then. Good to see you, Monroe."

She stares slack-jawed at him as he struts his towel-clad ass in the direction of my bedroom and the master bath.

I take a moment to appreciate the incredible physique of the man who just gave me more of the best orgasms of my life. His shoulders are broad and defined. His muscular back tapers into a V at his narrow waist. I didn't know it was possible for my mouth to water at the sight of a well-built man, but that's exactly what I'm doing right now.

"Holy shit," Monroe whispers as soon as he disappears from sight. She cuts her attention to my face. "You sure as hell snagged yourself one *fine* man."

I nod, one eye still trained on the doorway through which he disappeared. "I know. I've never lived with a guy before, so this is going to be a bit of an adjustment—but a really, really, really good one, I think."

"Wait. Hold up. You're *living together*? When did that happen?"

I hold up a finger. "Let's put that on pause while you tell me what's wrong."

Monroe shakes her head. "Mine can wait. When did he move in? Oh my God, who else knows? What is your dad going to say? Scar, this is huge. Like a massively big move." She goes on to list everyone I know to see if I've told anyone. Obviously, that answer is *no.*

Part of me wishes she'd taken my suggestion to talk about her issues instead of bringing up all the people who are no doubt going to freak out when they find out Gabriel is living here.

While I'm thinking of a way to redirect the conversation, Monroe snaps her fingers in front of my face to get my attention. "Girl. Spill. Now."

I go to my mug rack and grab two. "You want some coffee?"

"What I want is answers."

My annoyance is rising, but I don't know why. Monroe's acting like I can't decide anything by myself without first consulting everyone else in my life, and it's kind of pissing me off. I also don't know how much to tell her about what happened at the club, so I go with the basics.

"No one knows. We decided last night. We're just testing it out, seeing how we like it."

Her golden-brown eyes seem to widen even further. "This is a big move. Like . . . huge in relationship terms. Are you sure you know what you're doing?"

"Absolutely. I like being around him. He makes me feel safe. He makes me happy," I tell her. Even though the situation is supposed to be temporary, there's another question running through my mind—*what if I don't want it to be temporary?*

Monroe bursts into tears, and in a split second, she goes from standing to crumpling into one of my kitchen chairs, sobbing with her head in her hands.

"Monroe!" Her name comes out more like a yell, and footsteps and nails click against the floor as Gabriel and Roux come rushing into the kitchen.

Gabriel's got his razor in hand, but freezes when he sees the crying woman. "What happened? What's wrong?"

Roux sniffs along her side before returning to sit at Gabriel's feet.

"I think I'm ruining my marriage. It's probably over. And it's all my fault."

Gabriel's blue gaze locks onto mine over Monroe's head. I drop into the chair beside her and scoot closer, throwing an arm around her shoulders.

"Honey, no. It's not over. Your marriage isn't ruined."

"You . . . don't . . . know . . . that." Monroe snuffles each word through sobs.

I grab a handful of tissues. As Gabriel slowly backs out of the room, Monroe's head pops up and she looks right at him with tear-filled eyes.

"You're a man. You know how this works. You tell me."

I have to give Gabriel credit. His expression looks more *deer in the headlights* rather than horrified.

"What's going on?" he asks, even though he has no clue what he's getting into.

Monroe takes the tissues and uses them to dab at her tears. Even when breaking down, she's as elegant as it gets. "I went to his away game," she says with a sniffle.

"Harlow said you thought he was cheating. What happened?" I know that information is supposed to be locked in the double vault, but this is an emergency.

Monroe's lip quivers, and a few more tears spill out over her lashes. "I didn't tell him I was going."

"*Oh fuck*," Gabriel whispers, reading my mind exactly.

"What happened?" I ask again.

She swipes at her nose and takes a steadying breath. "I saw

him at a bar with the team. Talking to a woman while he was getting a drink."

"Okay . . ."

"And then when some of the guys left, he went with them, and so did she."

My heart clenches because I'm scared of where this is going. In her defense, it looks bad.

Monroe keeps going. "She went up the elevator with them too, so I waited a few minutes . . ."

I'm dying to know what happened next, but I don't dare interrupt.

"And then I pounded on the door to his room, and when he opened it, I shoved inside. I thought I was going to catch him red-handed with that slut in his bed. I searched the whole room, while he just stood there by the door."

Oh shit, I think, catching a glimpse of Gabriel from the corner of my eye. He shakes his head slowly as I picture Monroe ripping open closets and screaming as she searched for the woman.

"But she wasn't there," Gabriel says quietly.

Monroe jerks her head toward him. "How did you know?"

His face goes soft. "Because he's married to you. He doesn't need a skank from the bar when he's got you waiting at home for him."

Monroe bursts into another round of sobs. "Why didn't I trust him? What is wrong with me?"

"Oh, honey." I squeeze her tighter against my side. "You were scared and—"

"I ran out of the room and took a red-eye home. And when he got back a little while ago, Nate said he didn't want to see me. He told me to leave, or he would."

My stomach twists into a knot. "Shit. I'm so sorry. God, Monroe."

"I deserve it. He's going to divorce me. He told me we have nothing if we don't trust each other."

I don't know what to say to her, but thankfully, Gabriel drops into a crouch beside my friend.

"How many times have you been cheated on?"

Monroe lifts her head. "Too many."

"He know that?"

She doesn't respond right away, but I have a feeling I know the answer.

Monroe's always dated and married athletes. Not a single relationship has ended well, and yet . . . she keeps trying. I can't imagine she'd show Nate that crack in her armor, though, because she'd think it would make her less desirable for him to know that other men have been married to her and banged those bar skanks without a second thought.

"No," she whispers. "I was ashamed. I didn't want him to know."

"Well, hell. You gotta tell him," Gabriel says in a soft voice that makes me love him even more because he's being so gentle with my friend when she's fragile. "A man needs to know what kind of shit is going to set off his woman. I guarantee he'd be a fuck of a lot more understanding if he knew that you've been down this road before, and that it's not really just him you don't trust. It's men in general."

Monroe's tears slow. "You think he'd listen to me if I tried to tell him now? Because he was *so mad*. Some of the guys from the team came out of their rooms and saw it all. It was so bad, Scarlett."

She turns to me, her face splotchy from her tears. "So. Bad. God, it was like I was standing outside my body, just watching myself freak out. I was embarrassed for myself, but I didn't know how to stop. *I love him*, and now I'm going to lose him."

I wish I could tell her she's not going to lose him, but I don't know Nate well enough to say that. Instead, I hug her tighter.

Thankfully, Gabriel says exactly the right thing. "Ask him for five minutes. Tell him you need to explain something. He'll listen.

You might only get this one chance, so don't waste it. Be real. Be honest. Tell him why you went crazy. Lay it out and explain."

She snuffles one more time. "You think he'll forgive me?"

Gabriel shrugs. "No clue, but it's worth a shot. Talking about your shit goes a long way toward avoiding situations like this."

Monroe nods slowly, and Gabriel and I lock eyes over her head. I'm almost positive that he's thinking about his past, and what he needs to tell me.

Whatever it is, Gabe, we've got this.

Besides, after last night and Moses, I'm getting caught up to speed pretty damn quickly already.

Monroe straightens her shoulders, as if moving one muscle at a time until her spine is straight and her chin is lifted. "I can tell him. I can do this. He'll listen to me. I can apologize. This can work." Her words sound like a mantra.

I squeeze her hand. "You've got this, babe. Do you need some time to pull yourself together before you go?"

She shakes her head. "No, I need to do this before I lose my nerve. I'll text you. Hopefully after the makeup sex," she adds with a watery smile. "I really do love him. I've got to make this work."

"You will. Love you, girl."

She presses a kiss to my cheek. "Love you too. And we're not done talking about you and him." She jerks her chin at Legend. "Take care of my girl, okay?"

"Yes, ma'am," he replies with a hint of that Southern drawl that slips out every now and again.

"Okay, now I'm going straight home before I wuss out."

Monroe dashes away as quickly as she arrived, leaving me, Gabriel, and Roux in the kitchen, staring at the door as it closes behind her.

TEN

"She's like a hurricane, isn't she?" I say as Scarlett walks toward me and threads her fingers through mine.

"Something like that. You give damn good advice, ace."

I smile at her nickname attempt. "I thought we were going with *stud?*"

She smiles. "I'm still working on it. I'll find the perfect one. Just wait. But, seriously, I couldn't have given Monroe that advice. You told her exactly what she needed to hear."

"I've got a dick." I shrug. "I know what I'd do if I were her man. But since she doesn't have a dick, I shared some insight to help her see the bigger picture."

"Well, you nailed it. This might be the one thing that could actually save their marriage." Scarlett's head tips to the side and she beams up at me, looking sweet as pie in her robe.

"I hope so. But if not, she'll learn for the next time, hopefully."

"I don't want to think of Monroe heartbroken and going through yet another divorce. So I'm going to be optimistic."

"You do that," I tell her, leaning in to kiss her nose.

When I pull back, Scarlett meets my gaze. "You know you can

tell me anything, right? Nothing you say to me will change how I feel about you."

I study her face, framed by strands of blond hair floating down from her messy bun, and instantly, the thought that popped into my head when I was talking to Monroe Grafton comes back to the forefront.

"I believe you, and I do need to tell you something. I would've last night, but I honestly fucking forgot with everything that happened."

"What?"

"That Lucy chick from the fundraiser thing . . ."

Scarlett's expression tightens. "Oh God. What did she do? Did she hit on you? Because she already made it clear that she's interested. And just so you know, I might not be well-versed in how to cut a bitch, but I would learn if she said anything nasty to you."

A grin stretches my face at the feistiness underlying Scarlett's words.

"I believe you, ladybug. But you don't need to cut her. I lied to her to get her to stop bidding on your mom's necklace."

Scarlett's brows shoot toward her hairline. "Lied to her how? About what?"

"I let her think that I'd fuck her."

My girl's jaw drops. "What?"

"She needed encouragement to leave the bidding alone, so I gave her some. But you gotta know, I would never fucking—"

Scarlett's entire face lights up as giggles spill from her lips. "Oh. My. God. This is epic. Holy crap. Lucy is going to lose her mind when she finds out you made a fool of her!" Scarlett doubles over and slaps the table. "And she won't be able to tell anyone either! Because it'll make her look too desperate. This is priceless."

When Scarlett meets my gaze again, tears turn her eyes glassy. I'm so damned glad they're tears from laughter and not something else.

"You are a genius!"

A smile tugs at the corners of my mouth. "I'm really fucking glad you're not mad."

"Mad? Are you kidding? I got my mom's necklace because you played on Lucy's biggest weakness—a man she's not supposed to have." Her humor fades for a moment. "Chadwick slept with her while he and I were together. I guarantee she thought you would too. What an arrogant see-you-next-Tuesday."

"Baby, you know you can say the word and not spell it, right?"

Scarlett shakes her head. "Nah, she's not worth it. And don't worry about Lucy for another second. If she comes back, I'll handle her."

"My ferocious ladybug," I say as I pull her into my hips. "You're amazing, you know that?"

Scarlett shrugs. "I'm just me."

"You're fucking perfect is what you are. But I need you to know that I won't ever do something like that without talking to you if I can avoid it. And no matter what, I will do whatever it takes to make sure that nothing connected with me ever blows back on you. Moses will never fucking hurt you. I won't allow it. Just like last night, I'll stand as your shield. I will gladly take any bullets so that nothing ever touches you. I swear it on my life."

She reaches out and digs her fingers into the towel wrapped around my waist, and her expression is grave.

"I don't want you to take any bullets, Gabriel. Not for any reason. If there is any way you can get Moses to take money, you have to swear to me that you'll take it from me. *Please*. I can always get more money. But even with all the money in the world, I'd never be able to find another you."

I move one hand to cup the back of her hair and press a kiss to her forehead.

"I promise that I won't let my ego or my pride get in the way of asking for your help if I truly need it. I swear."

I left my girls curled up on Scarlett's bed. Roux was snoring at the foot while Scarlett tapped away on the keys of her laptop.

I didn't want to go, but she kissed me and sent me on my way, but only after I got the log-in info to her security camera app for the building. I told her it was for Hal so he could see inside the stairwells and store, but I'll be checking it all the fucking time too.

Scarlett made me promise I'd drive instead of walk, and that I wouldn't take any unnecessary risks. I agreed, because I've got a whole hell of a lot of reasons to live a long and happy life, and I'm not letting Moses take that from either of us.

Hal's out front, keeping an eye on the place. He sent a text to notify us that Monroe was coming up the sidewalk earlier, but I didn't read it until after she left. After giving him strict instructions to notify me of anything he saw that caused concern—on the street or on the cameras—I head to the club to meet Q and go through our own security footage.

Moses weighs heavy on my mind.

Is he watching me right now? Could he really have popped me at any time?

I already know the answer to that is *yes*. Moses didn't get to the top of the Biloxi crew without being clever and ruthless.

Underestimating him won't happen again.

I park in the alley and head inside the club, thinking about how we're going to have to hire more security for Scarlett and Curated. Someone will have to take turns with Hal, because the old boxer won't be able to stay awake around the clock for much longer. I need to figure out where the money's going to come from, but that's less of a concern. We don't have a choice.

I shoot Hal a text to ask if he has anyone he would trust with his life who could trade shifts with him.

HAL: Let me ask my brother. He's between jobs. Only man I'd trust with my life.

LEGEND: Thank you. I appreciate it more than you know.

HAL: We both know I owe you big. Consider this a long overdue repayment, and if you try to slip me cash, I'll consider it an insult.

I stare down at my phone. *Well, shit, at least I won't have to come up with the money to pay Hal.* One problem solved off my long list. I'll fucking take it.

Next up, to figure out if the cameras caught any footage of Moses inside Legend.

ELEVEN

Q is in his office when I make it inside, and he's already got camera feeds up on both of his monitors.

"You see anything?"

"Not yet, but I only vaguely remember what he looks like from that picture you showed me years ago. Fuck, now I feel like I should've had it framed on my desk so I was ready."

I shake my head. "I'm so fucking sorry, man. I brought this to our door—"

Q waves me off. "Stop. I've known since the beginning that tying myself to you could mean that I'd find myself in this situation. I know what I signed up for, Gabe."

I pull one of the extra chairs around the side of his desk and sit down beside him. "Regardless, it's eating at me. I should've handled my shit all those years ago."

Q turns, and his dark gaze pierces mine. "You were a scared-as-fuck kid back then, and it doesn't make you less of a man to admit it. I wouldn't have gone after him either, if I'd been in your shoes."

"So, what do we do now?"

Q releases a long breath. "I don't know. Because if this fight really comes together and you win . . . we're still fucked."

"I will win. Losing isn't an option."

"So we find out where the fuck Moses is holed up and take him out ahead of time." Q leans back in his chair. "Or get a million and a half from someone who isn't your girlfriend."

I shake my head. "No one is giving me that kind of cash to pay off a gangster from Biloxi. I hate to break it to you, but I don't have a fairy godfather."

Q grunts out a laugh. "No shit. Because we wouldn't be in this position if you did. He'd be turning piles of dog shit into stacks of hundreds instead of pumpkins into carriages."

"You've been watching cartoons with your nieces again, haven't you?" I ask him.

He points at me. "So what if I did? You going to judge me for it, after going to a gala with the richest assholes in town?"

"No judgment." I raise my hands in surrender. "But I'm still going to give you shit about it."

"Whatever. Back to Moses. Even if we spend hours going through security footage, it's not going to help us find him now. You got any idea where he'd go?"

I shake my head. "None whatsoever. Could that PI buddy of yours take a look?"

"Eduardo? He's fucking crazy. You know he only takes payment in cash up front, and we're not exactly rolling in it . . . which brings me to another question. If your plan is to bet on yourself for the fight and win big, where the fuck are you going to get *that* money, man? I assume you're not asking Scarlett for that either."

It's a question that's run through my mind more than once since I came up with this plan to pay off the investors after I win.

I lean back in the chair and cross my arms, ready to put it out there. "I've only got one idea right now, and you're really not going to like it."

"Tell me."

"Putting the club up as collateral with a loan shark."

Q bursts out of his chair so fast, it tips over backward. "Are you fucking shitting me? Gabe, what in the actual fuck? If you lose, then we're fucked on every goddamn level. Not to mention, Cannon Freeman and Creighton Karas will probably have you offed by the fucking mob if you do that. And guess who most of those loan sharks are in bed with? That won't work."

"What other option do I have?"

He jams his hands into his hair. "Fuck. Me. This isn't the conversation I wanted to be having right now. Goddammit, Gabe. Swallow your pride. Ask your girlfriend. She's got the money, and she's a hell of a lot safer than a New York City loan shark."

I know he's right, but everything in me is screaming *no fucking way am I asking Scarlett for the money*, even though I just promised her I would swallow my pride and ask if I really needed the help. I might have to, but I'm not ready to go there yet.

"Let's table this for now and deal with it later, okay? We'll come up with something. I just need to let it simmer for a few more days."

Q shakes his head. "This shit is going to age me before my fucking time. Whatever you do, please swear to me that you'll tell me first, before it happens, so I can be prepared for the fallout."

"I fucking swear."

After scanning a few hours of video, I spot Moses. Bold as brass, he walked right into my fucking club and ordered a drink before he left . . . only to show up again in my office and hold Bump at gunpoint.

I have to take him out. That's my only option. But I've got no fucking clue where to find him.

As I'm leaving the club, Q sends a second text to Eduardo, the crazy PI, and I pray he'll help us on good faith alone. It's the only chance we have, because I can't lose this fight. It's not in me to take a dive.

After I'm forced to park a few blocks away from the gym, I sit in the truck for a few minutes to get my head right. This workout might not be with my fancy new coach, but it's the first one where battle needs to be at the forefront of my mind. I'm preparing for the fight of my life, the odds are stacked against me, and I have no choice but to win—despite Moses's threats or the fact that I don't have a signed contract in hand making the event official.

The fight will happen.

I close my eyes and picture the signed contracts on my desk and Q nodding in approval. *The fight is happening, and I'm going to win.*

I have no fucking clue how I'm going to pull all of this off, but I have to believe I can. If I don't, there's no reason to walk into the gym.

"I got this. All of it. I can do this." I say the words out loud to myself, psyching myself up until I can speak it with such confidence that I believe it.

It's a trick I picked up early in my fighting career, the first time I was going up against a nasty opponent who'd killed a guy in the ring earlier in the year. I pictured myself standing over his body as the ref raised my hand in victory. I lived that vision over and over and over until I was certain of exactly how the fight would end.

I took him out with a brutal TKO from a ground-and-pound finish, and he was still on the canvas when the ref raised my hand in victory.

This is how winners think, I realized.

Two years later, I'd earned enough to start Urban Legend. From the goddamned day I was born, the odds have been stacked against me. It's nothing new. I haven't let it stop me yet, and I'm sure as hell not starting now.

"Let's do this." I hop out of the Bronco, shoulder my bag, and head inside. I walk differently, with more purpose.

I barely see the other people in the gym as I go to the lockers and get ready to train. It's like tunnel vision, but different and hard to explain. Regardless, when I finish my warm-up and start working the bag, I'm in the zone. My muscles remember every damn move and combination that's been drilled into my head since the first time I put on gloves. I savage the bag, switch to jumping rope until I can barely breathe, and chug some water before doing it all over again and again and again.

It's as familiar to me as breathing. Hell, sometimes I think this is what I was meant to do with my life. Train, fight, and overcome battle after battle. I understand this world. I know how to win. But for so many years, I've had Jorie's dreams in my head, and those are what drove me to open my underground club, and then Legend.

Is that really what I want? I push the question away and return my focus to the bag.

I'm drenched with sweat and grinding out one last combination when I sense someone behind me. I finish and grab the bag to steady it and myself.

"What do you want?" I ask before I haul in a deep breath of oxygen, hoping to make the black spots dotting my vision disappear.

"Damn, man. I haven't seen you train like that in . . . a long fucking time."

Hearing Rolo's familiar voice makes me stand upright and turn to face him. "Seems like one hell of a coincidence I keep seeing you here, what with the odd training hours I've been keeping and all."

Rolo crosses his arms. "We could pretend it's a coincidence, but we both know it's not. I got people. They let me know you were here. I've been wanting to talk to you."

The last thing I want to do right now is have this conversation, but just like I thought before I got out of the car—if you don't deal with shit, it keeps coming back until you do. And it always returns bigger, meaner, and more prepared to take you out.

"What's on your mind?" I ask him.

The older man sighs and shakes his head, his chin dipping close to the gold chains around his neck. "You and me both come a long, long way, boss. We've always been a damn good team."

I know where he's going with this. No doubt he's heard the rumors about the fight that are apparently already all over the city. I wait, and he continues.

"We both made a lot of money together too."

"I know," I reply.

"I'm the one who came to you about the rematch with Black, so imagine my surprise when I hear my boy, my *partner*, is cutting me out of the action and making that fight happen without me, after everything I did for you. That's some cold shit, man. Really fucking cold shit."

I expected Rolo to be pissed—*really fucking pissed*—but the betrayal in his tone takes me by surprise.

Other than Q and his family, Rolo did more for me than any other person in New York or Jersey. He believed in me when I didn't believe in myself. He got me fights that people thought were insane, because he believed I could win.

Now, don't get me wrong—he was in it for the money, and if I hadn't been as good as I was, he wouldn't have done all he did. But back in the day, it was more than that. We were friends.

When I was broke and needed help getting Bump into a doctor because he was sick, Rolo fronted me cash, knowing he'd make it back from the next purse I won. I'm not the kind of guy who turns his back on the people who helped him get where he is, and from Rolo's viewpoint, that's exactly what he thinks I did.

"I'm sorry you didn't hear it from me first, man. That was shitty of me, but in my defense, nothing is for sure yet. Until I have a signed contract in my hand, I don't have much room to talk about what is or isn't going down."

Rolo's entire posture seems to hunch forward like he just absorbed a blow. "But it is true that it's in the works. You and Black. Sanctioned fight. At your club."

I bounce on my toes and smack my gloves together to keep my muscles warm. "I'm in a tough spot, Rolo. This is my way out. If you were in my shoes, you'd do the same thing."

His dark eyes sharpen on me. "I wouldn't cut you out, man. That's where we're different. Don't sign the contract. Do it underground. Fewer rules. No taxes. Whatever tough spot you're in, I'll help you out. We'll make it happen *our way.* Fuck those guys who want contracts and assurances. That's not how we roll."

I inhale slowly and then release the breath. "I can't do that. Sanctioned is the only way I'm fighting Black. Neither of us are dying in that cage, because that's not how it should be either."

Rolo shakes his head at me. "That new woman of yours don't want to go slumming. That's what it's really about, ain't it? She ain't the type to go to an underground club and be able to hold her own."

I don't like hearing him talk about Scarlett. Not one fucking bit. But what he said is true.

"If you were me, you wouldn't risk exposing her to shit like that either."

"I guess times are a-changin'," Rolo says with another long sigh. "Never thought I'd see the day when I barely recognized this city anymore. New players coming into the game every day, and here I am, just trying to hold on to our measly slice of the pie. You and me had a good thing going, Gabe. Real fucking good. Pretty soon, I'm just gonna be like one of those high school quarterbacks, reliving my glory days from the sidelines because the best ain't yet to come. It's already gone and passed me by. Hell of a reality check, man."

"Shit, Rolo. It's not like that. You've still got plenty of action. Your new fighter you were with the other time I saw you? Sounds like he's a solid prospect." I don't know why I keep the conversation going. Guilt, I guess. Because I hate seeing Rolo look so damned depressed and beaten down.

"He's all right. He ain't you, though, because he ain't got this." Rolo reaches out to tap his finger against the side of my head. "That brain of yours was always six steps ahead of everyone else. That's why I pushed so hard for this fight with Black. You can win. The only person who's ever been able to beat you is yourself, Gabe. That's the damn truth."

My chin dips, and I stare at the spatters of sweat dotting the mat beneath our feet. An idea hits me, and I look up at him. "You ever thought about going legit? Giving Uncle Sam his cut of your take?"

Rolo's head jerks back. "Now, why would I want to give the government a fuckin' dime? They didn't work for that shit. Ain't no one robbing me of what's rightfully mine."

"Just think about it, Rolo. Maybe if this fight goes well at Legend, I could start up my own thing—but legit. High-end fight nights. Bigger money. Bigger gate. Do it right. I'd need someone to help make it happen." I can't believe what I'm saying, because I rarely speak without thinking things through— or talking them out with Q—but the fucking guilt is crushing me right now.

"You'd do that for me? Bring me in on your action?" he asks, scratching the back of his neck.

"Let's see how this fight goes, and then we'll sit down and talk about it. How's that?" I'm dodging his question, but at least I don't feel like such a piece of shit.

Rolo shifts on his feet and cracks his knuckles, which sport heavy gold rings. "Yeah. You and me will sit down and talk after this is over. I miss you, man."

I step in, and we give each other a half hug, slapping backs. I'm covered in sweat, but that's nothing new for Rolo.

When we release each other, I shake his outstretched hand. "Thanks for understanding. I'm really not trying to fuck you over here. I just don't have a choice. I have to do this."

"Yeah, Legend. I'm getting that. I'll see you again soon. You got my number. Don't be a stranger."

Rolo leaves the gym, and a sense of relief washes over me as he disappears from sight.

Everything's going to work out just fine. Those contracts will be on my desk and signed this week. I'm going to take out Moses, beat Bodhi Black, make Scarlett happy, and save the club.

I got this. Somehow.

TWELVE

Scarlett

Gabriel and I are both working on our laptops when there's a knock on the interior door Monday morning. "Amy's here. Crap, I lost track of time."

He stands up. "I'll get out of your way then. I've got an office of my own, after all."

I've been struggling with the idea of him out there in the world where Moses can get to him, while I stay at Curated with security out front.

Hal's half brother, Pat, also a former boxer, is alternating shifts with him until this entire thing is over. When I asked Gabriel if I could pay their salaries, we had our first official living-together argument. It ended in my bed, with both of us naked, so I'm calling it a win.

We agreed to split the cost of Pat's time, since Hal won't take any money, but only because I told Gabriel it wasn't fair to expect me to sit back and contribute nothing when his money could be better spent elsewhere, like on the club.

"Stay. Take the bedroom. We won't be long. Maybe a half hour. It's usually a super-quick rundown of the week and any employee issues."

He tucks the laptop under his arm and kisses my cheek. "I'll be on that fancy little couch of yours then. That is, if it can hold my weight."

I squint at him, not really offended at his quip. "The settee is solid. I promise."

"We'll see about that."

He heads for the bedroom as I let Amy in. Her eyes expand to the size of dinner plates as she looks over my shoulder and watches him shut the door.

"I thought I heard a man's voice in here. I'm sorry." She glances back to my face. "I didn't mean to interrupt. You didn't say anything about changing the time of our meeting, but we can reschedule."

"It's fine. No need to change anything. Come sit down."

Her gaze cuts to the closed bedroom door again. "Does this have something to do with the black SUV out front that hasn't moved since Sunday?"

"How do you know it hasn't moved since Sunday?"

"I thought it was suspicious, so I went back and checked the security feeds. What's going on, Scarlett?"

"I needed to increase security. Ryan and Christine were pushing me to do it when the troll first surfaced, but I didn't want to overreact. Now . . . I think it's time."

Her eyes grow wide again. "This is because of the troll?"

"Not quite. But it's important."

"Before I fully freak out, is there some other threat I need to know about? Are you in danger? Because of him?" Amy's gaze darts to the bedroom door as it opens.

Gabriel comes out with his gym bag over his shoulder. "I'm not trying to step on your toes here, but I'm guessing it would help if I explained what's going on to Amy."

"Yes, please," Amy says, nodding rapidly.

Thankful that he's going to deliver whatever information we can share, I smile. "That would be great. Let's all sit down."

I move to the kitchen table and pull out a chair, and Gabriel and Amy do the same. When we're all seated, Gabriel starts.

"Scarlett's safety is my number one priority."

"Perfect. That's a great start," Amy says, brushing her coppery curls over her shoulder, and then she sits up straighter to give him her full, undivided attention.

"We have reason to believe that someone could possibly target her due to her relationship with me. And since I'm not going to let that happen, there will be a guy in that SUV who can handle himself and whatever might come up for as long as there are any security concerns."

"Oh my God. This sounds bad. Really bad." Amy's gaze cuts to mine. "Should we call the police? They'd probably send someone to sit out there too."

I shake my head. "No, that's unnecessary. You know that the paps would find out, and then we'd have stories leaked and it would be a big mess. We're keeping this quiet. You know how much privacy means to me."

A crease forms in Amy's brow. "But your safety . . ."

"Scarlett's safe right where she is. I'm staying here with her, and no one's ever going to make it through me to get to her. Understand, Amy?"

"Yeah. I think so." Poor Amy looks like she's about to faint or freak out, so I'm relieved when Gabriel smiles at her.

"It'll all be fine. But I'm going to get out of your hair and head to my office," he says, rising to his feet.

"You sure?" I ask, my apprehension climbing.

Gabriel leans down to press a kiss to my cheek. "I'm positive. Do your thing, ladybug. I'll be back before you know it."

"I love you," I whisper.

"I love you too," he says quietly, but I know there's no way Amy missed it. "I'll text you to let you know what I've got going down today. Let Hal know if you need anything."

After I agree, he heads out the back door, leaving Amy staring after him.

"You're in love with each other," she whispers, and tears fill her eyes. "That was the sweetest thing I've ever seen. I'm happy for you, Scarlett."

I take in my manager's face, overcome with pure joy, and I'm grateful I have her in my life and on my team. "Thank you. He makes me really happy."

"I'm glad." Her expression loses a bit of its luster. "But this security thing scares me. Are you sure you're safe? Is *he* safe? Does he have any security following him around?"

"I think Gabriel is more than capable of taking care of himself, but I understand what you're saying. It's all new to me too. The only thing I can hope for is that it'll all be over soon."

I straighten the place mat in front of me, pick up a crumb, and flick it away. "Now, what do we have on the agenda for this week?"

THIRTEEN

The contract is waiting in my email by the time I get to the club—just as I envisioned. *Maybe there's even more to that visualizing shit than I thought.*

"We got the fucking fight," I yell to Q, whose door is open one office over.

"Fuck yeah!" he yells back, and he's in my doorway a few seconds later. "Thank fuck. I swear to Christ, I was about to have a goddamn coronary waiting for the thing to come through. How does it look?"

I scan the document, catching the highlights and the numbers. The first contract is for the venue, and what we agreed upon for the gate percentage is there in writing. That's a damn good sign. I open the second one, the contract for me to fight Bodhi Black. Again, nothing looks out of order to me.

"It looks half-decent, but it's not like I'm used to dealing with contracts for fights," I remind my best friend.

"The lawyers are going to want to go through it with a fine-tooth comb to make sure we're not getting screwed anyway," Q says as he sits in one of the chairs across from my desk. "We'll need to have them rush it and only push back about the most important things. We can't drag this shit out by negotiating forever, or fuck, take the chance that they'll find another venue who'll just sign the damn thing as it is."

If I could understand all this legal shit and knew what I was signing, I'd have my signature on the thing as fast as I could scrawl it out, but I know we can't take any unnecessary chances. Even though the biggest payout for me will come from the betting, this is too important to fuck up.

"I hear you. I'm sending it your way, and you can explain to the lawyers that they can't go crazy on this thing. Just make sure we're not getting screwed. It's not the time for them to shine by pointing out every damn detail that could go wrong."

"Got it. I'll deal with the lawyers. Good thing I'm already in a shit mood." He strides out of my office, his footsteps slapping against the floor.

I check the time. Less than an hour before I need to meet my new trainer.

There's no way I'll be able to concentrate on anything in this office with the prospect of the fight so close I can practically taste it. *Fuck it*. Might as well head to the gym early.

I grab my bag and head for the door.

When I arrive at the address Bohannon texted me, which is around the corner from the gym I keep seeing him at, there is a sign that reads PROFESSIONAL COMBAT COACHING.

I open the door and head inside, knowing that today has the potential to be brutal. I have less than thirty days to be ready to face Bodhi Black, and I'm going to need every single one of them to be in top shape.

When we fought three years ago, he was the hottest prospect in the city. He tore through one guy after another, leaving dozens of opponents permanently injured. Most retired from fighting immediately afterward, including me.

I didn't lose, but I took a beating and sustained serious damage that took months to heal. I was lucky, though, because none of the injuries were major.

Unlike Bodhi's knee.

Destroying it wasn't my plan, and I still have guilt riding me over what happened. But it wasn't a dirty move. He wouldn't tap out.

I knew if I let go of the heel hook before he tapped, there was a damn good chance he was going to win, and the money from that fight enabled me to have a real shot at leveling up. Urban Legend was a great underground club, but it served its purpose, and that wasn't the crowd I wanted to be surrounded with for the rest of my life. I may not have been raised with much, but I do know that you become like those around you.

Staying in the shadows would have meant getting sucked into action that I didn't want to touch. Which is why I made what most people would consider a terrible decision—killing the cash cow and putting every cent I had on the biggest bet of my life . . . going legit.

I'd been a criminal since I was eight, the first time I shoplifted. At sixteen, I was running with men twice my age, watching them get picked off one at a time by bullets or the cops.

That's not the life I wanted for myself or for the people I loved.

Which brings me back to the here and now, and the doorknob I'm holding, preparing to step into a strange world that exists between the one I know and one that's totally foreign. My fights have always come with more risk than a sanctioned fighter would possibly face, because death was never out of the question. But this one . . . I may not be walking away under my own power, but at least I won't be going out in a body bag.

At least, not if I can take out Moses first.

It'll happen. That's the way it has to be.

In the meantime, I need to be ready for anything.

I jog up the stairs with my bag slung over my shoulder and open the sleek glass door at the top. Inside is the sweetest training setup I've ever seen. It must take up the entire floor of the building.

Two different cages are set up at opposite ends of the space. One quarter is all weight lifting and cardio equipment. The last section is dedicated to heavy bags, speed bags, mats for grappling, and everything else you could possibly need to train.

A man with salt-and-pepper hair walks away from the two guys currently sparring in one of the cages and meets me where I stand near the door.

"Gabriel Legend in the flesh. It's a pleasure to meet you." He holds out his hand to me. "I'm Jeb Goodwin."

I shake his proffered hand. "Nice to meet you. Thanks for doing this."

"For Bo, we'd do damn near anything, but when we heard the favor he wanted, we jumped in with both feet. I've been watching you for a long damn time. You've got skills, but with our program, you're going to be a monster in the cage. Our gym will probably be at capacity after word gets out you trained here."

It's always surreal to hear when people have watched my fighting career through all those YouTube videos, but that's the magic of the internet. It makes the world a hell of a lot smaller place.

"I appreciate it more than you know. Bodhi Black is training with my old coach. I'm definitely working from a disadvantage, because Johnson knows how I move and think."

Jeb shakes his head. "That's some real shady shit on the part of your former coach, but smart if you're Black. Don't worry, you're gonna look like a completely different fighter when we're done with you. Even your old coach won't recognize the new and improved Legend."

"That's a big promise with less than four weeks to go until fight night."

Jeb grins. "Just wait. You'll see. I'm damn good at what I do. Don't start thinking this is for pansies because I train movie stars. They're just the only ones who can afford me on the regular. I know my worth."

I don't even want to think about how much this costs, but I know one thing—I'm not going to waste a goddamned minute of the time I have here.

"Then let's get to it. I'm ready to warm up."

"Perfect. Let me introduce you to your new sparring partners. You're gonna be best fucking friends by the time that fight rolls around."

FOURTEEN

I've plowed through a ton of work in the few hours Gabriel has been gone when my phone chimes from a text. At the same time, it buzzes with a notification from the security app connected to the camera and intercom at the front door. Given everything that's going on right now, I don't ignore either of them.

The text is from Hal.

HAL: Guy with brown hair at the front door. Older man with him. Sending a photo for ID. I'll take care of them if you want them gone. You won't even have to open the door.

The picture comes through a few seconds later. *Chadwick and my father.*

I drop my head into my hands and release a long sigh. Chadwick is the last person I want to deal with today, and I have absolutely no idea why he's here with my father. I was sure that after I saw my dad at the gala, I wouldn't be hearing from him again for a long, long time.

Apparently, I was wrong.

What could they possibly want?

I tap out a reply to Hal.

SCARLETT: *That's my ex-boyfriend and my father. I'll deal with them.*

HAL: *You sure? Because I'm happy to take care of this, Ms. Priest.*

SCARLETT: *Thank you, but I've got it.*

HAL: *Okay. I'm notifying Legend. He'll want to know.*

I hope like hell that Hal's text won't disturb Gabriel, but I'm glad he's keeping him in the loop. It makes me feel safer. Regardless, my goal is to get them out of here as fast as humanly possible.

I pick up my phone and tap the app that allows me to see who is at the door and talk to the person. "Hi, Chadwick. Dad. Is there something you two need?"

Down at the front door, Chadwick glares at the unit where he knows the camera is located, blocking my view of everything but my father's shoulder behind him.

"This is bullshit," Chadwick shouts. "I don't know what the fuck you told the cops, but this is complete and total bullshit."

"Scarlett." My name sounds like a curse on my father's lips as he steps around Chadwick and comes into full view of the lens. "This is unacceptable. Whatever you told the police, you need to retract it."

They can only be talking about one thing—the information I gave the detective last week about the online stalker. The police must have finally questioned Chadwick. However, I'm not retracting anything. It's illegal to give authorities false information, and I did no such thing. They're only looking into possible leads, and where there's smoke, there's usually fire.

I pinch the bridge of my nose and shake my head. *My father didn't even ask me if what I said was the truth. He doesn't care that I'm being harassed and potentially stalked. He just wants me to make it go away.*

"Good to see you too, Dad. So glad you could stop by in the middle of the day. I know you're incredibly busy, so I'll keep this short. I told the police what happened, and they're handling the investigation as they see fit."

My father's face pinches with annoyance. "I am not having this discussion with you while we're standing on your damn doorstep. Let us in, Scarlett."

The camera angle is wide enough that I can see Hal walking up the sidewalk behind them.

"If Ms. Priest wants you to go, gentlemen, then go. *Now.*"

Both my father and Chadwick turn around to face him.

"I don't know who you are, but if you're another one of my daughter's *men*, then I suggest you leave immediately. This is a family matter, and you are not involved," my father says to Hal, who stands in the middle of the sidewalk with his arms crossed over his barrel-shaped chest.

"If by men, you mean one of Ms. Priest's security guards, then that's correct. I'm one of her men. And unfortunately for you, you're on private property, sir. If she wants you gone, you're gone." From the tone of Hal's voice, it's clear that he means business if they resist. "I'm more than happy to remove you myself, or we can call the police. I'm sure they'll be interested to hear of your visit."

Shit. A scuffle right in front of Curated is the last thing I want to happen. Plenty of paps cruise by the building on the regular, hoping to get a shot of me or my celebrity clients coming or going. If they catch a fight going down, that publicity is *not* going to be ideal.

"I'm coming down," I say into my phone before rising from the kitchen table.

A few minutes later, I unlock the dead bolts on the front door and stand face-to-face with my father and Chadwick.

Chadwick lunges toward me. "What the hell did you tell them? That I was harassing you? Because that's bullshit, and you know it."

"Calm yourself, Chadwick," my father says, in a tone I've always considered patronizing as hell, before meeting my gaze. "Scarlett, if you're upset about how your relationship ended, then you should've stayed in counseling. Telling the police you think Chadwick is bothering you is not how we handle things in this family."

I blink at both of them for at least thirty seconds because I'm utterly stunned. "Excuse me? You think I'm upset about how our relationship ended, and that's why I went to the police? Did you just come from a five-martini lunch?"

"I'm not drunk," Chadwick snaps with his lip curled. "And I do not appreciate being treated like a criminal. The police can save that for your trashy new fuck boy. I'm sure he's used to it."

It never hit me until this very moment that Chadwick looks a bit like an irritated opossum when he's angry.

From behind them both, Hal speaks up again. "Mr. Legend is on his way. You should clear out, gentlemen."

Based on his emphasis on *gentlemen*, it's clear Hal thinks they're nothing of the sort. I feel the same way about them confronting me like this without any concern for the threat I reported to the police.

Chadwick whips around to glare daggers at Hal. "Fuck him, and fuck you."

My father comes closer to me, and I step back out of instinct.

His eyes narrow. "What in the world is going on with you? Is this his influence? You're looking at me like I'm a stranger and not your father."

I choke on the audacity of his words and let out a cough-laugh. "Are you serious right now? You . . . *you* may be my sperm donor, but you've never been a real father. God, why didn't I see it before? You don't give a damn about me if it doesn't directly impact your life or your bank account. If you were really a father, you would've been at the hospital when I was having surgery—"

"I was busy," he says with a sharp tilt of his head. "And it was just your appendix. Stop trying to make a big deal out of something so inconsequential."

I blink at him again. "Do you even hear yourself right now? What is wrong with you? You haven't even asked me what I reported to the police, or why I feel like I'm unsafe enough that I had to report *anything* to the police. Have you ever cared about me, Dad? Or does that only happen when it's convenient for you or to your benefit?"

"Are we going to play twenty questions then, Scarlett?" Chadwick says, interrupting. "Or maybe you should just tell us and stop acting like a spoiled brat with a secret. Did someone hurt your poor feelings?"

His mocking tone makes me want to slam the door in their faces and never open it again. *Acting like a child? Oh, I could show them immature.*

"Go fuck yourself, Chadwick. If you're the troll who has been harassing me and stalking me, then I hope they catch you red-handed so it's easier for me to press charges. Because I won't let you try to crush me with your threats."

From Chadwick's wide-eyed expression, it's clear I've shocked him. "That's why the police questioned me? Because someone's threatening you, and you think it's me?"

I lift my chin another inch. "I dumped you, and you didn't take it well. That's what the police call motive."

"This is ridiculous," my father says. "Chadwick doesn't have time to threaten you. He's busy working, Scarlett. I can't believe you'd waste our time with some petty little matter."

My lower lip trembles. *Petty little matter. My father thinks my safety is a petty little matter.*

I look over his shoulder to Hal, who has one hand tucked underneath his suit jacket. I'd be willing to bet that his fingers are resting on the grip of a gun.

But I don't have time to say anything because the roar of an engine fills the air, just before Gabriel's Bronco charges down the street and screeches to a halt in front of my building.

When he jumps out, he's shirtless, shiny with sweat, and *running* toward us.

FIFTEEN

Both men spin around, staring at me like I'm Tarzan, about to beat my fists against my chest. Good, because that's exactly how I fucking feel right now seeing them standing between me and my woman.

I was exhausted after training, but as soon as I got that text from Hal, it was like mainlining adrenaline.

These two assholes, two men who should have protected Scarlett, are standing on her doorstep, and according to Hal, yelling at her.

Not on my fucking watch.

"Hey!" I yell as I point to the younger one. "You got no reason to ever come near this building or Scarlett again. Get the fuck out of here while you're still able to walk, or I'll remove you in a way that ensures you never will again."

At least the shithead has the sense to step away from her and throw his hands in the air. "I didn't do anything. I didn't touch her. I swear."

The older man, Scarlett's father, steps in front of Chadwick. "I don't know who you think you are, but this is a family matter, and you are not family."

Oh, this motherfucker.

"*Family?* Family shows up when your girl is in the hospital getting cut open and sewn back up. *Family* is there to make sure she gets home safe and is taken care of. *Family* is there for her every fucking day while she's recovering, making sure she takes her meds and isn't in pain. I don't remember seeing you here while I was doing all that, old man. So step the fuck down and don't tell me any goddamned thing that has to do with Scarlett isn't my business. She's my woman, and if you so much as make her shed another fucking tear, so help me God, I will make you regret that decision for the rest of your life."

A cold, calculating gleam comes to life in his gray eyes, which are the only damn thing he gave his daughter. "If you touch me, I'll make sure you spend the rest of your worthless life as a guest of the State of New York. I hear Rikers is lovely this time of year. Don't test me, because I will bury you."

"Dad!" Scarlett comes forward a step, but I don't need her to shield me from her father or his threats.

I open my mouth, about to tell him exactly how things are about to go, when I notice the wet spot on the front of Chadwick's tan suit pants that's growing larger by the second.

Instead of yelling, laughter booms from my lips.

"Are you fucking kidding me? You pissed yourself? Jesus Christ, I knew you were a piece of shit, but I didn't realize you were a gutless coward too. Makes sense how you could stoop to harassing her online. Too big of a pussy to say a goddamned word to her face."

Scarlett sucks in a breath as Hal laughs beside me. Chadwick's face turns a mottled red as Lawrence Priest whips his head to the side to look at his crotch.

An expression of complete and total disgust crosses his face. "Whatever Chadwick is, he is not *harassing* my daughter. I provided his alibi to the police for the time periods in question."

"Was he even with you, Dad?" This comes from Scarlett, her

words rife with betrayal. "Or did you just cover for him because that's what you do for your buddies? Even when it's your *daughter* who is being threatened?"

Scarlett's father turns so that he's able to see both of us, and I decide I'll make it even easier for him. I shove past him and take my position next to her. He shifts with a sneer on his face, recognizing the move for what it is—a power play.

With Hal at his back and me next to Scarlett, there's not shit he can do.

"Chadwick isn't behind any threats. He's much too busy with company matters to bother you. Whatever the police think, you need to tell them they are mistaken."

"Scarlett doesn't take orders from you, old man. And she wasn't fucking mistaken about anything. If your boy here didn't do anything, then he's got no reason to be pissing himself." I look pointedly at the wetness on Chadwick's pants and shake my head. "You might think I'm shit, but, man, you gotta recognize that your daughter leveled up."

I take a step toward him, and impressively, the old man doesn't back away. "Because I ain't pissed myself since I was in diapers, and it would take an army to get between me and my woman. Whatever you came here for, it ain't happening. So you better leave before we call the cops and have them question you again right now."

Lawrence straightens and his jaw rocks from side to side. He cuts his attention from me to Scarlett. "I don't even know who you are anymore, Scarlett. Come on, Chadwick. We have business to take care of. This was obviously a waste of time."

SIXTEEN

Scarlett

My father turns and strides down the sidewalk with his head held high and not a single care in it for me.

My knees go weak, but Gabriel's arm wraps around my waist, and I lean into his strength. Never before has a man stood up for me like that . . . and it kills me that it had to be Gabriel defending me from my own father.

"Let's go inside," he whispers into my ear.

I nod woodenly. "Okay."

He walks me in the front door of Curated and leads me to the sofa. I collapse onto it, but the tears don't come like I thought they would. I'm just . . . empty.

Gabriel waves at Hal and says something to him, but the white noise in my head drowns them out.

My father doesn't give a damn about me. I might as well be a stranger on the street.

It hurts, but the parts of my heart that used to feel like they would bleed from that knowledge are numb. Or maybe they're getting harder? Either way, I couldn't cry if I tried.

Gabriel locks the front door and comes to sit next to me on

the couch, pulling me onto his lap. He holds me there, rocking me against his bare chest, while I sit in silence for long moments.

"Did he break me?" I whisper the question. "Because I can't cry."

Gabriel shifts and tilts my chin up toward his face with his knuckles. "No one could break you, ladybug. Not your ex. Not your father. Not me. No one. You're too fucking strong to let any man do that. You hear me? You are a fucking warrior, and this shit might hurt like a motherfucker, but it will not break you."

I swallow, processing his words. "How is it possible not to care about your only child?"

Gabriel looks down at me with knowledge in his gaze that stabs at the unguarded part of my heart.

"I don't know, but if we get to the point where we have kids, they will never know anything but love from both of us. They will never feel the things we've felt, ladybug. The cycle ends here. I swear that on my life."

SEVENTEEN

I'm beyond sore after two days of training, but I'm so fucking excited about Jeb's plan of attack for taking on Bodhi that I don't even mind. I welcome the burn and the ache. It means *progress.* Getting ready for a fight this big in such a short period of time felt overwhelming until I had a team on my side that knew how to win and wouldn't stop at anything to get me where I need to be. Protesting muscles aside, I feel amazing when I walk into my office at the club.

Except, I don't even make it through an hour of work before Q is in my doorway.

"You've got a meeting you need to take."

"When?"

"Now. You're being summoned."

I look past him, into the hall, but I don't see anyone else. "By who? What the hell are you talking about?"

He rolls his bottom lip between his teeth. "There's a black car out front that's here to take you to the Upper Ten to meet with Creighton Karas."

I lean back in my desk chair and shake my head. "That's not

how shit works. I'm nobody's lapdog. I don't come when I'm called."

Q shoves his hands in the pockets of his slacks. "You really want me to send him away and tell him you're too busy?"

The very idea of being *summoned* pushes all my fucking buttons. Then I remember—I did this to myself when I asked for other people's money. I may walk around thinking I'm beholden to no one, but that's not the truth. Not once I brought on investors to make the club happen.

I look down at my sweats and T-shirt. They're clean since I changed into them after my shower at the gym, but they sure as hell aren't up to the dress code of Legend or the Upper Ten, the most exclusive cigar bar in the city, run by none other than Cannon Freeman.

"This is some shit, man. But if he wants me, then he's going to get me." I push off the arms of my chair and rise to my feet. I take a few steps toward Q, and he holds up a palm.

"Tell me you're not going like that. You've got a suit here somewhere. I know you do."

"No. This is me. If that's not good enough for Creighton Karas, then he can go fuck himself."

Q pales beneath that swarthy Puerto Rican skin of his. "He's a fucking billionaire and one of our biggest investors, Gabe. You've got to at least pretend to show him some respect."

"Like he's doing by sending a car to pick me up like I'm a kid at day care? I don't think so."

His head falls to the side, and his shoulders slump. "They won't even let you through the front door of that place in sweats. It'll be a wasted trip."

"We'll see." I clap a hand on Q's upper arm. "If he's got a problem with it, then he should've made a fucking appointment like anyone else." I glance over at Roux, where she's curled up in her bed in the corner. "You wanna come, girl? That'd make a statement."

My dog shoves her snout farther into the cushion. *I'll take that as a no.*

I leave my best friend and my dog staring after me as I stride out of the office.

You want to see me, Mr. Karas? Well, here I fucking come.

EIGHTEEN

"It's a pleasure to welcome you to Curated, Meryl." I open the door myself to greet her and let her inside.

As Meryl steps across the threshold, I watch her face for reactions to the main floor of the store. With bright eyes, she scans the room and grins. "This is lovely. And it's all for sale?"

"Almost everything. Some of the furniture is from my personal collection and not available for purchase."

She wanders inside and turns in a circle, stopping to look more closely at a pair of sterling silver ballet slippers sitting on the end table. "My daughter would love those. She's in her fourth year of ballet."

"According to our records, they used to belong to one of the members of a dance company in Moscow."

Meryl smiles. "In that case, I must have them." A light laugh follows. "And to think I was resistant about coming. I've hardly made it through the front door and already found something I can't live without. This is going to be dangerous, isn't it?"

My grin is so wide, it almost hurts. "I'm not sure what you were expecting, but we pride ourselves on having a unique collection of one-of-a-kind items that will tempt you unmerci-fully because once they're gone—they're gone forever."

Amy hovers a dozen feet behind Meryl, at the antique desk where we process payments from the general public when we're open on Fridays. She's been even more anxious than I have for this appointment, because she knows how much I've wanted Meryl as a customer for months. Even though I promised I could handle it on my own and Amy could take the afternoon off, she stayed to see exactly how it went.

"Would you like to follow me upstairs? The third floor is where all the newest items are displayed."

Meryl glances around the room. "Do I get to come back down and pick from all of this as well? Because I've got my eye on a few other things, and we've barely scratched the surface."

"Absolutely. The entire store is your playground for the after-noon, Meryl. We can take however long you want."

She squeezes her hands in front of her, and I wonder if she's secretly trying to stop herself from clapping them together like a kid standing in front of a bakery case. "All right. Show me the way."

"If you'll follow me."

We reach the third floor, and Meryl's mouth drops open.

As soon as she called on Monday afternoon to make this appointment for today, I pulled out all the stops in our restock-ing. Did I go a little overboard? Maybe. But I don't care. I want to impress her—*need* to impress her. I'm not sure why I care so much, but it goes deeper than me seeking her approval.

I think . . . I think I want her friendship, and this is the best way I know how to start. There's just something about Meryl Fosse and her commitment to her causes and her convictions that inspires me to grow and evolve.

Curated can't just be about creating the perfect social media feed, and I'm starting to realize that it never was. It has always fed my need to make sure that unique and beautiful items aren't lost and forgotten in our world where everything seems to be disposable and nothing is built to last anymore. I want people to appreciate amazing workmanship, and the time and effort it took to craft so many of our pieces by hand.

"Oh my word, it's like Ali Baba's cave—full of treasures," Meryl says in a soft voice as she turns in a slow circle.

She walks toward the curio cabinet with mismatched hand-painted pieces of china displayed on delicately tatted lace. But before she reaches it, she stops next to the sofa and studies a blown glass lamp in the shape of water lilies.

"Scarlett . . . this, this is incredible."

She stares at the lamp in awe, reaching out to touch it, but stops before her fingertips make contact.

"You can touch it. It's delicate, but not that breakable. It makes me think of Monet."

Meryl's head turns toward me. "I learned how to paint by studying the water lilies. This takes me right back to my teenage years when the only thing that made any sense was a brush in my hand and paint on my smock."

"I didn't know you were an artist."

Her fingertips gently skate across the green glass. "My mother told me I'd never make a living at it, and I'd be better off putting my efforts into finding a husband. She was probably right that I couldn't make a living at it, but I wish I hadn't packed up my paints quite so soon." She retracts her hand and turns to face me. "I have a wall at the center that needs a mural, and I was going to commission someone to paint it for me. But this . . . this makes me wonder if I still have any skills left to do it myself."

"All you can do is try," I say with an understanding smile. "I'm sure the kids would love to see your work."

Her eyes light up. "They're the most wonderful group of children I've ever had the pleasure of meeting. Did I tell you we have a carnival Sunday afternoon? It's open to the public . . ."

I know what she's getting at. She wants us to bring Bump, and I think it could be amazing for him. "I don't think we're busy. I'll talk to Gabriel and Bump, and see if we can make it work."

Meryl's teeth flash pearlescent white as she beams at me. "Excellent. Now, time for me to shop."

NINETEEN

When the Escalade Creighton Karas sent rolls to a stop in front of the building housing the Upper Ten, the driver climbs out of the front to come around and open my door, but I can manage myself. We meet on the sidewalk as I shut it behind me.

"I'll show you up, Mr. Legend."

"I can find it," I tell him.

The suit-clad man produces what looks like a credit card from his breast pocket. "You'll need this to access the top floor of the building. If you leave with it, it'll be deactivated within hours."

"I'll leave it with Karas. Don't worry, I won't be in a hurry to come back. This isn't exactly my scene," I say, glancing down at the sweats I've shoved up around my calves and the running shoes on my feet.

"Understood, sir. I'll be out here to return you to Legend once Mr. Karas is finished with you."

It's on the tip of my tongue to tell him not to worry about it, but my promise to Scarlett won't let me. *No taking unnecessary chances with my safety.*

"Thanks."

He inclines his head, but I'm already striding toward the doors. Inside, the building looks like it's been restored to its glory days of the Roaring Twenties. It definitely gives the right vibe for a high-end cigar club that even I can appreciate, although cigars have never been my thing.

The keycard gets me up the elevator, and the hair on the back of my neck stands up when I hit the top floor. *They've gotta be watching me.* I don't look for the telltale signs of security cameras, though. There's no point. They're definitely here.

The elevator lobby leads to two massive wooden doors. I haul one open and find myself in an entryway with a high ceiling and a fancy-looking clock in the corner. One wall is glass, and through it I can see the crown jewels of the Upper Ten—boxes upon boxes of cigars in a big glass room that must be temperature and humidity controlled. Rumor on the street is that they've got millions of dollars' worth of tobacco in this place, which seems fucking crazy to me. *To each their own.*

A man who is built a hell of a lot like Bodhi Black stands between me and the next set of doors, which lead into the Upper Ten. I have to give him credit, though. His eyebrows don't go up when he sees me wearing gym clothes.

"I'm here for a meeting with Creighton Karas."

"Of course, Mr. Legend. Please come with me."

Without introducing himself, he turns and pushes open the door, and I step into the hallowed halls of Cannon Freeman's club. I didn't expect to feel instantly jealous, but that doesn't change facts. Anyone who runs a club like this knows what they're doing and has his shit together. I can't deny how nice that would feel.

Fucking hell. This place is *swanky.*

I try not to meet any of the curious eyes that lock on me as Team No-Neck leads me across carpet so soft that my shoes sink into it. It even smells expensive up here, like I shouldn't be breathing the air. Something about its rich man's old-world library atmosphere makes me feel even more out of place than my clothes.

I'm not built for this life, which is a real kick in the ass, because Scarlett is. *I can't give her this. I wouldn't even know where to start.*

Except . . . then I see Da Real Ting, a rapper who got his start on the streets slinging drugs, sitting at a table in the corner next to a guy in a sharp suit. Ting, wearing black jeans and a black T-shirt, gives me a chin lift, and I feel oddly more at ease.

Maybe it doesn't matter where you come from when you're rich as hell and don't give a fuck what anyone thinks of you. Maybe then, you just know you belong, because no one can tell you to leave. I have no idea what that feels like, but I'm pretty sure I'd like to.

I return the rapper's silent greeting and follow the big man from the entryway back to a hallway with heavy wooden doors every several feet. He stops in front of one and knocks.

"Enter," a muted voice says from inside.

Instantly, I pull my shoulders back and stand tall and proud. I may be wearing forty-dollar sweatpants, but I'm not walking in with shit posture.

Team No-Neck swings the hefty door open, and I step inside to see Creighton Karas wearing a three-piece suit and holding an unlit cigar in one hand.

"Mr. Legend. Thank you for joining me on such short notice." Karas, a dark-haired man with gray starting to lighten his temples, smiles as he rises from the leather club chair.

I step farther inside, and the door shuts behind me. "I was under the impression it wasn't a request I should refuse."

He holds out a hand, and I firmly shake it.

"I appreciate your flexibility, Mr. Legend. Have a seat."

"It's just Legend," I tell him. "No mister."

"Right." Karas nods as I claim the other big leather chair.

"Legend. You've really made that name work for you over the last few years."

"I'm just getting started." The words come out without any forethought.

His jaw rocks as if he's holding back a chuckle. "I like your attitude. How's the training going?" he asks, motioning to my clothes.

"Good. I'm just getting started with that too. Great coaches. Best I've ever had." I rub my hands down my thighs, just for something to do with them.

"I heard Silas Bohannon pulled a few strings and set you up. He's a good friend to have, or so my sister tells me. She and her husband are quite close to him." He taps the unlit cigar against the high-end table beside him.

"Bohannon seems like good people. I'm not real sure why he's helping me, but I appreciate it more than he knows."

"Yes, I would imagine," Karas says as he leans forward, the leather creaking beneath him. "And Bodhi Black's using your old coach to prepare for the fight. That had to be a blow to your confidence."

I study him with narrowed eyes. "How the hell do you know all this?"

Karas smiles, but it's not an expression of pleasure. It's more like what you'd imagine if a shark could grin. "It's my business to know things. Information is one of the most valuable commodities a man can possess."

I don't know what it is about this guy, but his presence demands respect. He's on a different level, one I doubt I'll ever be familiar with.

"So, is that why I'm here? You want information?"

Karas gestures with his cigar. "You want a stick before we start discussing business? It's on me."

It might be the one shot I ever have to smoke something that costs more than a used car, but I shake my head. "Can't. Gotta get my cardio up. Fifteen minutes in the cage is a fucking eternity if you're not prepared."

"Fair enough. I should've known. I'll abstain then. I wouldn't want the secondhand smoke to damage your chances of beating Black." Karas sets the cigar down in a lined box and closes the lid. "I'll save this one for later."

"With all due respect, Mr. Karas, can we just cut to the chase? I don't know what you want, but I've got shit to do, and I have no idea why I'm here."

Karas leans forward again, planting his elbows on his knees and lacing his fingers together out in front. "All right then. Your lawyers—have they sent the contract back for the venue or the fight?"

His question makes my head jerk back a few inches. "So you don't know absolutely everything that happens in this city?"

"I'm aware you got the contracts. The reason I called you here at the last minute is because I don't want you or your legal team to fuck them up. Call it protecting my investment."

I run my hand over my hair and scratch the back of my neck. "Your stake in my club is a drop in the ocean of your money. This shouldn't even take up a minute of your time. So, why is it?"

A faint smile ghosts over his lips. "I'm intrigued by you, Legend. You don't quit, even when the odds are unfairly stacked against you. You seem willing to do anything to save what you've built, including putting your own ass on the line to possibly take a massive beating. I invested in your club on a whim, but I've been fascinated by what's happened since then."

He relaxes in the chair and leisurely crosses one custom-suit-pant-covered leg over the other. "I'm not sure what to make of you because you don't fit any molds, and that intrigues me enough that I've taken a personal interest in the city's new *Legends*—the man and the club."

Part of me expected to be greeted with an ultimatum from Karas—win the fight or lose the club completely because he would pull the plug on the investments. But this . . . this is something totally different.

"I'm not sure what that means, Mr. Karas."

"Crey. That's what my friends call me."

It takes all my self-control not to stare at him slack-jawed in shock. "I wasn't aware we were friends, Crey."

That shark-like grin comes back. "We're not, but we will be. Now, let's talk about your plans for bailing out the club with your winnings from the fight."

TWENTY

Scarlett

So far, Meryl has chosen over a dozen pieces she can't live without. Amy has been carefully taking each one out of the rooms to be wrapped, crated, and delivered to her Upper East Side home tomorrow morning.

When she's finished her sweep of the third and second floors, we descend to the first so she can make a loop around it. I hand off the sterling slippers she spotted upon entry to Amy as Meryl picks up a small travel clock and then a watercolor framed in filigreed silver.

"This place is truly wonderful, Scarlett. I am so sorry for how I treated you when you first approached me about it. I was completely wrong about what you're doing. There's nothing fake about these treasures. This place matters. What you're doing matters."

The warmth of her approval makes me glow. "I know it's not the same as changing kids' lives, but I'm really proud of what I've built."

"You should be. I can see why you've been so successful." After taking a deep breath, she says, "I'm sorry I was so judgmental. I really didn't consider you had no idea about the tension between your mother and me. I shouldn't have transferred that to you. It was unfair. She'd be incredibly proud of what you've done with her space."

This time, my smile wobbles. "I like to think she would be too. She knew I didn't have her passion for fashion, but I love beautiful things and helping them find new, appreciative homes." I pause, mostly because discussing my mother with Meryl feels awkward. "By the way, I never did ask you how the silent auction and gala turned out. Did you raise the money you needed?"

Meryl's entire expression shifts. "It turned out wonderfully well. We'll be able to start construction on the new section of the center in a few months, exactly as we had hoped. I really do appreciate your contributions. Through them, you're helping change those children's lives too."

"That's wonderful news—"

A knock comes at the front door, interrupting my train of thought.

Amy bustles out from behind the counter to answer it. Given what happened the last time I had an unexpected visitor, I go quiet until the door swings open.

"Flynn?"

My former stepsister stands outside. Wearing leggings and a hoodie, she looks even younger than twenty. Amy lets her in, and I move toward the entry.

"Are you okay? Is something wrong?"

Flynn sees Meryl behind me and shakes her head, but I don't believe her. Meryl must pick up on the vibes, because she smiles at all of us.

"Scarlett, I'm finished for now." She glances at her wristwatch. "I've taken up more than enough of your time today. Thank you so much for letting me play. I'll just pay for everything and be on my way."

"It was my pleasure. You're welcome to come back as often as you like. Amy will handle the payment details and arrange to have everything delivered in the morning."

"I'll see you soon. Thanks again. Have a wonderful day."

I wish her the same and then lead Flynn upstairs.

As soon as we're out of earshot, she whispers, "Isn't that the lady you've been trying to get in here for months? Shit, Scar. I didn't mean to run her out."

"You're totally fine. She's been here for hours, and I'm sure she was ready to go." I open the door to my apartment and let her inside. As soon as the door closes behind us, I study her face, which seems paler than normal. "What's going on, Flynn?"

She rapidly shakes her head and then rubs her hands over her arms. "I don't know, but I got a really weird comment on my social media today."

Instantly, my entire body tenses. I've never seen Flynn rattled before, and that's exactly what she looks like now. "What kind of comment? From who? About what?"

"About you. From some private account. I couldn't get any more info. It . . . it wasn't nice, Scarlett."

"Please tell me you screenshotted it."

She slides her phone from her pocket and holds it out to me. "I did. Here, I'll show you."

I scan the screen, and the nasty words that normally cut like knives cause me to glare in rage instead. I've seen too many variations of them calling me a whore, a slut, worthless, fake, etc. to be shocked by them anymore.

But how dare this awful online bully come at me through Flynn? That is *not* okay. And yet there their horrible words are.

You're a cunt and a whore like that bitch Scarlett. You deserve what she's going to get.

I reach out and yank Flynn to me, wrapping my arms around her and squeezing tight. "I'm so sorry this happened to you. You shouldn't have to deal with this."

She grips me hard and doesn't let go for a few seconds. "Wait, why are you apologizing to me?" she asks as we loosen our holds. "You didn't do this. Some ass-clown with a toxic attitude and no fear of getting punched in the damn face did. So, what are we going to do about it?"

I think of all the screenshots I've sent to the detective who is handling the case, and the only thing they've managed to do is question Chadwick and get him riled up enough to come at me in person.

"I don't know. We've had cops looking into it, but they've found nothing. The accounts are all impossible to trace. I guess I should try something else, because this isn't working."

Flynn sassily careens back. "Damn right we need to try something else. You need a hacker to track this asshole down."

"That'd be really awesome, but I don't exactly know how to go about finding one of those."

"I'll ask around with the techy kids at school and see if I get any bites. I'm really getting sick and tired of you having to deal with this crap. And I'm sorry that I'm here adding to it."

I hug her to me again. "You shouldn't be apologizing either. This is neither of our faults. But I do appreciate your offer. If you find someone who can look into it, I've got a lot more accounts that they can dig through too. It's like this jerk starts a new one every damn day at this point."

Flynn plops down on the sofa and stares up at the ceiling. "Who would do all that? And why?" Her gaze cuts to me after a few moments of silence, because I don't have any answers for her. "Did the cops have you make a list of your enemies?"

I shake my head. "I told them about the messy breakup with Chadwick. They questioned him. He and Dad showed up here, indignant . . . but I don't think it was him. I honestly have no idea who else would spend their time doing this crap. It makes no sense."

Flynn reaches for her phone and taps the screen. "Let's start a list. Shitty suppliers. Angry customers. Men you wouldn't sleep with. We have to do something, Scarlett. This asshole can't keep coming at you. I won't have it."

Since the very first time the troll threatened me, I feel a wash of relief. We're nowhere closer to finding out who it is and putting a stop to it, but Flynn's concern fills me with warmth and gives me a new sense of hope.

This might not get us anywhere, but if it makes her feel better, then it's worth it.

I drop onto the sofa beside her. "Okay, let's make a list."

TWENTY-ONE

Creighton Karas decided we're going to be friends.

I have to say, that's the first time a billionaire has ever been interested in a goddamned thing I do, and it's a little weird. Not unnerving, because I don't get shaken by shit like that, but just . . . strange. And now he wants my plan.

I have two choices. I can give him the "I'm going to win; your investment is safe" speech, or I can tell him the truth.

Fuck it. I might as well go all in with my new *friend*.

"I'm going to win the fight, but I'm also betting big on myself. If everything goes according to plan, I'll make enough to pay off all of you investors, and the club will be mine free and clear."

This time, Karas's brows go up. "Interesting. That's how you made enough to open Urban Legend too, isn't it?"

This guy really does know everything, which is also fucking creepy.

"Yeah."

"How much are you betting on yourself?" he asks.

"As much cash as I can put my hands on."

"Where are you going to get it?"

I lean back in the leather chair and cross an ankle over my

knee. "I don't know yet. I was thinking about putting up the club as collateral with a loan shark."

Karas squints and strokes his clean-shaven chin and jaw. "Considering we've invested in your club, you're a ballsy son of a bitch to even consider it. You really think that's smart?"

"I don't have a choice. I have to win, and win big. I'm taking a massive risk just by winning."

"What do you mean?"

Karas picks up on the abnormality of what I said, and I shouldn't be surprised. I mentioned it for a reason. This shit with Moses is weighing heavy on me. I don't know what the fuck I'm going to do, because Eduardo flat-out refused to look into Moses after Q explained who he was.

"Someone from my past showed up Saturday night. He's betting against me. Wants me to get the odds right, and then—"

"He wants you to lose," Karas says, finishing for me.

My head falls forward, and I blow out a large puff of air. Even hearing it from his mouth sounds like shit. "Yeah, and I can't do that either."

"Jesus Christ, Legend. You've got yourself into a hell of a mess, haven't you?"

My shoulders feel like they're weighed down with bags of concrete, but I meet his gaze anyway. "Damned if I do, damned if I don't. That is, unless I can find Moses first and get rid of his threat."

"Moses?"

"Moses Buford Gaspard. A gangster out of Biloxi."

With his face dead serious, no bullshit in sight, Karas asks point-blank, "What'd you do to him?"

"Fifteen years ago, I jacked one of his trucks of electronics and fenced it for fifty grand. He wants his money back, with interest. One point five million."

"Well, hell." Karas laughs and pinches the bridge of his nose. "He's really turning the screws on you."

"That's nothing. His crew killed my girlfriend and shot her little brother in the head. Bump will never be more than a kid, no matter how old he gets. I won't let Moses take another thing from me. Especially not another person I love or my fucking club. Not happening."

Karas leans back and crosses his arms over his chest. "Let me get this straight. Your plan is to find a loan shark who'll front you a shit ton of cash, kill your arch nemesis, bet on yourself, win the fight, and walk away to live happily ever after with your new socialite girlfriend? Because that sounds like a hell of a lot for one man to carry."

"I don't have a choice. I gotta do what I gotta do."

"You always have a choice, Legend. But, even more, you need to learn how to ask for help. It doesn't make you less of a man. And right now, you need all the fucking help you can get. Today's your lucky day, because for some reason, I like you. I think you're a smart guy. You work your ass off. Your people are loyal as hell to you, and that tells me they respect you. But you can't do this alone." His fancy leather shoe kicks my sneaker to get my attention and so I'll meet him eye to eye. "You need me in your corner to pull this off."

"What do you get out of it?"

Creighton leans back in his chair, opens the box, and lifts the cigar once more to sniff the tobacco. "It's been a long time since I've had anyone try to tell me what to do, other than my wife and the tiny terrorist we made together. I don't run into many problems anymore. And you know what? Sometimes, a man needs a little excitement to keep life interesting."

I blink at him, trying not to gape. "You want to help me because you're bored?" *Fucking rich people sure have ass-backward problems.*

"And because you're an interesting man who is going to give me a great return on my investment—*years* sooner than planned. Now, let's discuss this Gaspard character, because Cannon's connections are going to find your gangster and deal with him so you don't have to."

Holy shit, he's going to put the mob on Moses? I lock my shock inside, fighting to keep my expression placid. "I'd appreciate that."

"I know. And then we're going to run the numbers and figure out exactly how much money I'm going to front you to bet on yourself and get out of this hole. No loan shark, just me."

"What if I don't win?" I don't even want to voice the thought, but I have to. What will Karas do to me if I can't pull this off?

That predatory smile comes back over his face. "Simple. I'll own you."

TWENTY-TWO

Scarlett

*O*h *my God. All I want to do is rip his clothes off and ride him. Holy hell, I had no idea this would be so freaking hot.*

It's Friday night, and instead of going to the club, I volunteered to go with Gabriel to watch him train at his new super-fancy fighting gym. Having watched his fights on YouTube and been shockingly turned on by them, I've been curious about what goes on in the gym while he's training.

The first part of the evening was a little less exciting, mostly warming up and some drills. But once Gabriel started sparring with the other guys, it was like watching my fantasy come to life right in front of my eyes.

The leggings I have on are going to have a wet spot if I don't get my thoughts under control.

Gabriel shoots for a takedown, grabbing his opponent by both legs and yanking him off his feet. It's vicious, yet graceful. Violent, but elegant. When the guy slaps his palm on the canvas, Gabriel pops to his feet and offers him a hand up.

I'm salivating because *I* want to be the one to take Gabriel down and pin him there while I do all the naughty things running through my mind. Visions of that thick, hard cock sliding between my lips and then thrusting inside me are enough to have me turning away to look out the windows on the far wall.

Jesus Christ. No one told me I'd need a fire extinguisher to keep myself under control while watching this stuff.

Gabriel is setting up to continue sparring with a fresh partner, when Jeb stops next to me.

"If you're bored, you can always hit the bag. Gabe told me you want to pick back up on your self-defense training."

I have no idea how to tell the older man that I'm not the least bit bored. But in the interest of not making a fool out of myself by launching myself at Gabriel and mauling him, I take Jeb up on his offer.

"I'd love to. Just point me in the right direction."

"I'll get one of the other coaches to give you some instruction. It'd be our pleasure. We do women's clinics once a month for free, if you ever want to come to one of those too."

"Really? That's awesome."

Jeb shrugs. "It's a sad thing that we gotta teach women to defend themselves in this world, but ever since my wife got mugged coming home one night, it's been a passion of mine." He turns and calls out to a younger guy in red sweats a few feet away. "Charlie, come help Scarlett out. She's going to hit the bag. Give her some pointers."

Charlie, a sweaty trainer in his late twenties, waves and jogs over. "Happy to. Come over here with me, and we'll get your gloves on."

I glance at Gabriel, who is taking his one-minute break. He salutes me as he sucks back some water and listens to the other man whose name I forgot, but I think he's the Brazilian jujitsu coach. I point to the area where the bags hang and follow Charlie to an equipment locker.

Once my gloves are on, I smack them together. "I've missed this."

"Good deal. Let's get you going."

Twenty minutes later, I'm drenched in sweat and smiling huge. "Damn, that feels *good*."

"You're a natural at boxing. Some women are afraid to punch through the bag, and are more comfortable just tapping it. You've got more power than you realize."

I open my mouth to reply but am distracted by a woman walking across the gym floor . . . and straight toward the cage where Gabriel is fighting. Her perfectly coifed black hair tells me all I need to know about her identity—Lucy Byers. But *what the hell* is she doing here?

Charlie turns and follows my gaze. "You know that chick?"

"Oh yeah, but what I don't know is what she thinks she's doing here."

Jeb strides in her direction, hopefully to eject her skinny ass, but she grabs hold of the cage and shoves her face into the spot where Gabriel is leaning against it to catch his breath.

I remember what he told me about the "deal" he made with her at Meryl's gala to get her to stop bidding on my mom's necklace.

Oh, hell no.

I glance at Charlie. "I'll be back. I've got to take care of something."

Charlie's eyes widen, but I'm not paying attention to him anymore. My sneakers cross the floor silently, and I'm finally close enough to hear what she's saying.

"You promised me you'd make me scream, baby. There's no better night than tonight. I'm getting tired of waiting for you. And that's before I realized how *hot* you are when you're a sweaty beast. I'll even let you fuck me in the locker room. Just pin me up against the wall and nail me to it. You know you want it."

Gabriel lifts his gaze over Lucy's shoulder, and those vivid blue eyes lock with mine. There's an apology in them, but he doesn't owe me one. This is all on Lucy.

I stop behind her and tap her on the shoulder with my glove.

"I'm busy, as you can see—"

I jab her in the shoulder the second time, and she whips around to face me.

"Scarlett! I had no idea you were—"

"Shut the hell up, Lucy."

Her eyes narrow into slits. "Don't you talk to me—"

"Quit talking and listen, because I'm only going to warn you once. You're never going to approach Gabriel ever again. You're never going to come to my store again. You're never going to breathe my name or his name to anyone in this town or on this planet ever again. Do you hear me? You are toxic, and I don't ever want to see you or hear about you for the rest of my life."

Her glare intensifies, and something malevolent gleams there. "You stupid bitch. I'm here because your precious Gabriel wants *me* and not you. Shouldn't be too much of a surprise, since your last boyfriend wanted me too. I can't help it if you can't keep a man satisfied, Scarlett. You're just an uptight prude who wouldn't know what to do with a big dick if it slapped you across the face."

I see red as the words *see you next Tuesday* flit through my brain.

I don't know what happens in that moment, but I snap. I haul back and my glove slams into Lucy's left cheek.

She stumbles back, falls against the cage, and lands on her ass before unleashing an unholy screech. "She hit me! Call the police! You're going to jail, you bitch. I have witnesses!"

No one moves. Not me, not Gabriel, and not a single one of the other men in the gym. Everyone stares at Lucy on the floor.

From just behind me, Jeb speaks first. "I didn't see anything. Anyone else see anything?"

The men around the room all speak up, one by one.

"Nope."

"Not me."

"Didn't see nothing."

"She must've tripped and fallen."

Gabriel stands tall in the cage and stares down at Lucy. "Don't ever come looking for me again. I didn't promise you shit . . . except that you'd scream. Looks like I followed through on that. Get the hell out of here."

Lucy sucks in an angry breath as she climbs to her feet. Whipping her head in one direction and then the other, her glare lands on the unfriendly faces of every man in the room before finally stopping on me again.

"You just made the biggest mistake of your life, Scarlett Priest. I'm going to ruin you. Just wait. I'm going to enjoy this."

Given what I've been through lately and everything we still have to navigate, her threats don't register.

"You're just a mean girl who never should've left prep school, Lucy. If you come at me, I'll bury you. Don't tempt me."

She screeches again before stomping out, shoving past the trainer near the center of the room. As soon as the door closes behind her, a slow clap starts. Gabriel and the other men join in.

I walk toward the cage as Gabriel opens the gate and comes down the stairs. He wraps me in a hug and picks me up off my feet.

"Team Scarlett for the win," he whispers, and the gym fills with cheers as he kisses me.

Jeb grins at Gabriel. "I think you're done with your workout for the night, Gabe. Get cleaned up and then take this girl out for some dinner. You both could use a good steak tonight."

Charlie yells, "And watch out for her right hook."

Gabriel holds me tighter to his chest, and I'm overwhelmed with the moment.

"I punched her. In the face. I've never punched anyone before, let alone in the face."

"And you did a damn good job, ladybug. I'm proud as hell." He lowers me to my feet and drops a kiss on the tip of my nose.

"How about we both shower? I've got some sweats you can wear home."

My earlier thoughts about how hot it was to watch him spar come rushing back. *Shower with him? In the locker room?*

"That sounds like a great plan."

TWENTY-THREE

I'd never expect Scarlett to fight a battle for me, but damned if I'm not turned on after watching her haul off and punch Lucy Byers right in her arrogant face. It was fucking perfect.

With that bitch out of my mind, the only thing I care about is getting Scarlett's gloves off and hurrying her into the empty locker room. As soon as the door closes, I throw the dead bolt on the inside of the door.

Scarlett grins. "Are you thinking what I'm thinking, stud?"

I have no complaints about the nickname, especially because I'm thinking *exactly* what she's thinking. "You and me. Right here. Right now."

Scarlett's tongue darts out to swipe across her lips, and her chest heaves as she draws in a deep breath. "I thought you'd never ask."

We collide in the center of the locker room, intent on tearing off each other's sweaty clothes. As soon as I've got her naked, I circle my hands around her waist and lift her into the air to drag her perfect tits across my chest.

"You were a warrior out there. That was so fucking hot," I tell her as my lips skim over her skin, tasting the saltiness from her sweat.

"I should be saying that to you," she whispers, tugging my jock strap and cup off. "Because I seriously thought I might lose it when you were wrestling in the cage. I wanted to come in there, mount you, and ride you until I made us both see stars. Or maybe wrestle with you and let you pin me and take me any way you want."

My cock, already hard, stiffens almost to the point of pain.

"Fuck, I love you, woman."

I adjust my grip and throw her over my shoulder, slapping her on the ass as I carry us both toward the showers. I flip on the water and wait a few beats until it starts steaming. Backing into it, I check the temperature before lowering Scarlett down under the spray and pinning her to the wall.

"I'll take you however you need me to. And if you want to mount up and ride, I'm your fucking stallion, ladybug. Whatever you want, you get it. You never have to wonder, because I'm on board for every fucking thing you can possibly imagine."

Her gray eyes glow, the hunger highlighted by the flickering fluorescent light. "Right here. Right now. I can't wait."

Her orders come out like breathy moans, and my cock bounces against my lower stomach.

"Fuck yes. Wrap your legs around me."

She doesn't hesitate. My cock presses flush against her pussy, and Scarlett grinds against it, her hips rocking as if she's trying to push me inside.

"I got you, baby. You're gonna take me right here."

I separate our bodies enough to wrap my fist around my dick and angle it so the head breaches her entrance. Hot, wet, tight heaven grips the head, and I press forward an inch.

Her body softens as her eyes close. "Oh God. More."

"As you wish." I slide inside, inch by hard fucking inch, until I'm balls deep. "This is gonna be rough and rowdy. Hang on."

With her arms around my neck and her nails digging into the muscles of my shoulders, I grasp her waist and lift her off my cock only to slide her back down, impaling her with each stroke. Her clit grinds against me, and the sound of Scarlett's screams fill my ears. The whole gym will hear us, but I can't find it in me to give a single fuck what anyone thinks.

This, right here, is everything.

Scarlett's head slides back and forth against the tiled wall of the shower, and then I feel the hard pulse of her inner muscles locking down on my cock. She comes so fucking hard that she nearly traps me inside.

My balls tighten, and lightning shoots down my spine. There's no chance in hell of keeping my roar at bay. It booms and echoes off the walls until my head finally drops forward to rest on the cool tile beside her head.

"Holy. Fuck," I whisper. That was a goddamned religious experience if I've ever had one. My legs shake and my arms feel like rubber, but that was *incredible.*

I open my eyes and brush my lips over her forehead. "You okay, ladybug?"

Her eyes flick open, and the gray is hazy and soft. "I'm more than okay. Actually, that's the perfect way to end a workout."

My laughter booms, echoing the same way our cries did. I can only imagine the ribbing Jeb and the guys are going to give me about this later.

Worth. Every. Fucking. Second.

"Come on, baby. Let's get you cleaned up and go home. We'll order in steaks. God knows, I could eat a damn cow."

Scarlett presses a kiss to my lips. "That sounds perfect too."

TWENTY-FOUR

I'm shocked to see Harlow and Monroe when Pat parks the SUV in front of Dolly's on Saturday morning.

"You're both early!" I dodge a few pedestrians on the sidewalk and rush forward into their open arms.

"I told you she'd be shocked," Monroe says to Harlow with a giggle as they both hug me.

"More like I thought I was being punked." I pull back and scan Monroe's face. She looks a million times better than she did at my kitchen table, freaking out about losing Nate. "Are things better?" I ask quietly.

I've only heard from Monroe once since she came to my place —after I checked in with a text. She replied with a simple, *I'm okay. We talked. I'll fill you in later.*

With all the craziness going on in my life and Gabriel's, I haven't had a chance to talk to her and get caught up, so I was thrilled when Harlow suggested brunch this weekend to our group chat. I need some quality time with my girls.

"I am, actually. I'll tell you everything that went down when Kelsey gets here," Monroe replies with a genuine smile that calms some of the anxiety I've been carrying for her.

"Fair enough. Flynn should be here soon too. I'm glad you girls are welcoming her into the fold. I know she's young, but—"

"Psh. That girl is more mature than I am," Monroe says, waving off my comment.

Harlow squeezes my hand. "We love the little firecracker too, you know. If she wants to roll with our squad, then she's more than welcome."

"Here she comes! Hey, street racer." Monroe waves Flynn over to us. "We were just talking about you, Little Miss Badass. Did you win any cool cars last night?"

Flynn stops next to me, and I throw an arm over her shoulder to pull her into my side for a quick embrace.

"No to winning a car. Someone tipped off the cops about the race. We heard it on the scanner and bolted. Total letdown. I was supposed to be going up against some guy with a beast of a Chevelle, and I've *always* wanted one of those."

I lean my head against hers. "Do you have any idea how hard it is for me to listen to you say stuff like that without telling you to be careful, and maybe consider racing at tracks where it's legal from now on so you'll be safe?"

Flynn rolls her eyes my way and smiles at a guy about her age in a suit as he passes by us on the sidewalk. "Since you just told me that anyway, I'm assuming it's incredibly hard. Likely impossible."

"She's right, kid. That shit is dangerous. You need to be careful," Harlow says with concern in her voice.

"Who needs to be careful about what?" Kelsey asks as she comes up the walkway from our right.

Flynn and I spin around to face her. "This one. Running from the cops last night."

"To be fair, I didn't run from the cops. I simply drove away like I wasn't there for a street race. It's not as if any cop who pulled me over would even think I was part of that scene. I'm a college student, out late, grabbing more coffee to study for a test."

Kelsey looks her up and down. "You might look like that right now, but not when you're dressed in black leather from head to toe."

"Can we move this inside? I'm starving," Harlow says, patting her belly. "I'm practicing eating for two, because Jimmy and I decided we want to try to get pregnant."

"Oh my God!" Monroe squeals.

"Holy shit." Kelsey gasps. "That's like . . . serious shit."

Warmth floods my system, and my cheeks hurt from how wide my smile stretches as I stare at Harlow in wonder. "That is officially the best news of the entire day. I am so excited for you both."

She gives us a tiny shrug. "I'm excited, but also terrified. Can you imagine me as a mother? I have absolutely no idea what to do with a baby, but I can't seem to shake this feeling that I need to do it."

"You'll be an amazing mom, Har-har. I know it," Monroe says with a look of absolute bliss. "And I'm going to spoil the shit out of this baby and be the best auntie ever."

"Thank you, guys. I'll tell the hostess we're all here," Harlow says.

As soon as we're seated at the table, placed our orders, and have talked about all things baby with Harlow, Kelsey glances in my direction.

"I heard Curated was bananas yesterday after Meryl Fosse posted a pic of something she bought for her daughter. I literally danced in my kitchen when I saw it. I know you've been trying to get her as a client forever, Scar. That's so huge."

I wipe my mouth and take a long sip of water before replying. "She came by after the gala, and we really hit it off. I had no idea the reason she was so resistant to Curated was because she and my mom had *tension* before my parents were married."

Monroe smiles and waves to our server, her bloody mary almost gone. "No shit?"

"Yeah, I guess my mom thought my dad was into her or something. And it's quite possible he was."

"Talk about red-flag warning for your mom about your dad," Harlow whispers with her eyebrows rising. "But, obviously, I'm glad they still got together, because we got you out of the deal."

My smile comes and goes. "Definitely, but it was hard to hear from someone who wasn't a big fan of my mom. I feel like I've been putting her up on a pedestal since she passed, making her seem like a saint, when she was only human like the rest of us."

"Oh, honey." Kelsey reaches across the table to cover my hand with hers. "Of course you have been. That's what we do with good people we lose too soon. Your mom was an awesome woman who changed all of our lives through her work. She was an icon. Whatever flaws she might have had are irrelevant at this point. You're honoring her legacy, and that's exactly what you need to keep doing."

"Agreed," Harlow says with a sympathetic pout. "Besides, it doesn't matter anymore if you and Meryl are straight. You should remember your mom exactly the way you want to."

I make a mental note to bring it up with Dr. Grand at my next appointment, even though it's not really her specialty. Then I change the subject.

"Okay, Monroe. You're up. How did the conversation with Nate go? I've been dying to hear good news from you all week, but you've been quiet."

All eyes cut to Monroe, and hers lock on me.

"Okay. So . . . your boyfriend gives the best relationship advice in the history of the world, as far as I'm concerned."

I press my palms together like I'm about to pray. "Thank God."

"Wait, catch me up," Flynn says before she pops a chunk of potato into her mouth.

"I thought Nate was cheating on me. I went to his away game, followed the team around, and saw them leave with a woman."

She grimaces, but I urge her on with a wink. "Then I barged into his hotel room and searched it for her . . . but she wasn't there. Nate told me if we didn't have trust, we didn't have a reason to be married."

"Ouch," Flynn whispers in response to Monroe's matter-of-fact recitation of what went down.

"Yeah, it sucked a big fat donkey dick, and I thought my marriage was over. So I ran to Scarlett's and found Gabriel in her kitchen—in a *towel, because he just moved in with her,* I must add—and he gave me the best advice ever."

"What advice?" Kelsey asks as she reaches for her water.

"To be honest with Nate and tell him why I'm such a nut job."

"You're not a nut job," Harlow says with a shake of her head. "You've been hurt before. It's understandable."

"You told him everything?" I ask.

Monroe nods. "I told him *everything.* All six times I've been cheated on since I started dating at fifteen. Why I'm afraid he'll cheat on me too." Her typically perfect posture slips as her emotions begin to show. "That I really love him and I don't want to lose him, but I'm afraid he's going to find some younger, prettier model and trade me in like all the others have."

My heart clenches in response to Monroe's statement, because I never realized how much she's kept her scars hidden from us. She's always been the fun girl, the life of the party, the one willing to do anything on a dare. But inside . . . I can't help but think she's been looking for belonging and security all along.

Then again, aren't we all?

"Oh, honey." Kelsey rises from her chair and walks around the table to wrap Monroe in a hug. "I'm so proud of you for putting it all out there. No matter what happened, that was brave of you, and totally a bold move."

"I know." Monroe's lower lip wobbles. "Nate was pretty shocked too, but he was incredible. I cried, and he held me and told me I never had to worry about that with him, because he doesn't want anyone but me, exactly as I am. He loves me so much, you guys. I had no idea because I've always told myself that he's just saying it because he was expected to. But he *really* loves me. He told me he'd retire from baseball if that's what I wanted."

My mouth drops open. "You're kidding."

Monroe sniffs and looks up, blinking away her unshed tears. "No, for real. He said that he knows as long as he keeps playing, the job will put a lot of strain on our marriage, and he loves me enough to walk away from it all."

Tears stream down Harlow's cheeks. "Goddammit, you'd think I was already pregnant. What the hell is wrong with me?"

Kelsey slings her arm around Harlow's shoulder too. "You're a great fucking friend, that's what's wrong with you. God, you guys. Look at us working out our problems like adults and shit. I'm so proud of you, Monroe." Kelsey kisses her on the cheek and then straightens to pull a tissue from her pocket and hands it to Harlow. "It probably has some concealer on it, but you're still leaking, so use it."

Harlow dabs at her cheeks. "Is he going to retire then? Did you two decide?"

"I'm not going to let him walk away from doing what he loves because of me. Not until he's ready. Besides, I like being a player's wife. It might be even more fun now that I'm not worried that he's going to pick up a cleat chaser at every game if I'm not there."

"Good, and I'm not saying that just because Jimmy would be devastated because Nate's arm has plenty of good years left," Harlow says.

Monroe smooches the air at our friend. "Har-har, I love you. We'd better all be co-godmothers to that little rug rat you're going to have."

Kelsey returns to her seat with a laugh. "No offense, but I wouldn't even know what to do with a godchild until she's old enough to play with makeup. So you don't need to worry about me."

Harlow's gaze cuts to me. "Don't think we missed the part about Gabriel Legend moving in with you, Scarlett. Is that for real? Is that why you've got a beefy new security guy instead of just your normal car service?"

I glance out the front plate-glass windows to where Pat sits in the parked SUV. "Uh, well . . . that's complicated."

All four women stare me down. *Apparently, Monroe's out of the hot seat and it's my turn.*

"You didn't tell me Legend moved in," Flynn says with an accusing undertone. "And I was just at Curated. Are you keeping it a secret or something?"

"No, it's just . . . well, with this fight coming up, we had to shore up security."

Kelsey narrows her eyes on me. "I feel like there's something big you're not telling us."

I think about the scene from last week in Gabriel's office when Moses had a gun to Bump's head. *Do I tell them? Don't I?*

I make the decision on the fly. "Someone from Gabriel's past came back and threatened him. We're not taking chances right now. That's all."

"Shit," Harlow whispers. "The fight has been getting a ton of publicity now that the deal has been inked. That makes perfect sense."

I'm not going to correct her or elaborate on her assumption.

"Are you safe? Like really safe? Or do we need to be worried about you?" Monroe's acrylic nails tap nervously on the Formica table, and the waitress appears with our refills.

We're all quiet as she replaces our empties, and we thank her when she's finished. As soon as the waitress is gone, all eyes are on me again.

"I'm fine. I'm not worried."

Harlow still looks skeptical, but they don't push me any further on that subject.

"We're here for you, babe. Whatever you need. And just so you know, Jimmy is getting us two tickets to the fight, so I'll be there if you need me."

I could hug her for her solidarity. "Thank you."

"Wait, I want to come too," Monroe says.

"And me." Kelsey raises her hand. "Actually, I need two. My brother will be all over this shit."

"This is bullshit that you have to be twenty-one to get in," Flynn grumbles. "I have a fake ID. Just tell that tall, dark, and asshole side-kick of Legend's to let me into the club. I shouldn't have to miss it just because an accident of birth makes me a few months too young."

I bump her in the shoulder. "I'll see what I can do."

"Do we have a look planned for fight night?" Kelsey asks. "Because you're going to need to be straight-up fire for him."

"Gunter is making me a dress. He called yesterday and insisted. I was kind of shocked, to be honest."

Kelsey claps her hands together. "Hell yes. Gunter won't steer you wrong. This is going to be fabulous."

"If you get me a ticket and promise me I won't get kicked out, I'll give you the number of the hacker I got last night," Flynn blurts out.

My chin jerks in her direction. "You found someone?"

"Wait, why do we need a hacker?" Monroe whispers to Harlow.

Flynn crosses her arms over her chest. "Because Scarlett's troll came at me this week, and it's time to bring that asshole down. No more screwing around. If the cops can't find him, we will."

"Thank God," Kelsey says as she forks up a bite of pancake. "I'm so damn tired of that piece of crap ruining Scarlett's day."

Flynn smiles at her, and it's all teeth. "Not for much longer."

After we finish breakfast, we all spill out of the restaurant onto the sidewalk with lots of hugs and promises to do it again next week at the same time and same place. I'm totally free for that, considering Gabriel is training like crazy.

Flynn hugs me good-bye and heads off down the sidewalk, and then Harlow and Monroe hop into Harlow's town car, leaving Kelsey and me alone near the entrance. Pat is already out of the SUV, waiting by the door, and I hold up a finger to let him know I'll be a moment.

"Are you sure you're okay? Because I don't like the idea of you needing security and not telling us how serious these threats are."

I meet Kelsey's deep brown, almost black, gaze. "The guy that came back from Gabriel's past is pretty scary, Kels. I don't know what he's capable of, but we know that he's probably not going to do anything before the fight."

"How could you know that?"

"Because he's betting on Gabriel to lose."

Kelsey's eyebrows shoot to her hairline. "Legend's going to throw the fight?"

I shake my head. "No. He's not. Which is why we have to be prepared for whatever happens next."

"Shit, girl. This is heavy stuff. Why didn't you tell me sooner? You know I'm always here for you."

"Because it's not really my stuff to tell. And I didn't want Monroe or Harlow to spread it around. They wouldn't on purpose, but . . ."

"I remember what happened last time. I get it. I do. But, still, that shit is scary. You have to be careful. If there's anything I can do to help, all you have to do is ask."

"I know, and I love you even more for that. Come on, let me and Pat give you a ride home. Gabe's training all day, so I've got time."

"Oh . . . training. That sounds sweaty and deliciously hot."

The memory of what happened in the gym after I put Lucy in her place blasts into my brain. "Oh, girl, you have *no idea*."

TWENTY-FIVE

Bump is practically vibrating with excitement in the back of the SUV as we head to a carnival at the center for kids that Meryl Fosse runs.

I was on the fence about Bump coming along, but Scarlett made a good case for bringing him with us.

"What if he can have a positive impact on the lives of some of those kids? Meryl wouldn't keep inviting him if she didn't see potential in him. He loves working for you, but it would be cool for him to have something of his own too."

Give Bump an even more well-rounded life than he currently has? Yeah, it wasn't hard to get me to agree to that.

"You think they'll have Skee-Ball? Will it be like the arcade? I'm really good at Skee-Ball, remember?"

Scarlett shifts in her seat to smile at him. "I'm sure they'll have all sorts of games. Even if they don't have Skee-Ball, you'll find one that you're really good at."

"I hope so. But, mostly, I want to know if they have good prizes. What's the point of working hard to win if the prize isn't good?"

Bump's succinct view on effort and winning knocks a chuckle

loose from me. "Yeah, Bump. You're right about that. The prize has got to be worth the hustle."

"I'm a good hustler. Isn't there a song about that?"

I reach for Scarlett's hand and squeeze as we take the tunnel from Jersey and are officially back in Manhattan.

"Yeah, bud. There is. Why don't you tell Scarlett what you've been doing with Mike and Joanie?"

"I've been doing *so much stuff.* Big Mike let me push the button to crush a car yesterday. I worked really hard all week, and he finally said I could do it. You should've heard the crash. It was *awesome.* And Joanie made enchiladas last night and let me eat a whole jalapeño. It was *so hot.* I thought my mouth was on fire. I didn't eat any more after that. But Big Mike told me that I'd learn to like them; I just need some more Puerto Rican blood." His brow bunches, but he's wearing a half grin. "I don't know how I get that, but I sure do want it."

"Ah . . . I don't know how you get that either, bud. You're gonna have to ask Big Mike," I reply, but Bump is already on to the next topic, and it reminds me of how damn much I love this guy. This is the longest we've been apart in over fifteen years, and I've missed the hell out of him.

"I wish Roux was here. I miss her," Bump says with a slight frown. He's been away from her all week, and I wondered how he'd do with the separation. "She misses me too, doesn't she?"

"Of course she does," Scarlett says. "She's been my shadow every day she's with me. Whenever I move from one room to another, she comes with me."

"Roux is a good girl. I'm glad she's with you a lot. She'll keep you safe. Moses won't get you if Roux is there. Not like he got me."

A stab of regret rips through me when he says Moses's name. I'll never forgive myself for leaving Bump vulnerable to Moses for the second time.

I turn in my seat and face the back. "Are you sleeping okay? Have you had nightmares?"

"I had one, but when I told Big Mike, he knew how to cure it."

"What did he do?"

Bump bites down on his lip and speaks through a closed mouth. It comes out a mumble, but it sounds like, "*I can't tell you.*"

"Did Big Mike ask you to keep it a secret?"

Bump nods three times. For a second, I think he's going to hold out on me, but he can't do it. He opens his mouth and blurts out, "He took me to a titty bar, and I got a lap dance, and then I didn't think about anything but Kitty's pink pussy after that."

Hal chokes in the driver's seat as Scarlett slaps a hand over her mouth to cover her laughter.

I close my eyes for a beat and send up a prayer to the heavens for the Quinterro family. I owe Mike and Joanie a ton for keeping an eye on Bump, and even more for treating him just like he's one of their own.

"You're not gonna tell him I told you, are you? Because I really want to go back. Kitty was so pretty, Gabe. She had brown hair, and even though I couldn't touch it, it smelled so good."

"I'm not gonna tell him you told me. You know I got you, Bump."

His grin threatens to split his face wide open. "It was even more fun than Skee-Ball, and that's a lot of fun."

Scarlett changes the subject back to the carnival, and Bump latches onto it and leaves the stripper talk alone—for now. I have a feeling we'll be hearing more about it sooner rather than later. There's no way in hell he gets his first lap dance from a stripper named Kitty without wanting to go back and do it again . . . and again . . . and again.

Big Mike might have just created a monster, but I'm not going to fault him for it if it got Bump's mind off Moses.

Hell, I might as well just go change a hundred for a fat stack of ones just in case he has another nightmare. Maybe Big Mike is a goddamned genius.

By the time we roll up to the Fosse Center, the carnival is in full swing, from the looks of things. There's a small park across the street packed with big inflatable bounce houses, and a stream of kids and adults heading into the building.

"I am *so* ready," Bump says, cracking his knuckles. "Let's do this."

We climb out of the car, and I pause next to the driver's door while Hal rolls down his window.

"I'll park and come in. I can help watch over Bump."

I scan the street and note at least a half dozen officers in NYPD uniforms helping control traffic and keeping an eye on the park.

"This place is crawling with cops right now. Moses is too smart to try to make a move in a place where he'd be this exposed," I say, then rethink it. "But, yeah. Find a place to park, and I'll text you our location. I'm not taking any chances with either of them."

"Sounds good. I'll be back as soon as I can. Maybe go inside first. It'd be harder for him to go unnoticed in there."

I give him a nod. "That's exactly what I was thinking. Thanks, man. For everything."

"It's my pleasure. Be right back."

I push off the car and head for Scarlett, who is standing in between two inflatable towers near the door, getting our tickets.

"I could've gotten those," I tell her.

She swivels her head with a smile. "Not necessary."

"She got me so many tickets, Gabe! I'm going to play all the games!"

If the woman at the ticket counter thinks it's weird to hear a grown man sound like a child, she doesn't even blink.

We head inside and follow the big red footprints stuck to the gray floor, toward a gymnasium filled with carnival games. The first thing Bump does is grab Scarlett by the hand and drags her along after him while he checks out every one of them and the prizes they offer.

I follow behind them, noticing kids in wheelchairs, and a few who look like they've had it rough, just like Bump. But every single one of them has a smile on their face right now.

Well, shit. Maybe Scarlett is right about wanting to see if Bump would like coming here. Maybe he'd be able to help keep those smiles on their faces. Maybe it would keep a bigger one on his.

Bump does have a gift for it, and sharing it would probably make him happy as hell.

Before I can think any more about it, Bump spots a basketball game in the corner. Four hoops are mounted on a plywood board, and there's only one person playing.

"We can all play! Come on, guys."

Bump's enthusiasm is contagious. We all step up to the game and hand over the correct number of tickets.

"Is this a good time to tell you that I was never good at basketball in gym?" Scarlett asks with a giggle. "Because I was *terrible.*"

"You don't need to be good at basketball," Bump says, bouncing from foot to foot as we watch the other player finish his game while the attendant sets up ours. "You only need to be good at shooting baskets. No dribbling. No other players. Just you and the ball. Focus, Scarlett. You got this. I believe in you."

Scarlett's chin trembles, and a sheen comes over her eyes. "Thank you, Bump. I really appreciate that." I can hear the tears in her voice from Bump's ardent faith and encouragement.

"I'm still going to win, though," he says, shooting her a quick glance. "It's just how it has to be."

I look from one of my favorite people on earth to the other. This is what it's all about. No matter what happens during the fight or after it with the club, as long as I have these two, everything else will be just fine.

TWENTY-SIX

Scarlett

"I'm trying really hard not to be stunned that you beat Bump," I say with a pink stuffed bunny clutched to my side.

Gabriel glances at my prize. "It's not a salt-and-pepper-shaker set, but it'll do. *For now.*"

I grin at his mention of my salt-and-pepper-shaker addiction. *I love that he remembers the little things.*

Bump has Hal at his side, and the two men walk ahead of us. Bump declared he has to take another walk around the gym before he decides what to play next. He uses his hands as he talks to Hal, and warmth fills my chest. I'm so happy we came. I've missed Bump, and I know if I have, Gabriel must be feeling the separation acutely.

When we walk past a water-target shooting game, Gabriel pauses. "Do you see what I see?"

I jerk my head around toward the game and look. "What?"

He points to the upper right-hand corner. "There. It's black and red and white."

I search through the mass of stuffed animals until I spot it. "A ladybug!"

Gabriel's lips form the half grin that I love so much. "You

know I have to win that for you, right? Hal can stay with Bump for a few."

With a glance in their direction, I see Bump stop in front of a temporary tattoo station with a line of six people ahead of him.

"I think Bump's about to get tattooed, so you might have enough time to win that ladybug for me before he's done."

"Want to make a bet about how long it'll take me to win?" he asks with a dazzling blue wink. "Because I'll totally wager sexual favors any day of the week with you, ladybug."

"I already know you're going to win it."

"How?"

I lean in and press a kiss to his lips. "Because you're unstop-pable when you set your mind to something. Bump might believe in me, but I believe in you even more."

Gabriel's face goes soft. "Thank you. I needed to hear that. It means a hell of a lot."

"Whatever happens with this fight, we're going to be fine. I've already decided. Okay?" Who knows why I'm bringing it up now, but I need to hear him say it too. Win, lose, or draw, what he and I have is solid. We're going to flourish, no matter what.

"Yeah, I agree with you there. We're going to be just fine. But, first, I'm going to win my ladybug a ladybug."

"Okay," I say with a smile I can feel all the way into my chest.

Meryl finds us shortly after we've rejoined Bump and Hal. She nods at the two stuffed animals in my arms. "It looks like you're having a good time."

"We're having a great time. Thank you so much for the invite."

Bump stares at his feet instead of talking to Meryl, and for a moment, I'm worried he won't want to speak to her.

"Hi, Bump. Remember me? I'm Meryl from the arcade. I'm glad you could join us today. There are some kids I'd love for you to meet, if you're interested."

Bump's head pops up. "I like kids, even though they make fun of me sometimes for looking old but sounding like them."

My heart breaks right then and there for whatever teasing Bump has endured.

"These kids are very special, and they know what it's like not to be like everyone else. It's like a club, and I think they'll be really happy if you hang out with them."

Bump's eyes widen. "Really? That could be cool. I'm good at basketball. And Skee-Ball. And I really like—"

I freeze, afraid the next words out of his mouth will have something to do with Kitty the stripper. Thankfully, Gabriel wades into the conversation.

"He really likes making new friends. It's good to see you again, ma'am." And there's Gabriel's Southern charm again, making the temperature in the room rise. "Thanks for inviting us. Bump's having a great time. This place is impressive as hell, but I can see why you need more room. Lots of good work going on here."

From the pleased look on her face, Gabriel just slipped right onto Meryl's good side with that comment. I applaud silently in my head.

"Thank you, Gabriel. It's my passion. I know I've been a bit insistent on Bump coming, but you'll see why in a moment. Come with me."

All four of us follow her across the gym to a corner where a ring-toss game is set up. There are two boys in wheelchairs, and they look like they're both around eighteen.

"Omar. Ashton. Do you think you've got room for one more player?"

One of them turns around and looks at us and Meryl. "Why you wanna know, Mrs. Fosse? You bringing in another stray?"

"I'm not a stray," Bump says, and the boy who spoke looks him up and down from the wheelchair.

"No, but you old. You ain't no kid."

I open my mouth to intervene and explain, before Bump gets offended, but Meryl dives right in.

"This is Bump. You three have something in common, Omar."

Omar looks to the other kid beside him and then zeroes in on the strip of hair missing from the side of Bump's head. "He take a bullet to the head too? Fuck him up like us?"

Bump's head bobbles. "That happened to you too? Dude . . . I'm so sorry. It was the worst thing ever, but I'm okay now. You look like you're mostly okay too."

Omar looks down at the chair. "I'm learning to walk again. Ashton ain't so lucky, but it don't matter. When I walk again, I'll take him everywhere with me. We're brothers from another mother."

Bump squats down to their level. "I bet you still kick my ass at ring toss. I'm shitty at this game."

Ashton finally pipes up. "Then come on. Let's put some money on it."

"Boys . . ." Meryl's tone comes with a warning note. "No gambling. Remember?"

Omar and Ashton trade shit-eating grins before looking back at her and saying in singsong unison, "Yes, Mrs. Fosse."

Meryl smiles at the three of them. "I'll let you boys get acquainted." She turns to me and Gabriel as Bump hands over more tickets to the person in charge in exchange for his rings.

In a low voice, she whispers in my ear. "Thank you for coming. It really means a lot to me. Omar and Ashton both have been through so much, and it's hard for them to relate to people who don't understand what they've experienced. When I saw Bump, I just had a feeling I couldn't shake. If he's not interested in coming back, I won't push. But if he is, we'd welcome him with open arms."

That's something for Bump and Gabe to discuss, but I'm not too worried. "We'll let you know, but I think he's already decided he loves it here." I turn to see the three boys flinging rings and cheering when the others miss and they don't.

Meryl nods. "I hope so. Make sure you check out the park

across the street too and get some food. It's all terrible for you, but it's delicious."

"We will. Thanks, Meryl."

As she walks away, Gabriel leans in. "What did she say?"

"She sees Bump, and she values him."

Gabriel turns to look at her back. "She seems like good people."

"I think she is."

Then Gabriel goes still.

"What?"

When he scans the crowd again, Hal and I whip around to do the same.

"Who did you see?" I ask. "Moses?"

I catch sight of a light-skinned black man walking through the crowd, but his eyes are all wrong to be Moses, and Gabriel relaxes.

"No. Not Moses. Not today, and hopefully never fucking again."

TWENTY-SEVEN

After Bump finishes playing ring toss with Ashton and Omar, I'm ready to get the hell out of the packed gym. I'm on edge in the crowd, but having Scarlett and Bump within reach and Hal keeping watch along with me helps a hell of a lot.

Karas and the mob are taking care of Moses, I remind myself, but the uneasiness won't quit creeping up the back of my neck as we head to the park across the street. It's busy, with over a dozen food trailers offering all your typical carnival fare, but not as crowded as it was inside.

Hal walks with us, not far from Bump, who is carrying a massive inflatable guitar he won during the last game of ring toss, and I force myself to relax and enjoy the day instead of looking for trouble. One thing I've learned the hard way—every time I look for trouble, I find more than enough.

We walk toward a trailer with a karaoke setup, and a kid who can't be more than thirteen is belting out AC/DC's "You Shook Me All Night Long" like he'd written it himself.

As soon as Bump hears the song, he stops, and a look of pure excitement takes over his features. "It's my song!" he yells, then breaks away from our group with his inflatable guitar.

The man running the karaoke freezes for a few seconds, and the kid misses a few words of the vocals. Bump climbs up onstage, but before they can stop the music, he starts rocking with the inflatable guitar like he was born to play. A smile stretches across the kid's face as he throws up the devil horns, and he belts out the lyrics even louder.

Hal and Scarlett watch with bemused expressions, but I can't stop laughing. It's pure Bump.

I wrap an arm around Scarlett and sing the words of the chorus in her ear. Her head swivels at my vocal performance—which isn't half bad, if I do say so myself—and she joins in. By the end of the song, a crowd has gathered in front of the trailer, and even Scarlett has her hands up in the air and is jumping with the beat.

As soon as the music dies, the crowd bursts into cheers and applause.

"Encore!" Scarlett yells, and the kid whispers something to Bump.

Bump nods and yanks a handful of tickets from his pocket and shoves them at the kid.

"What are they doing?" Hal asks, scratching his head and then scanning the area, never fully letting his guard down.

"Oh, Bump isn't done yet. The kid will play air guitar until the strings fall off, if you know what I mean."

Hal chuckles as the strains of "TNT" come through the speakers next. Scarlett claps and screams to cheer Bump on, and he *eats it up.*

Bump holds that inflatable guitar like he was meant for the stage. All those years of playing *Guitar Hero* definitely paid off.

When they hit the chorus, the crowd goes wild, and everyone sings along. Scarlett is bouncing on the balls of her feet, trying to see over a tall man who keeps bobbing in and out of her vision, so I pull her into my side.

"Trust me?"

It's a simple question, only two words, and her answer is just as simple.

Her gray eyes, bright with excitement, meet mine. "Of course."

Fucking hell. Hearing her say that without hesitation and knowing that I've earned her complete trust sends a charge through me.

"Up you go," I tell her, squatting down and pointing to my shoulders.

"You want me to get up there?"

I wave her closer. "Best view you'll get. You don't want to miss Bump in his element, do you?"

"If you think it's a good idea . . ."

"Come on, ladybug. I'll hold your toys and your purse."

She hands off her handbag and ladybug to me, and Hal takes her bunny. After a moment of adorable-as-hell trepidation, she goes for it, climbing onto my shoulders until her crotch is situated against the back of my neck and her knees dangle forward over my chest.

"Up we go," I say over the music and the people singing along to the lyrics. When I stand, she becomes the tallest person in the crowd.

After another verse, she gets more comfortable and releases her grip on my shoulders. I glance up, and all I can see are her arms in the air, proudly rocking the devil horns as she yells, "Go, Bump! You rock!"

Right in that moment, I fall in love with her all over again.

My sophisticated socialite knows all the words to AC/DC's "TNT," and she's not afraid to climb on my shoulders and cheer on the man who will always be a boy because of a bullet.

Before I met Scarlett, if anyone had asked me to describe my perfect woman, I wouldn't have had a clue what to say. If I'd have been pushed, I probably would have gone with a generic description, because I never thought I'd find one who was perfect for me. Not even in my wildest dreams would I ever have been able to describe Scarlett Priest.

On paper, we're all wrong. It just goes to show that how things look from the outside doesn't mean a damn thing. Life is messy, like Scarlett's favorite hashtag says. We don't always know what we need until it's right in front of our faces.

I almost fucked it up, but if I know Scarlett like I think I do, she wasn't going to let me. She's too smart for that. Thank God I caught on too, because Scarlett Priest is the best goddamned thing ever to happen to me, and I will never take her for granted.

I squeeze her thighs on my shoulders to make sure she's safe up there, and then together, the entire crowd belts out the last chorus. The cheers and applause are nearly deafening, and the cops have all gravitated toward the crowd.

Bump and the kid take their bows before jumping off the stage.

At least Bump didn't try to crowd surf, I think as he rushes up to us.

"Wasn't that so badass? Could you feel the energy? I was in the *zone*, man!"

I don't know if it's possible to get high off an air-guitar performance, but Bump looks like he's blissed out to the max.

I squat down to the ground, and Scarlett scrambles off my back and throws herself at Bump for a hug.

"You were *amazing*! Your stage presence is legendary!"

Bump smiles so wide, his face may split in half. "It's because I'm an honorary Legend."

When he releases Scarlett, I take my turn, giving him a back-slapping hug. "Killed it, bud. Damn fine job."

He fist-bumps Hal before looking at me with a hopeful

expression. "I'm so hungry after that set. Can I get a corn dog and fries? You know I gotta feed my inner rock god."

It takes everything I have to keep a straight face. "Yeah, bud. Let's go get you some food."

"I could be talked into french fries," Scarlett says with a grin. "Because I can smell them from here, and my stomach is sending out clear 'get in my belly' signals."

"Yes!" Bump plays another air riff before charging through the crowd. People slap him on the back and give him high fives, and he handles it like a damn rock star.

Maybe I should get him a real guitar. That thought is quickly followed up by a second one—*when I don't ever have to share a wall with him again.*

Why didn't I think of it before? Probably because I've been so worried about getting the club up and running and going legit, I've had tunnel vision for way too long. That's coming to an end.

"You want anything? Or . . . can you eat anything with your training?" Scarlett asks as she takes a step to follow after Hal, who is a few feet behind Bump.

"A few fries won't hurt me. I'll eat more broccoli later."

"Good. Let's get in line before Bump sweet-talks his way to the front using the 'I'm with the band' line."

I chuckle as she threads her fingers through mine and tugs me along behind her. My feet almost stay planted to the ground, though, because I'm staring at our hands. Scarlett looks back and then down at them.

"Something wrong?" she asks.

"No. Not at all. I just like holding your hand. I like it a lot."

The soft glow of happiness radiates from her entire face. "I like holding your hand too, stud. It's one of my very favorite things."

It's so different from the faint echo of my mother's voice in my head. *"You're too old to be holding my hand, aren't you, boy?"*

Something that's been inside me for a long damn time—a hardened edge, sharpened by my mother's abandonment—dissipates like mist rising off the surface of the Hudson.

I follow along behind her, feeling so fucking grateful for this day that nothing can possibly bring me down.

TWENTY-EIGHT

W
e find a picnic table in the middle of the park. Bump leans his inflatable guitar carefully against the side so he can devote his full attention to devouring the three corn dogs he ordered.

I fear for his stomach, but I can't say anything because he looks so confident and proud.

Watching him onstage was a riot. If that performance doesn't prompt Gabriel to buy him a real guitar and get him lessons after things settle down, I will do it myself. *I mean,* after we discuss it like adults and find him a soundproof place where he can practice. But in my head, I'm already trying to decide what color guitar he would want. Black or blue, maybe?

"I forgot how good these things are," Hal says with a moan of pleasure as he takes a bite of his own corn dog. *Brave man.*

As Gabriel takes over hawk-eye duty while Hal grabs a bite, he steals a few more rough-cut french fries out of the big bucket we've placed in the center of the table.

I lick salt off my fingertips, thumb through pinky. "This is better than any restaurant I've been to in the last month, bar none," I say with a wink. "Sometimes you just need potatoes, grease, and salt."

"And family. Family is the best spice," Bump adds, sounding like a wise man.

Gabriel reaches out to throw an arm around him and pulls his head against his side. "You definitely got that right, bud."

"So, does that mean you'll come to the barbecue next weekend at Big Mike and Joanie's? I told them you might be too busy to come, but Big Mike said I was crazy and that you wouldn't miss it."

I glance back and forth between the two men and watch as Gabriel's face softens. "Of course I wouldn't miss it. Big Mike's barbecues are the best."

Bump throws both hands into the air, sending a chunk of the cornmeal coating from his dog flying over his head. Thankfully, the projectile flings the opposite direction from my face, and I smile at Gabriel.

"I've never been to a barbecue . . ."

Bump's mouth drops open. "No way," he says in shock. "You are not living, Scarlett."

His comment, so straight to the point and innocent, like I've learned is typical from Bump, hits me right in the solar plexus.

He's right. I wasn't living. Not before Gabriel and Bump came into my life.

Gabriel reaches across the table and covers my hand with his. "Don't worry, you'll get your fill of them in no time. Mike would have one every Sunday if he could talk Joanie into fixing all the food that often. You'll love her. I promise."

"And you'll meet Dani and Tony and Carrie and Christopher . . . oh, and Melanie, and maybe more. It's *so much fun*. Gabe had to miss the last two, but Big Mike bet me he'd come to this one and I never bet against Big Mike because he's always right even when you don't think he could always be right." He heaves for breath after that mouthful and then gulps down half his bottle of water.

"Sounds like I'm coming to a barbecue then."

"This is *awesome!*" Bump throws his hands into the air again before lowering them and turning to Gabriel. "Can I have another twenty? I want to get a lemonade. You know, the kind that they squish the actual lemons into and then put a chunk in the cup? I saw it when I was in line, but my hands were full . . ."

Gabriel reaches into his pocket and pulls out another twenty-dollar bill. "Get your lemonade, dude. Rock gods can't be thirsty."

The look on Bump's face as he swivels and rises from the picnic table is priceless.

"I'll come with ya, Bump. I could use some lemonade to wet my whistle," Hal says, also rising.

"You want a big one or a small one? Because I'm getting a big one," Bump asks as the two men take off to the trailer with two giant lemons wearing ball caps on the side.

As soon as they're out of earshot, I grab Gabe's hand in midair, while he's reaching for another fry.

"You getting stingy?" he asks.

"No, but we have to get Bump a guitar. And lessons. And see if he likes it for real. God, Gabe. He looked so happy. Did you see how he soaked up the energy from the crowd?"

Gabriel nods. "I saw it. I was thinking the same thing." He tangles his fingers with mine. "I don't know how it'll go, but it'd be worth it just to see if he enjoys it."

"Okay, good. So we need to find someone who knows about guitars, and get the right one for him. I'll talk to some people."

Gabriel's shaking his head while I'm talking.

"What? Am I moving too fast on this?"

"No, you're fucking perfect. I can't stop thinking about how damn lucky I am that Bump decided to steal you for me."

My cheeks stretch with my grin. "I know. It'll never sound

normal, but I'm so glad he kidnapped me. Just thinking about missing out on all of this would level me."

He brings my hand across the table and presses a kiss to the back of it. "And my life wouldn't be nearly as good without you. It's still early with all this, but I know what I want, Scarlett."

"What?" I whisper as my heart thuds impossibly hard.

"You. For as long as I can possibly have you."

My eyes burn instantly with happy tears. I know how he feels about me, but when he puts it like that . . . *instant melty puddle*. "I know the feeling, cowboy."

Gabriel's shoulders shake with laughter. "I thought we decided on *stud*?"

My grin widens. "How about *mine*?"

He closes his eyes for a beat, and when he opens them, I caption the expression on Gabriel's face as *When I Make Him Happy*.

"That's perfect, ladybug. Absolutely fucking perfect."

TWENTY-NINE

I push the bucket toward Scarlett on the picnic table with a smile on my face that feels like it'll never come off. "I better leave the rest to you, or Jeb is going to wonder what the hell happened to me tomorrow."

"If you insist," she says before diving into the rest of the delicious fries.

Before she can pop another one in her mouth, Bump comes rushing back to the table, and he looks like he's seen a ghost.

Instantly, I bolt to my feet, all systems on alert. "What happened? Is everything okay?"

"I . . ." He huffs out a few breaths while he tries to find his words. "I . . ."

"Sit down. Are you okay? Where's Hal?" I press Bump down onto the bench, his back to the table, with my hands on his shoulders.

Scarlett jumps out of her seat and rounds the table to sit beside him. "What's wrong, honey?"

"I . . . I saw him."

My stomach twists into a wicked knot. Even though I'm 99

percent sure who he's talking about, I ask the question anyway. "Saw who, bud?"

Bump shakes his head back and forth with tiny, fast movements.

I spin around to look for Hal, but the man is nowhere to be seen.

Fuck. If Moses is here . . . I'm wishing I had a nine tucked into the back of my pants, but I didn't exactly think that would be welcome at a community center carnival. I scan the crowd, locking in on every face that could possibly belong to Moses, but none of them are him.

I turn back to Bump. "Was it Moses?"

Scarlett pulls him hard into her side with her arm wrapped around his shoulder. "You're okay. He can't get you. Not here. Not now. I promise."

"He was here. I saw him. He looked right at me with those creepy eyes. Evil eyes."

Fuck. Moses's eyes are definitely the most distinctive thing about him. They seem to glow an unearthly greenish gold.

"Where did you see him?"

"By . . . by the lemonade. I got mine, and I dropped it. Hal ran after I yelled."

I lay a hand on Bump's knee and squeeze as I push to my feet. "I'm so fucking sorry, bud. Goddammit. I'm done letting him fuck with us."

Scarlett looks up at me, and instantly, I quiet down. Now isn't the place or time to lose my temper over Moses. We need to wait for Hal, get the situation from him, and then get the fuck out of here so we can figure out a new plan.

Because if Moses can get close enough that Bump can see his eyes . . . he's close enough to kill.

A shaft of fear shoots through me at the thought. *No one hurts Bump again. No one touches Scarlett.* Those two things are nonnegotiable in my life, and I'm not going to let Moses change either of them.

I spot Hal coming through the crowd. His chest rises and falls faster than it did before, so I know he was running. "You lose him?"

He nods slowly. "Got into a car on the street and hauled ass out of here. I wasn't close enough to get a plate number. I'm so fucking sorry, Gabe. I should've gotten a plate. I should've gotten *him*. I feel like I fucking failed you."

"No," I say, shutting down his shame with a shake of my head. "Moses is smart. Wily. Always has been. He knew we were here. He wanted something, probably to shake us up and let us know he can still get to us. Checking on me would be right up his alley, and he said he would."

"Can we go home now, Gabe? I want to go home. I want Roux." Bump's voice sounds so weak after all the excitement it's been charged with this afternoon, and it makes me want to take out Moses right then and there.

No one gets to steal Bump's happiness.

"Roux is at my house, Bump. Do you want to come have a sleepover? You remember when you came before?"

Bump perks up, and I could kiss Scarlett for the suggestion. Her building is secure as hell, and Bump would be in a new, different place, so he'd be more likely to be excited and curious than terrified all night. At least, that's the outcome I'm praying for.

"Your house? The big house?" Bump's eyes are wide.

"You can see the whole place. Have a tour. But I only live upstairs, where you saw."

"Can we make a pillow fort again?"

"If you want," Scarlett says gently. "Or you can have your own room, and make one for you and Roux in there."

Bump turns to me. "I don't want to go home. I want to go to Scarlett's house."

I ruffle his hair. "Okay, bud. Then we'll go to Scarlett's house." I glance at Hal, and he motions toward the street.

"Car's a few blocks over. You want to wait until I pull up at the entrance to the park?"

"Yeah. That'll be good."

Hal heads off to get the SUV as we toss the remains of our food and the containers.

Bump picks up his air guitar and clutches it to his chest. "Why did Moses come back, Gabe? I thought we were done with him?"

The question makes me feel like a damned failure. What the hell are Creighton Karas's guys in the Casso family doing, and why the fuck haven't they locked onto Moses yet?

"He probably was just making sure I look like I've been training for the fight."

"He wants you to lose," Bump says with a frown. "I don't want you to lose. You need to win. It makes you happy to win."

This fucking guy. I swear to Christ, Bump gets how I think and feel better than anyone. He's totally attuned to my moods in a way that even Q isn't after fifteen years of friendship.

"Let's not worry about Moses or the fight right now," Scarlett says with a forced smile. "Why don't we make our way over to where Hal is picking us up? I'm sure Roux is going to be so excited to see you."

Bump forgets about Moses as soon as Scarlett mentions Roux, and I could kiss her for distracting him. He starts chattering about all the treats he's going to feed her, and how he's going to let her sleep on the bed—if that's okay with Scarlett.

By the time we reach the entrance and Scarlett has caved about letting Roux cuddle him on the bed, Hal is just pulling up in the SUV. We all pile in, with Bump taking the far back seat.

We're quiet for a few minutes, before Hal flips on the radio station and "Highway to Hell" is playing. A shiver rips up my spine, but Bump breaks out his air guitar and starts singing. I try not to take the words as a bad omen, but that only lasts as long as it takes for the ringing to start.

"Is that your phone?" Scarlett looks at me with a questioning expression on her face.

I shake my head. "No. Not mine."

"Mine's on silent," Hal says.

"Mine too," Scarlett adds.

"It's coming from your purse, though," I tell her as I point to her red handbag.

Scarlett shakes her head but digs into her purse anyway. "I don't have a ring tone that sounds like—" Her words cut off when she pulls out what looks like a cheap prepaid cell phone. "This isn't mine."

I snatch it out of her hand and hit the TALK button, but I already know who is going to be on the other end before I answer.

"What do you want?" I ask.

"Gabe . . . you're looking real fine. The training is already showing. You been workin' hard, haven't ya?" Just like I knew it would be, Moses's accented drawl comes through the other end of the line.

"What do you want?" I whisper through clenched teeth, even though everyone in the SUV can hear me.

"Nothin' much. Just wanted to see how you were doing. Can't I keep tabs on my old friend Gabriel *Legend*?"

I stay quiet, fighting the urge to yell and tell him how the fuck I really feel about him terrifying the shit out of Bump, *again.*

"Nothing to say to me?" His tone shifts, turning harder and more serious. "That's fine, Gabe. I don't need to say much to you either. Just wanted you to know that I'm watching you. Might even call it watching *over* you. Making sure nothing happens to my prizefighter so fight night goes off without a hitch. You stay healthy now. Eat your vegetables and keep training hard. And think of your old buddy Moses here and there if you need any motivation to make this shit count."

"Stay away from my people," I grind out as sweat collects on my forehead from all the rage I'm bottling up inside.

"You'd like me to promise that, I'm sure. But I don't take orders from you, *Legend*. I give them. Now, you and your new little family have a nice afternoon. Tell your lady I like her purse. She's got style."

My eyes lock on the red leather bag Scarlett pulled the phone out of. Moses wants me to know he was close enough to touch her.

The old me would lose my goddamned mind and threaten to kill him if he ever came anywhere near her again, but I can't do that right now, not in front of her and Bump. The kid's been through enough, and Scarlett doesn't need to hear it either.

"I hear you, Moses. Everything is coming through *loud and clear*."

"Good. That's real good. Now y'all go get some real food. Because you can't be training just on french fries. I am glad to see you finally found a woman who ain't afraid to eat, though. I always like me some meat on them bones."

Wrath is threatening to burst from every pore of my body as my temperature rises higher and higher.

"Don't look at her again. I promise you'll regret it."

His snicker is dark and twisted. "Then stay the course, boy. You know what you gotta do."

The call goes dead, and I drop the phone on my lap.

"It was him," Scarlett whispers.

My entire body feels like it's been filled with concrete. I don't want to move a muscle, because I'm afraid I'm going to do something stupid like punch through the window to my left with my fist.

I'm not going to let him dictate how the fuck I feel too, I tell myself, fighting for control over my rioting emotions. Moses Buford

Gaspard knows how to push all my fucking buttons, and I won't allow it to keep happening.

"I need to make a call when we get back to your place," I tell her.

"Okay, whatever you need."

I note her pale complexion and wide gray eyes. "Alone."

She nods slowly. "Okay. I'll take care of Bump, and you take care of business. We've got this, Gabe. Whatever it is, we've got it."

I sit quietly in my seat, staring out the window as we drive back to Curated, wondering what the fuck I've gotten myself into, and how the hell I'm going to get us all out.

I replay the call with Moses in my head a half dozen times, grappling with my anger. When we get out at Curated, Hal walks us up to the front door and checks every room in the entire building to make sure it's secure.

By the time we reach Scarlett's apartment, something occurs to me.

"He doesn't know about the mob," I whisper to myself.

"What?" Scarlett says from beside me.

I glance at Bump to make sure he can't hear us, but he's on the floor of the living room, letting Roux cover him with welcoming doggy kisses.

"I'll go outside with them so the dog can take a walk," Hal offers, and I nod. As soon as the door closes, I meet Scarlett's gaze once more.

"Moses didn't mention the mob."

After my meeting with Creighton, I filled her in on where everything stood, so my mentioning the mob is not a surprise to her.

"That's a good sign, right?"

I nod slowly, my confidence rising again. "Moses loves being the smartest guy in the room. He craves it. Even back in the day, he never missed an opportunity to show off how sharp he was. If he knew the mob was on to him, he'd have thrown that in my face and taunted me about being smarter than all of us. But he didn't. He doesn't know."

"Oh, thank God." Scarlett releases a breath with her palm pressed to her chest. "If he doesn't know . . . then that means there's still a good chance they can find him and—"

"Take care of him before the fight. Yeah. That's exactly what I'm praying for, ladybug. Because I don't know what the fuck else to do otherwise."

She comes to me and wraps both of her arms around my waist. "We'll figure it out. He's not going to hurt us, no matter what he says. We won't give him the chance, Gabe. I trust you."

I press a kiss to the crown of her head. "You're right. We've got this. There's no other alternative I can live with."

"I wish he'd just take the money," she whispers.

Instead of my ego brushing her off, I say the one thing I never thought would come out of my mouth. "If I get a chance to talk him into it, I'll do it. You have my word."

THIRTY

Legend

While Scarlett's getting Bump settled, I pull out my phone to call Creighton Karas.

When a billionaire tells you that he's going to take care of something, and that something pops up in the form of a prepaid cell phone in your woman's bag, the billionaire has some explaining to do.

Shockingly, he answers. "Hello, Legend. What can I do for you this Sunday evening, when I normally wouldn't answer calls from anyone?"

"Apologies for interrupting your weekend."

"I assume it's important."

I sit down at Scarlett's kitchen table, the prepaid cell in my hand. "Moses is still alive."

"Yes, he is. Did you expect otherwise?"

My eyes narrow on Scarlett's wall of salt and pepper shakers, like they could substitute for Karas somehow. "I thought you said you were going to have him taken care of?"

"I did. And I meant it."

I shake my head, and my knee bounces underneath her tablecloth. "Anytime soon? Because he made sure to get in my head today."

"What happened?" Karas asks, his tone still conversational, like this doesn't stress him out in the least.

"We were at a carnival. He dropped a prepaid cell in Scarlett's purse. Wanted me to know that he can still get to me—or her or Bump—anytime he wants."

"Ah . . . he must be getting worried that you're not going to play his game."

I shrug, even though Karas can't see me. "Apparently. But I've got less than three weeks left until this fight, and if you want your money back, then I need him out of my head. Out of the fucking city. Out of the fucking picture."

"Are you giving me orders, Legend?"

I hear the warning tone underlying his words.

"I'm just asking if you've got a plan, and if you do, what's the timeline on it? Because I need to know my people are safe." I tap my finger so hard on the tabletop that I'm probably leaving pockmarks in the wood. "You said we were friends, *Crey*. So you gotta understand that my people are my whole goddamned life. They're *all* that matters. I need this covered, or I'll cover it myself."

Karas is silent for several seconds. "There's a plan. It's in motion. I'll make a call and give you an update when I get it. But for now, business as usual. You work. You train. You go home to Ms. Priest. Forget about Moses."

I stare skyward, from his lips to God's ears. "You make it sound like it's easy."

Something clinks over the phone line, and it sounds like Karas is pouring himself a drink.

"It is. Focus on what's important. Don't get distracted. Have a good night, Legend. I'll be in touch."

The call ends, and I'm left sitting at Scarlett's kitchen table without any more answers than I had before I dialed his number.

Do I trust Karas? His father is Dominic Casso, who was the head of the Casso crime family for the last twenty or so years. *Do I have the choice to do anything* but *trust him?*

I think of my other options.

Eduardo, Q's PI buddy, refused to look into Moses. I don't have another PI who's even crazier, so that leaves me and Q doing the legwork. But it's my problem, not Q's, and he's got enough on his plate right now with running the club without much help from me because of all the hours I'm putting in at the gym.

So that leaves me. Hunting Moses. On my own. While trying to train, keeping Scarlett safe, and making sure I spend time with Bump. On top of all that, I don't have a damn clue where to start.

I lower my phone to the table as Scarlett walks into the room.

"Everything okay?" she asks with a crease forming between her eyebrows. "You look—"

"Like I'm wrestling with a problem I don't know how to solve?"

"Yeah," she whispers. "What can I do to help?"

I glance over her shoulder toward the living room, listening for sounds of Bump.

"He's all settled into his pillow-and-blanket fort with Roux. I gave him a flashlight and a notebook, and I think he's planning his career as a rock star."

That brings a weak smile to my face, but I don't reply immediately.

Scarlett pulls out the chair adjacent to mine, sits down, and covers my hand with hers. "You can tell me anything. I assume this is about the cell phone and the call."

My jaw rocks as I contemplate what to share. I want to be honest, but I don't want to frighten her when Karas assured me everything is fine.

"Yeah. I just called Karas to find out what the hell is going on. He said he'll look into it and give me an update." I drop my chin and shake my head. "I hate waiting and wondering. There's too much at stake."

I wait a few beats before I raise my head, because I can't imagine the look on her face is going to be excited. When I do meet her gaze, those gray eyes are contemplative.

"What can I do? Do we need to hire someone else to find him? Because I can pay for that, Gabriel. There's literally nothing I wouldn't give to make this man go away so we can go back to living our lives without looking over our shoulders every day."

Her offer is generous, just like Scarlett always is, but her concern is like a blow to my chest, knocking the air from my lungs. I hate that my bullshit has spilled over to affect her life. It's the one thing I never wanted to happen.

"I can go after Moses myself," I say quietly.

Scarlett's spine goes stick straight. "What?"

"That's the only other play I've got right now if I don't think Karas can pull it off."

Her jaw tenses, and she stares at me as she takes several long, slow breaths without speaking.

"You don't like that idea."

"Should I?"

I shake my head and stare at the centerpiece that she's perfectly arranged in the middle of the table. "No. Because I don't know what'll happen. Fuck, I really wanted to believe that Karas had this under control."

Scarlett reaches out to cover my hand with hers. "Did he say they *didn't* have it under control?"

"No. He just said it's in motion, and he'd give me an update when he got one."

She tangles her fingers with mine. "I know that relying on other people isn't your favorite thing, but sometimes we all have to. Let's think about it rationally. If you set out to find and handle Moses yourself, something else in your life is going to suffer— like your training."

"Or my time with you. Or Bump. Or my time at the club," I add.

Scarlett swallows. "Whatever you decide to do, I will support you, but I also think that you should give it another week. Keep training. We'll all stay vigilant. If a billionaire and the mob can't bring Moses down, then we'll find bigger guns together, okay?"

Hearing her refer to Creighton Karas and the Casso family as something less than the *biggest guns* around tugs at the corner of my mouth. She's doing a hell of a job calming me down and wrapping her head around this completely foreign world I've dragged her into.

"Okay. We give it another week, and then if nothing changes, we'll talk about those big guns." I lift her hand to my mouth and press a kiss to her knuckles.

"Good. It's all going to work out, Gabe. I have faith. You should too."

Later, as I lie in bed listening to the sound of Scarlett's even breathing next to me, I work on searching for my faith. It's been a long damn time since I believed in anything or anyone but myself and Q, but times are changing, and so am I.

Then again, maybe faith is like trouble, and it finds you.

THIRTY-ONE

Scarlett

A s we ride out to Jersey the Sunday after the carnival, Bump tells me all about Big Mike and Joanie, and Q's three sisters and their families.

From what I've been able to commit to memory, Big Mike was born in Puerto Rico and came to the States with his parents when he was young. Joanie was the first child her parents gave birth to in America. They met in high school, and Big Mike proposed the day after graduation. Joanie's parents wanted her to marry a doctor or a lawyer, not a guy who worked at his parents' scrapyard, but Joanie couldn't be talked out of her love for Mike.

They got married that summer, and Dani, their oldest daughter, was born nine months later, followed by Carrie, Zoe, and then Q.

It's hard for me to imagine the reserved Q growing up with three older sisters who apparently liked to dress him up in makeup, wigs, and jewelry, but I have to admit it makes me like him a little more. He's Gabriel's best friend, but he and I haven't really broken the ice since the day we met—except for when he agreed Gabe should move into the city.

I'm not sure if he's waiting for me to decide if this is more than I can handle and bolt, or if there's something else I did to piss him off. Either way, he's supposed to be at this family barbecue we're attending.

A family barbecue. I still can't believe this will be my first ever.

As excited as I am about it, I'm a little worried about all the women. I've met Zoe and adore her, but her older sisters and mom are supposedly very protective of Gabe, according to Bump. He told me that they liked that he didn't date because women always caused problems. They also advised Bump to stay single for as long as possible, because no woman could ever be good enough for him.

In Bump's case, I have to agree. But I'm hopeful I pass whatever test they have to see if I'm good enough for Gabriel. I know how much this family means to him, and I'd never want to cause problems.

Thankfully, since the carnival, we've had a whole seven days of life that seemed relatively normal. No more cell phones that weren't supposed to be there ringing in my purse. No more signs of Lucy, which did surprise me a little because I definitely don't think I've seen or heard the last of her.

Things at Curated are going better than ever, and we're selling out faster than before. We're even discussing opening on Saturday for the general public as well. The demand is so high that we had to stay open an extra two hours on Friday, and still sent almost fifty people home who didn't make it into the line before we closed it. It's a good problem to have, I suppose, so I'll roll with it. Our new warehouse space is officially organized, making our restocking quicker and easier, which means that we really could support the extra day open.

Last night, I talked Gabriel into letting me make an appearance at the club with Monroe and Kelsey. Attendance has been up every night, and it was amazing to see the dance floor packed with people having an incredible time. Legend is truly on its way to becoming everything Gabriel had dreamed of.

Harlow is officially trying to get knocked up, so she stayed home with Jimmy, and we sent them text messages all night asking if they'd made a baby yet. I'm pretty sure she wants to kill all of us today, but she'll forgive us eventually.

Gabriel's training is going well, at least from what I can tell. He comes home exhausted, and I have a food service preparing meals to fit his specialized diet so all he has to do is pop them in the microwave and devour. His muscles are even more defined now than they were before, and I'm secretly excited that we're heading into the last two weeks before the fight, because the workouts are going to slow in intensity so he's not as depleted at night. But the man has been running all over Manhattan with his training partners, working on cardio.

I know next to nothing about fighting, but apparently part of his coach's game plan is to make sure that Gabriel is able to fight hard and fast for the full three rounds without tiring. They don't think Bodhi will have that kind of stamina and will be exhausted by the end of the second round, since he's never had a fight that lasted any longer than that. From Gabriel's comments about the training plan, it's a solid one. Although, I get the sense that he wants to take Bodhi out in the first round, so he takes fewer chances with everything that's riding on this fight.

As much as I loved watching those old videos on YouTube before, I'm not entirely sure how I'll feel about watching someone try to punch Gabriel in the face right in front of me.

I can do this. He'll be fine.

That's what I keep telling myself, anyway. Like I told Gabriel last Sunday, we have to have faith.

Practicing what I preach, I've spent a few extra minutes each day letting the universe know exactly what I'm putting my faith in. I believe in hard work. Staying the course. And Gabriel.

One thing is going extremely well, however, and that's the tickets for the fight. They sold out almost as soon as they were offered for sale, and that has Gabriel breathing easier.

Now if we would just get the word that Moses is out of the picture, we could all relax. Creighton called with an update a few days ago, but it wasn't exactly what Gabriel wanted to hear. Moses is still alive, but the mob knows where he is, and they've given their word that they won't let him get near any of us. Every time he moves, they're on him.

It's something, at least, but we're not sure why they haven't *whacked* him. There has to be a legitimate reason. According to Gabriel, he thinks that they want Moses alive to use him to their advantage, or to take a fall for some mob-related crime later. He says that's how they work, so I have to take his word for it.

Considering that I'm not used to being in a position where I'm waiting to find out whether some bad guy is still alive or has met his maker, I don't have a problem with them babysitting him and making sure he can't hurt us.

To me, that's like finding a spider inside your house and using a piece of paper and a glass to trap and remove it rather than squashing it. I'm pretty sure Gabriel and I have differing opinions on how to deal with spiders, though. Which is fine.

Stop worrying about everything, Good Scarlett hisses in my brain. *You're going to this family barbecue, and you need your head in the game. Time to impress the only family Gabriel really has.*

The reminder comes at just the right moment, because we're passing the service station and slowing down to turn into the driveway of the white house at the other end of the long green fence that conceals the scrapyard from the road.

"We're here! Time for football!" Bump claps from the back, and Roux shoves her head between the two seats in the middle where Gabriel and I sit.

Bump has been staying at Big Mike and Joanie's about half the week, and the other half with Gabriel and me. It's been a bit of an adjustment, but I know it's exactly as it needs to be. Even with the mob babysitting Moses, neither Gabriel, Q, nor Big Mike feel comfortable letting Bump go back to his apartment alone at night.

The front door of the house flies open as soon as Hal puts the SUV in park, and a girl who looks to be about middle school or early high school age stands there waiting.

"It's Melanie! I've missed her! She's going to be so happy to see you, Roux. You know that, girl?"

Thanks to Bump, I now know who she is. Q's oldest sister's daughter.

We all climb out of the SUV, and an older woman joins the girl in the doorway.

"You're just in time. Mike has only started devouring the guacamole. You might be able to get some before he finishes it," the older woman calls.

Gabriel holds my hand as we head up the walk, and Roux slides by us and dodges right between the two women, making her way into the house. The younger girl giggles as Roux's tail slaps her leg.

"Bump! I brought my Xbox so we can play after Grandpa's game is over. Aunt Zoe set up a giant screen in the backyard so we can watch outside, and the players will be as big as you!"

"No way! As big as me?" Bump high-fives her, but the girl's smile disappears when she sees me, and a look of apprehension sneaks over her features.

Wait. What'd I do? I hope I didn't mess up this family barbecue thing already. Did I?

"Joanie and Mel, this is Scarlett. Scarlett, meet Joanie, Q's mom, and Melanie, his niece."

"It's a pleasure to meet you both. Thank you so much for inviting us today." I hold out my hand, but Joanie ignores it and wraps me in a hug.

"I'm so glad to finally meet you, Scarlett. You have no idea how long we've been waiting for one of these boys to meet someone we could invite over."

"Mom . . ." Q's voice comes from behind the two women, who are still blocking the doorway.

"She knows what I mean, Marcus. It's not like she wasn't aware of Gabe's reputation when she started dating him." Joanie turns her attention back to me. "Please, come in. It's probably not what you're used to, but it's our home, and we hope you like it."

The younger girl bites down hard on her lip, and I think I see a little of what's going on here. *They know exactly who I am.*

Sometimes, being well-known is a double-edged sword because people have all sorts of opinions and expectations about you before you even say hello. So I do the only thing that I can think of to reset things to even.

"I've never been to a family barbecue before, so you're going to have to tell me if I'm screwing something up. I don't know how to cook, but I am *really* good at setting a table and washing dishes. Please, put me to work. I've got two hands, and they're at your disposal."

The girl's eyes go wide. "*You* wash dishes? No way. Seriously?"

I wiggle my very capable hands in the air, spirit-finger style. "Of course. That's what you do after you get them dirty, right?"

"But you're Scarlett Priest. You're like a bajillionaire celebrity. If you still have to do dishes . . . what hope is there for me?"

Thankfully, her teenage exasperation breaks the ice, and everyone, including Gabriel, Q, and Joanie, starts laughing.

"Poor kid. She was really hoping that when she's a rich and famous YouTuber someday, she won't have to cook, clean, or do laundry," Joanie says, wiping a tear from her eye. "Her dreams are crushed."

"You're a YouTuber?" I ask Melanie.

She shrugs. "Not really yet. I make a ton of videos, but Mom and Dad won't let me post anything. They're worried that people are going to make fun of me or say mean things, and that it'll hurt me. I have to wait until I'm sixteen before I can start posting." She rolls her eyes. "Like age is going to make it easier to take."

I can't argue with her parents being protective or waiting until she's a little older, but she certainly has the personality for it, at least from what I've seen and heard so far.

Joanie moves out of the doorway and ushers us inside. "Come on, get your appetizers while the food is hot. Mike will eat everything in sight if you don't claim them quick. The man is a garbage disposal. Luckily, it doesn't take away from that cute butt of his, so I haven't put him on a diet yet."

Gabriel kisses both her cheeks. "You know you'd never put him on a diet. You love making all that food and watching him devour it."

"Ain't that the damned truth? But, still, go get you some before it's cold. Carrie and Dani are out back with Zoe. The men were trying to tell her how to set up her projector, and I'm surprised no one has lost a limb. They've officially been forbidden from touching anything with a cord for the rest of the day."

Gabriel chuckles. "Sounds like Zoe. Tony and Chris should've known better."

"Damn right! Zoe's the best," Bump says, craning his neck to see inside.

Joanie narrows her eyes on him. "Watch your language in this house, boy. You know the rules."

"If I want to eat, I can't cuss," Bump singsongs with a heavy sigh. "You know how hard that is to remember? Because your food is so f—"

"You better be saying freaking," Melanie says quickly.

"Yeah, freaking good," Bump says, finishing with an angelic smile.

"Mm-hmm. I know what you're trying to do. Butter me up so you can ask me what I made for dessert. You'll have to wait with the rest of them, Bump. Now, go on." Joanie swats him with her towel.

This is what a real family looks like. My heart is full as Gabriel lays his hand on the small of my back, and I precede him into the house.

Once we're all in the backyard, I'm introduced to Q's other sisters and their husbands. Dani and Tony and Carrie and Christopher seem nice, and I feel lucky I've got everyone's names memorized so I don't make a blunder that way.

When everybody starts moving through the line to get food, Melanie situates herself at my side. Gabriel smiles at her and shoots me a wink before walking up to the grill to grab a burger from Big Mike.

"How do you deal with it?" Melanie asks as I scoop fruit salad onto my plate.

I glance at her, and she dips into the potato salad. "How do I deal with what?"

"People everywhere knowing who you are. Dealing with the mean things they say about you. The nasty comments on your posts."

I think of the troll that's been the bane of my existence for the last several months. "It's not easy sometimes, but it's part of the deal."

"Like you get so big that you don't have a choice but to have assholes come at you?"

I turn my head, almost sure Joanie's going to hear her swear, and somehow we'll both get yelled at. But Joanie is bustling back into the kitchen, no doubt for more food.

"Yeah, pretty much. Anytime something or someone is popular, the haters come out."

"It's even worse online than in person, isn't it?" Melanie asks.

"It can be. People don't think as much about what they say when they type a quick, nasty remark on your post like they would if they were saying it to your face. There's anonymity and safety behind those little avatars on our screens."

Melanie's mouth screws into a pout. "This is why we can't

have nice things. Because people are dicks. It's so annoying. I'm over it."

"Is someone being mean to you?" I ask her, feeling my protective instincts rise.

She shrugs. "Most people know who my uncle and Gabe are, so only the real idiots bother me."

"But there is someone?" I probe further, wanting to make sure that the girl isn't beating around the bush if there's a real problem at hand.

"A few guys. I told Gabe all about them. They make fun of me because I'm still a virgin."

A chunk of honeydew rolls off my plate and lands on the red-and-white-checked plastic tablecloth.

"And what did Gabe do?"

"Threatened to come to school and kick all their asses. Thankfully, it hasn't come to that yet."

I can totally picture him doing exactly that. Part of me wants to smile, but I keep my expression neutral. "Is there anything I can do to help?"

Melanie blinks at me. "You're Scarlett Priest. I just met you like ten minutes ago, and you already want to help *me*?" She says it skeptically.

"Of course. If I can help, I'd be more than happy to."

Melanie nabs the rogue melon and pops it into her mouth. After she's done chewing, she points a serious expression in my direction. "How old were you when you lost your virginity?"

Oh God. This is not where I expected this conversation to go. I'm panicking inside and hoping like hell it doesn't show on my face.

"That's probably a good subject for your mom to handle," I say quietly, and hate when Melanie's young face falls.

"She told me to wait until I was in love and wanted to marry the guy. I don't want to get married. So I guess that means I should stay a virgin forever, and I can tell you I'm not thrilled about that idea at all."

I reach for the spoon in the baked beans and pause. "I was twenty and in college, and I was tired of being a virgin when everyone else was out hooking up all the time." I cut my eyes to Melanie. "I wish I'd waited for someone special, but I'm really, really glad that I didn't have to see the guy every day in class for the rest of my college career, because he graduated shortly after."

I'm trying to make a point without saying it directly, because I'm totally out of my depth with this subject. Melanie's a pretty smart girl, though, obviously, and she picks up what I'm not saying in so many words.

"Oh my God. You're right. What if I did have sex with one of them, and he dumped me right after, and I had to see him every day until graduation? *Ew*. That would *suck*."

My head slowly bobs as realization floods her face. "Yeah, that would really suck. And you know what, Melanie? I've only known you for about fifteen minutes now, but I think it's safe to say that you're a bright girl, and you'll know when it's right. Don't listen to anyone else. Not your friends, definitely not the boys. *You* will know, and who cares if you're as old of a virgin as I was. Guess what? It didn't hurt me any to wait longer. It was my choice, and I was good with it."

A smile spreads across her face. "I make the decision. No one else. Just me."

"Exactly."

"Thanks, Scarlett. You're way cooler than those assholes on your social media say in the comments."

I choke out a laugh. "Thanks. And I have pretty thick skin, so I don't even worry about what they call me."

Her grin grows wider. "I like you. Gabe did good. I was totally prepared for you to be a stuck-up bitch, but you're totally not. I'll even let you do my share of the dishes," she says with a giggle. She has charisma in spades.

"I heard that, little girl! You know better than to put your chores off on guests. Guess who's doing *all* the dishes now?" Joanie says as she sneaks up behind us.

"Nooo. That's not fair."

"Welcome to being fourteen," her grandmother says in a singsong tone. "Life isn't fair."

THIRTY-TWO

Legend

Scarlett and Melanie have their heads together, as thick as thieves near the food.

I'm glad that Q's family is welcoming her with open arms. Part of me worried that Joanie and the girls would be standoffish because of who Scarlett is, but Scarlett broke the ice right at the front door by offering to do dishes.

Oddly, she fits perfectly into all my worlds. Who the hell would have guessed that would happen? Not me, but she's the best damn gift I've ever been given. Seeing her laughing and smiling with the people I love makes me fall even harder for her.

Once we get through this shit with Moses and the fight, Scarlett and I are going to have a serious discussion about our future. I already know I'm not going back to the service station. I don't want to live that far away from her. Shit, I don't want to live anywhere but right in the same damn place as her.

I've got it *bad.* She's it. The one. If I had the money to buy her the ring she deserves, I'd go get it tomorrow and put it on her finger. I want her and the whole world to know that she belongs to me, and I'm never letting her go.

But, first, I have to survive this fight.

My training is all on schedule. Jeb is a master of all aspects of MMA, but he's also a drill sergeant. I can barely lift my arms or climb stairs when I leave the gym, but it's all worth it. Every area I didn't have formal training in before has been shored up to the point where I'm confident about attacking with any of the skills in my arsenal. I can stand and bang, take him down, clinch, grapple, whatever.

We know Bodhi will be trying to take my head off to end the fight with a knockout, but I won't go out that way. I'm quicker on my feet than he is, and my footwork and head movement are top notch. If I'd had this level of training back in the day, there's no way in hell I wouldn't be a pro fighter on the biggest stages in the world right now.

But then you wouldn't have met Scarlett. It's the one thing that takes away any chance of regret.

She's . . . everything.

"You gonna just stand there and stare at her, or you gonna take some food and eat?" Big Mike asks from the grill next to me.

I jerk my head to the side and catch his narrowed eyes. "Sorry. Can't help it. Staring at her is my favorite thing these days."

The older man's chest bounces beneath his YOU CAN CALL ME BIG DADDY apron. "Damn, kid. Not even trying to be subtle about it, are you? No playing hard to get?"

I shake my head. "Nope. No games. Not with her. Just straight shootin'."

Bump waves Scarlett over to his chosen seat at the picnic table in the backyard, and she smiles and winks at him.

"I guess that's probably smart. Any games she'd play would be way out of your league anyway."

I cut my gaze to Mike's face, wondering what the hell he's getting at here. "If you got something to say about Scarlett, you might as well get it out, old man."

Mike flips a brat with his grill tongs. "Not really my business—"

"But you brought it up, so you've clearly got something on your mind. Might as well say it."

"Bump's getting pretty attached to her. You think that's smart?"

Out of the corner of my eye, I watch as Scarlett sits down across from Bump and playfully slaps at his fingers when he pretends to steal fruit off her plate. He throws his head back and laughs. He deserves someone good like her in his life.

"Why wouldn't it be? He's my family, and if all goes according to plan, she will be too before long."

The tongs smack against the grate, catching my attention. I glance back to Mike and take in the look of shock on his face.

"Seriously? You're in *that* deep here?"

I nod slowly. "She's it, man. I know you've got your reservations, but Scarlett is good people. The best."

"She comes from a totally different world, son. That kind of barrier is hard to navigate, even for someone as smart as yourself."

I've always loved it when Big Mike calls me *son*. It makes me feel wanted. Like I belong. The Quinterro family didn't just save Bump's life; they saved mine too. Without this family, I don't know where I'd be today.

Because of the bond we share, I don't take offense to Mike's questions. He's looking out for me the same as he would for one of his own kids, and that kind of concern isn't something I take for granted. I know all too well what it's like to have no one give a shit about me, and I'll take this any day of the week.

"We understand each other," I say, reaching out to stab a burger with my fork off the plate he's loading up. "She's from a different world, but that's not who she is. She gives a damn about people. She loves Bump. She knows what it's like to get the shaft from family. Apparently, that's an experience not just reserved for people who come from shit like me."

Big Mike's bushy eyebrows knit together. "She got a crap mom?"

"Mom's dead. But her dad, he's a piece of fucking work."

Big Mike's expression turns thunderous. "I'll never understand parents who don't give a damn about their kids. They brought them into this fucking world. It's their responsibility to do their duty. Too many people have forgotten what the fuck that means."

It's a lecture I've heard more than once, and something I believe in to my bones. My kids will never know anything except how much I fucking love them, and how goddamn grateful I am that they're mine.

"Scarlett's cut from the same cloth as me when it comes to that, old man. She'll be fierce as fuck as a mother. I can only imagine what she'd do if someone riled her up."

A smile crosses Mike's face. "Good. That's what you need. Someone willing to go to bat for you and yours when it matters. If that's what you're getting from her, then you've got my wholehearted approval, son. Not that you need it, but you got it all the same."

Warmth fills my chest. "Thank you. Means a lot to me."

"Now, go take these burgers over to the table. We've got more if anyone's still hungry."

I take the plate, but Mike holds out the tongs to stop me.

"I know Mel talked to you about her bully problem. Thank you for giving her a pep talk. That girl is going to set the world on fire one of these days, if some stupid boy doesn't get in the way."

I give him a chin lift. "Anytime. That's what family does."

"Damn right. Now, go eat, Gabe. No letting these burgers and brats go to waste. Joanie'll kick my ass."

THIRTY-THREE

Scarlett

I've never been so full in my entire life, but I don't regret a single bite. Joanie and Mike laid out an amazing spread, and every bit of it was delicious.

True to my word, I volunteered for dish duty, but Joanie tried to turn me down in favor of making Melanie do them. However, I persisted, and now I find myself elbow deep in a sink of suds while I hear gasps and cheers coming from the backyard over whatever is happening with the football game. Since my appreciation of the game starts and ends with the fact that the players are wearing tight pants, I'm not too worried about missing anything.

Footsteps alert me to the fact that someone is heading into the kitchen. When I glance over my shoulder, I expect to see Joanie coming in with another tray of dishes, trying to shoo me out of the way, but it's not.

It's Q, and his expression is more serious than I'd expect to see at a casual Sunday cookout. I gesture to the plate in his hand with my elbow.

"You can set it on the counter. I'll wash it for you."

He comes toward me slowly. "What are you trying to prove

here? You're Scarlett Priest, Manhattan socialite, not some chick who washes dishes for a Puerto Rican family you barely know."

"Still not my biggest fan, huh? Despite what you assume, I don't think I'm better than you or your family. And washing dishes is my way of thanking your parents for inviting me into their home and treating me with such gracious hospitality." My tone thankfully remains unaffected, and I'm proud of that.

"You sound like you really believe that." Instead of sounding like a dick, Q's statement comes out confused.

I pull my hands out of the soapy water, wipe them on a dish towel, and turn around to face him. "Simple explanation for that —because it's the truth."

He walks to the counter with measured steps and slides his plate and silverware across it. "Gabe isn't just my best friend; he's my brother. Doesn't matter that we don't share blood. That bond is solid. I'm not going to lose him because of you."

I blink twice. "Why would you lose him? I'm not following."

"You're gonna want to change him to fit in with your life, and I'm not okay with that. If you can't let him be who he is, then you need to walk away. Now."

Q's words hit me hard.

"And you're here to what . . . threaten me into leaving him? Because I have to warn you, that's not happening."

He squints at me, like he's trying to solve an invisible puzzle on my face. "Why do you want him? Is it just for a walk on the wild side? To be able to say you brought Gabriel Legend to his knees? Is that the game?"

I put my hands on my hips and attempt to lock down my temper, but I'm only partly successful if my tone is any indication of what I'm feeling.

"Is that all you think your best friend—your *brother*—has to offer someone? A walk on the wild side? If that's the case, first, you don't know me *at all*, and second, you don't know him as well as you think you do. Gabriel is the most honorable, intelligent, thoughtful, kind, and loyal man I've ever met. Meeting him, regardless of how, is the best thing to ever happen to me. I love him, and there isn't a goddamned thing I wouldn't do for him. What do you have to say to that, Q? Is that good enough for you? Or do you think I have some other hidden motives here?"

He opens his mouth to reply, but I'm not done.

"Because I'll tell you another thing. I don't *need him*. I don't need any man. I'm strong, smart, savvy, and I've got boatloads of money. But you know what? I *want* him more than I've ever wanted anyone or anything in my life. He lights me up. He makes me laugh. He brings me joy. I love Bump, and Roux, and goddammit, Q, if you weren't such an asshole, I'd probably love you too."

I shrug, realizing my guts have officially been spilled. "*Eventually*," I add quietly with a sniffle at the end, clueing me in to the fact that I'm near tears with my speech.

From the doorway, someone breaks into a slow clap. I cut my gaze over Q's shoulder as he spins around. Joanie stands there with a wide smile and shimmering eyes.

"Thank God, because Gabe deserves someone who sees him for everything he is. And, Marcus, you need to get your head out of your ass and stop pretending there's something wrong with what they've got. They love each other. End of story."

Q shifts from facing his mom to me again. "I misjudged you. I owe you an apology, Scarlett." He holds out his big hand.

"You don't owe me anything, Q. But I'll take a hug." I open my arms, and he steps forward and embraces me like a real friend.

"Whoa. Whoa. What's going on here?" Gabriel's voice comes from the doorway behind Joanie. "Q, you better not be trying to snake my girl."

Q releases me, and I step back toward the sink, feeling like I've just racked up a major victory. My gaze locks onto Gabriel's blue eyes.

"I told Q he was an asshole, and he apologized. We're all good now."

The corner of Gabe's mouth tugs upward, but before he lets it fully spread across his face, he turns to Q and asks, "You sure?"

Q turns to face him. "You did good with this one, brother. I approve."

Gabriel shakes his head. "Didn't ask for it, but I'm glad you're starting to see what I do." They hug, slapping each other's backs. "But you better get out there and see if your dad needs CPR after the Jets fumbled that ball. I'll help Scarlett with the dishes."

"Oh no, you three go and watch the game. I'll finish up in here. Scarlett, you've done more than enough." Joanie waves at the drying rack full of clean dishes. "Please. I insist."

"It was nothing. Thank you for an amazing meal."

Gabriel holds out his hand and I walk toward him, but as I do, his phone rings.

He pulls it out of his pocket, looks down at the display, and up at me and Q. "It's Johnson. What the fuck would he want now?"

"Maybe he's going to apologize for leaving you high and dry while he coached Bodhi?"

THIRTY-FOUR

I consider not answering the call, but curiosity gets the best of me.

"You got Legend," I say in greeting.

"That's some real low shit, Gabe. I didn't think you'd take a shot that dirty," Johnson says in reply. Even though I don't have him on speaker, he speaks so loudly that everyone in the kitchen can hear him, and Q's head jerks back.

"What the fuck are you talking about? What dirty shot?"

"Trying to take out Bodhi's knee so he can't fight. I never would've thought I'd see the day. I feel like I don't even fucking know who you are anymore. First, shutting down Urban Legend without so much as a warning. Then pretending like you're legit —even looking the part too, with that rich chick you're parading around town, and now this? Yeah, I'm real fucking glad I'm not in your corner."

My brain is running riot, latching onto each statement with confusion, because I don't have any idea what Johnson's talking about.

I start with the first part. "Someone went after Bodhi? Is he okay? Can he still fight?" I ask, not sure whether I'm going to get an answer out of the pissed-off coach, but I figure it's my only shot to understand what the hell is going on.

"Don't act like you don't know."

Scarlett curls herself into my side, and I wrap my arm around her waist.

"Ron, I don't fucking know. I don't have a goddamn clue what you're talking about. I'm at a fucking barbecue in Jersey. Been here all afternoon. If someone came after Bodhi, it sure as shit wasn't me. I got a whole yard full of witnesses if you want to talk to them."

"I don't give a damn if you've got a convent full of nuns vouching for your whereabouts. You could've paid someone easy."

"Why the fuck would I want to take out Bodhi? I *need this fight*, Johnson. Think for a goddamned second."

"I am thinking, and all I can figure is that you're trying to pussy out of this fight. You're afraid you're gonna lose, so you're trying to save face. If Bodhi can't fight, your club still gets paid as the venue. You take part of the gate. You don't need to risk your ass getting handed to you in the cage to cash out."

I can see where he's coming from, but he's totally wrong. "I got nothing to gain by Bodhi getting hurt, and you don't know what the fuck you're talking about. I have everything to lose if he can't fight."

"Bullshit."

"Let me talk to him," Q says, holding out his hand for the phone.

"Is that your Puerto Rican sidekick? He got the same alibi as you?"

"Yeah, that's Q. And it's his family's house we're standing in right now."

Johnson huffs. "Let me talk to the prick."

I hand the phone over, even though I don't really want to.

"What the fuck happened?" Q asks him after he taps the

speaker icon on my screen. "And drop your accusations for a hot fucking second so we can discuss this like adults."

"Bodhi was leaving practice. Someone came out of the alley and went after his knee with a pipe like he was Nancy fucking Kerrigan. I saw the whole thing. Big dude. Black hoodie. Face covered. Could've been either of you."

Q rolls his dark eyes and takes a deep breath before he flies off the handle too soon. "It wasn't. We were both here."

"Then someone you paid."

"You know damn well that isn't like me, and it doesn't make any sense," I say before Q can speak. "You know I always bet on myself. That's exactly what I'm doing here. I need this payday, Johnson. Taking Bodhi out doesn't do shit for me. I need him in the cage where I can beat him and cash in on the odds."

Johnson goes quiet for a few seconds. Joanie shuffles her feet beside me, and I have to wonder if she's holding her breath.

"If it wasn't you, then who?"

"Someone who doesn't want the fight to happen," I say quietly.

"Yeah, and who the fuck would that be?"

Q and I lock eyes.

"*Rolo*. Rolo's got nothing to lose, and he doesn't want this fight happening. Not legit, anyway."

Johnson's growl comes over the line. "If that piece-of-shit motherfucker went after my fighter because of some beef he's got with you, then this is still on your head, Legend. You fucking fix this, or I'll tell everyone it was you."

Scarlett squeezes my arm.

"What do you want me to do?" I ask.

"Cover Bodhi's expenses at the hospital. They're letting him out soon. His knee is gonna be fine, just so you know. And we're not letting this stop us. He's going to beat you. You know he would've last time. You just got lucky."

Hearing that out of my old coach's mouth is like a dull knife to the back.

"We'll cover his medical costs. But only because I'm a decent guy. This isn't my fault. If this was Rolo, then he'll answer for it, but I'm not taking the blame. You start that rumor, then we're going to have some real problems, and that's on top of the fact that you bailed on me and went straight to the enemy. I never did get a straight answer on why that was. You care to fill me in here, Johnson?"

He goes quiet for a minute. "I got bills to pay, and he offered me a piece of the purse."

I tighten my hold on Scarlett. "Good to know your loyalty has a price tag. Tell Bodhi to heal up quick. I'm not winning because he's injured. I'm winning because I'm a better fucking fighter than him."

"We'll see about that," Johnson says before ending the call and leaving the four of us standing in the kitchen, staring at one another.

"Do we need to call a lawyer?" Joanie asks, lines bracketing her mouth.

"No." I meet Q's nearly black eyes. "But we gotta go find Rolo and figure out what the fuck is going on here."

THIRTY-FIVE

I left Scarlett in Jersey with a kiss and a promise to be careful. Then Q, Hal, and I headed out to track down Rolo.

The first two gyms we hit were a bust. No one had a fucking clue where he was. The third, the gym near my club in the city, turned up a little information, but not much.

"He moved out of his apartment a few weeks ago. Crashed on my couch for a couple nights," one of the fighters Rolo was promoting tells us. "I don't know where he's living now, though. He says he's setting up a big fight for me, and I've been training hard."

"He give you the name of who you're fighting?" I ask the kid who looks half-terrified after we cornered him.

"Nah, man. No names. You know how Rolo is. He keeps everything close to the vest. Doesn't want to put the word out until something is solid."

Fucking kid doesn't have a clue that Rolo is probably hustling him. Word at the first two gyms was that he hasn't put together a fight in over six months, and most of the guys there don't take him seriously anymore.

"Thanks, man. We appreciate the info. You see or hear

anything from Rolo, tell him Gabriel Legend's looking for him. He knows where to find me."

His head bobs eagerly. "Of course. You want me to call you too?"

"Sure. Give me your phone." He hands it over, and I type my number in and call myself. "You got my number. You see anything or hear anything, call me."

"It's a real honor to meet you, Legend. If you're really putting fights together at your club, I'd love a shot at getting on a card. I put on a real good show. Knockout power, but I can grapple too. Been wrestling since I was eight."

I give the kid another look, but with a different eye. He's shredded. Looks like he could step into the ring at any moment and be ready. "What did you say your name was again?"

"Jeremiah Knowles. I can fight lightweight, welterweight, or middleweight. Whatever you need, man. I always make weight."

I pull out my phone and tap the missed call on the screen. "I'm saving your number, kid. Keep training. Come to Legend in a few weeks, and we'll talk."

"Yes, sir. Thank you, sir. It was an honor, sir."

Q snickers as we walk out of the gym. "I'm surprised he didn't hit his knees and ask if he could suck your dick too."

"Shut the fuck up."

"*Yes, sir. Thank you, sir. It was an honor, sir. I'll swallow, sir,*" Q says in a singsong voice, and I punch him in the shoulder. It doesn't stop his ribbing, though. "Pretty soon you'll have a whole stable of hopefuls who'll be begging to call you Daddy."

"Again, shut the fuck up," I tell him as we approach the SUV, where Hal is standing by the passenger door at the curb, watching the sidewalk and the gym.

"Actually," Q says in a normal tone, "what if you did have a bunch of kids like that who wanted to fight under your banner at the club? We could actually make a go of this, for real."

I raise an eyebrow at him as Hal opens the door to the back

seat for me. "You really think that's a good idea? Sounds like a fuck ton of work to me."

"I bet there'd be good money in it. They're all hungry. I bet there are twenty of them dying to ask you the same question that kid did, and we haven't even hosted a fight yet."

I hop inside and think about what Q said as he climbs in beside me. Having a roster of young guys who think I can give them their big break wouldn't be a bad thing.

"Maybe. But, first, we gotta find Rolo and get through this fight. Then we'll worry about the future."

"Where to next, Gabe?" Hal asks from the driver's seat as he shuts the door.

"Rolo's old girlfriend's place in Harlem. She's gotta know something."

A half hour later, we roll up in front of a barely half-decent apartment building.

"How about I go up with you this time?" Hal asks, looking at the entrance dubiously. "I don't want to let you guys get too far out of my sight. Not if Rolo's running around with pipes and taking out fighters."

"We can handle ourselves," Q says, but I'm with Hal on this one. I made a promise to my ladybug that I'd be safe, and I aim to keep it.

"Come on up, Hal."

Q looks at me with his dark eyebrows shooting up to his hairline.

"What? I promised Scarlett I'd be safe." He knows I don't take it lightly.

My best friend shakes his head. "Can't believe you just said that."

"Being careful with two weeks left to go before a fight this big? Yeah, I'm a real fucking pussy. Besides, I thought you two buried the hatchet this afternoon."

"I'm not calling you a pussy. I'm surprised you're finally taking your personal safety seriously. It's gotta be a first."

I meet his dark gaze. "I got a hell of a lot to look forward to now, and I'm not letting some fight promoter with a grudge take it away from me."

He slaps me on the back. "Fair enough, man. Fair enough. Let's go."

THIRTY-SIX

An unknown number flashes on the screen of my phone, and I don't really want to answer it, but for some reason I do.

"Hello?" I say hesitantly, fearing that I'm going to be talking to the troll who's been terrorizing me on social media. But I'm wrong. Totally and completely wrong.

"This is a collect call from the Manhattan Detention Complex. Do you accept the charges?"

What the hell? Did they arrest Chadwick?

My mouth drops open, and somehow I manage to get out the word *yes*.

As soon as I do, there's a click and a familiar voice comes on the line. "Oh, thank God you answered the phone. Shit, Scarlett, I didn't know who else to call."

"Flynn? What the hell are you doing in jail? Jesus Christ. Did you get arrested for—"

"It was all a misunderstanding," she says, interrupting me before I can finish my thought. "And no, it's not what you think. I went out with the wrong guy, and we ended up at a party . . . anyway, that's not important. Can you come bail me out? Please?

I really don't want to call my mom because she'll never let me live this down."

"Are you okay? Did he hurt you?" I ask as my mama-bear protective instincts shift into overdrive.

I'm getting concerned looks from Q's family, but admittedly, it sounds bad.

"I'm fine. I promise. I just really need you to make bail for me. Jail is seriously gross. And dirty. Please get me out of here, Scarlett."

"Okay, okay. Tell me exactly where I need to go and what I need to do, and I'll be on my way."

It's a first for me, being called to bail someone out, but I suppose this should also fall under the heading of *#LifeIsMessy*. Also, possibly a new one—*#FirstsForScarlett*.

Flynn rattles off the information, and I commit it to memory before telling her I love her and hanging up. I flip open a note on my phone and am typing it all out in case I forget something, just as Big Mike comes over to the lawn chair where I've taken up residence while he watches yet another football game.

"Everything okay? You sounded upset."

"My stepsister needs me to bail her out of jail, and I don't have a clue what I'm doing."

"Oh shit." He whistles with a toothpick still hanging out of his mouth. "She must be a spitfire too."

"She's something, all right. I need to call Gabriel and tell him what's going on, but I don't want to distract him from finding Rolo."

"You can call him on the way. I'll take you. This ain't my first rodeo with bailing punk kids out of jail."

I stare up at the man, who looks like a bear compared to his much leaner son. "Really? Because I don't want to put you to any trouble."

He shrugs. "The Jets lost. And the only ones winning this

game are the refs. Besides, you're family now. Shit like this is what we do."

And just like that, this big burly man melts my heart. "Thank you, Mr. Quinterro. I really appreciate it."

"Big Mike. Or Big Daddy, if Gabe'll let you." He scrunches his nose and winks at his wife, who is already reaching out to swat him on the arm.

I break into a grin. "Thanks, Big Mike. I'll get back to you on that."

THIRTY-SEVEN

"**W**hat the hell are you doing here?" Francine, Rolo's on-again off-again girlfriend, stares at me through the inch-wide gap between the door and the frame, her beady eyes just above the chain.

"Why do you think? Looking for Rolo."

"He ain't here," she spits out, her voice full of venom.

"Would you tell me if he was?"

"Hell no. You bailed on him after you got what you needed. Real shitty, Legend. You know he thought of you like a brother? And then you turned your back on him. Not cool. Not at all."

"Listen up, Francine." Q cuts in, stealing her attention. "Rolo's got himself into some real bad shit, and it's gonna bite him in the ass. Unless you want the next time you see him to be in a closed casket, you need to tell us where the hell he is."

Her mouth screws up into a tighter frown. "Yeah, right. You ain't got the balls to kill anyone. You're just Legend's pussy errand boy."

Q smiles, and I've seen that ticking time bomb before—it's taking everything he has not to explode. "You better back the fuck up, Francine," he sings with an obviously over-the-top friendly voice and then waggles his eyebrows at her. Quinterros always seem to smile while they lose it.

She jerks away from the door just as Q kicks out and busts the chain right off it, sending the door flying open.

Francine screams curses at us as she stands back with her arms crossed over her chest. "You piece of shit. Both of you. And that old man with you too. You just breaking into people's houses now?"

I shrug as I walk right by her and check the kitchen before making a quick circuit of the rest of the apartment.

No Rolo, and no sign that he's been here in ages.

I come back to the living room and break through Francine's temper tantrum with a shout.

"Hey. Listen up. You know where he's at, you call him and tell him that he needs to get in touch with me. Bodhi Black says Rolo just tried to take out his knee to stop this fight, and Bodhi's on the warpath. You'd rather have me find Rolo first, if you know what I mean."

Her hands fly in the air, and it's clear from her bouncing tits that she doesn't find bras necessary. "Like I give a fuck about some random dude's knee. Get out of here before I call the cops. I'm gonna have to blow the fucking super to get this door fixed."

I shake my head at her. "Might want to clean up that crack pipe in your bathroom before you do any of that, Francine. And if you see Rolo, tell him we're looking for him."

Turning on my heel, I walk out with Q and Hal at my back.

My phone starts ringing as soon as the door slams behind us.

"You think Rolo knows we're here?" Q asks as I pull it out of my pocket.

"No way." I glance at the screen. "Besides, it's Scarlett." I tap the glass to answer. "Hey, ladybug. What's going on?"

"Well, I'm with Big Mike, and we're headed to the Manhattan Detention Complex to bail out Flynn. If you're not too busy, I'd appreciate you meeting us there."

All three of us freeze in front of the elevator.

"Come again?"

"Flynn got arrested. I'm going to get her out. You want to join the party?"

I look up at Q, who is shaking his head, and I can't help thanking God he already got some of his frustrations out on Francine's shitty door. "You're fucking kidding me."

"Nope."

"We're on our way," I tell her. "Meet you there."

"Thank you, stud. I love you."

"Love you too, baby." I hang up the call, and Q's eyebrows might as well blend directly into his hairline.

"You're fucking kidding me with this bullshit, right?"

"Fuck if I know. Come on. Let's go."

THIRTY-EIGHT

Scarlett

Gabriel, Q, and Hal meet us on the sidewalk in front of "the Tombs," which are made up of the four fifteen-story towers of the New York City Criminal Courts Building, and I pull an envelope of cash out of my purse.

"I didn't know how much to get out of the safe. Do you think ten thousand will be enough?"

"What the hell did she do?" Gabriel asks with a look of incredulity on his handsome face.

"I have absolutely no idea. She said she was on a date with a guy, and there was some kind of misunderstanding."

"Of course there was." This comes from Q, who is raking his fingers through his jet-black hair. "That girl is a damned menace."

"Hey, she's my sister. Be nice."

"I'm confused," Big Mike says, breaking into the conversation. "I thought you said she was your stepsister."

"Ex-stepsister, but I'm claiming her as family anyway," I say to clarify. "Thank you for the ride, Mike. You don't have to stick around. I'm sure Joanie would be thrilled to have you come straight home."

The older man waves his hands in front of his big belly. "No way. I want to meet this little hellion for myself. You never know, maybe she'll be exactly the girl I've been waiting to match up with Marcus. It's not like I haven't bailed him out a time or two. Isn't that right, Inmate 3775?"

Q's head whips hard to the side. "Dad. That was ages ago. And fucking Christ. The girl's only like eighteen."

"Twenty," I say. "And very smart for her age. She's put herself through college on her own dime."

"Street-racing cars," Gabriel adds with a grin. "She'd make a hell of a daughter-in-law, Mike."

Q grabs Gabe by the sleeve and shoves him in the direction of the double doors. "All of you, shut the fuck up. Let's get this shit over with."

I can't wipe away my smile, despite the circumstances. Q's face is way too red for me to stop grinning.

We head inside. Apparently, the process is much easier than usual since I brought cash, and we don't need to wait for a bail bondsman. Flynn is released a half hour later. I stand up as soon as I see her coming through the doors to the lobby wearing a black crop top, a little red skirt, and thigh-high black boots. A little risqué for a date, but okay.

"Flynn!" I rush toward her and wrap her in a hug, squeezing hard. "Please tell me you're okay. Nothing happened in there?"

She squeezes me right back, just as hard. "Thank you so much for coming. God, I'm so glad your douche ex-boyfriend sent you to that sex therapist, because I don't know what I would've done if I had to call my mom."

I wince, hoping not everyone heard her, but Flynn sounds as young as a twenty-year-old should, which is out of character for her. From the dark circles beneath her eyes, she didn't get any sleep. "What happened?"

She glances over my shoulder, and her eyes go wide. "Whoa. Did you bring *everyone*? And strangers to witness my walk of shame?"

I twist to see Gabriel, Q, Hal, and Big Mike all standing a few feet behind us.

"Flynn, meet Big Mike, Q's dad. We were at a barbecue at their house this afternoon, and he brought me here. Gabe, Hal, and Q met us."

She nods at them with color rising on her cheeks. It may be the first time I've ever seen her embarrassed. "Nice to meet you. Sorry about the trouble. It was a big misunderstanding."

Big Mike waves her off. "Always is."

"What'd they pick you up for?" Gabriel asks.

Flynn shakes her head. "Not here. Can we at least go out on the sidewalk? Because I need some fresh air like now, and I *never* want to come back."

"Well, you'll have to because I just paid your bond, and if you don't show up in court, I lose it."

"Come on. Let's go." Gabriel holds out a hand to me, and I take it and follow him outside.

Once we're on the walkway, Q stares down Flynn. "They impound your car too?"

Her shoulders go back, and her chin shoots up. "What makes you think this has anything to do with my car?"

"It's a logical assumption, considering what you've been doing."

Flynn shakes her head. "I don't really want to tell you. God, it's fucking embarrassing."

"What? I'm starting to freak out here, and I need to know what's going on before I make some crazy guesses," I tell her.

Flynn's gaze drops to the pavement. "They picked me up for prostitution. Okay?" Her head comes up, and her face is now completely red.

All four men near me choke. "What?"

Q bursts out, "Are you fucking kidding me? You're hooking now too?" He begins to pace.

"No! It was all a misunderstanding."

193

"Want to tell us what happened?" Gabriel asks, his tone gentle and not the least bit judgmental. I'm tempted to kiss him right here just for that.

"I went out with some guy, and we ended up at a frat party. I don't usually do frat parties, but I was bored and didn't have a race, and I don't know how to sleep at night much anymore. So I went. And when we were there, the cops busted the party because they got tipped off that prostitutes were there . . ."

"And they thought you were one too?" I stare at the tiny crop top she's wearing, and the skirt and thigh-high boots. Although they're designer and definitely not hooker wear, I can see how cops who are intent on scooping up everyone possible made a mistake.

Flynn shrugs. "Yeah. Talk about humiliating."

"What about this fucking guy who brought you?" Q demands, his expression like a thundercloud. "Didn't he vouch for you?"

Flynn presses her lips together and shakes her head. After a beat of silence, she says, "He ran. Left me there to get arrested with the actual hookers and a few other girls."

"Didn't they look at your student ID?" Gabriel asks. "I don't get how they could fuck that up so badly. They can't just raid a party and accuse all the females of prostitution."

"I didn't have it on me, and they didn't believe anything I said to them. They treated me like a criminal. It was awful." Flynn sounds defeated, which is light years away from her bubbly, confident self.

"Maybe you should remember how that feels the next time you decide to go racing," Q says, his tone sharp.

Flynn pins her shoulders back once more and glares at him. "Go fuck yourself. I don't need you to tell me how to live my life." She looks to me. "Can you give me a ride home? I really want a shower and to fall into bed and pretend the last fourteen hours of my life didn't happen."

"Why didn't you call me sooner?" I ask, aghast at the thought of Flynn sitting in a cell for fourteen hours.

"Take it up with the justice system and apparently every hooker in town. I got my phone call when they gave it to me. It was a really busy night up in this joint. Can we go?" She looks like a lost little girl, and I nod.

"Absolutely. Let's get you out of here."

"At least give her your damn sweatshirt, Marcus. For Christ's sake, the girl's probably freezing. Did we not teach you manners at all?" Big Mike says, looking at Q disapprovingly.

Q peels it off and hands it to Flynn. "Here. Keep it."

Flynn takes it from him with a quiet thank-you before slipping it on over her crop top.

Gabriel holds out his arm to point us in the direction of wherever Hal must have parked. "This way. Q, you want me to drop you off at the club, or are you going back to Jersey?"

Q's gaze is glued to Flynn in his sweatshirt, and he has to yank his attention away to meet Gabriel's eyes.

"Uh . . . I'll, uh . . . go with my dad. I got some shit to do at home." His focus returns to Flynn and hangs there for a long moment before he finally nods at his dad. "Let's go to Jersey."

"See you tomorrow, man. I'll call you if I hear anything on Rolo," Gabe says, and Q gives him a salute in return. As he and Big Mike take off down the sidewalk, we go in the opposite direction.

But as we're walking, I notice Flynn glancing over her shoulder.

Hmmm . . . I'm not sure what to think about that.

THIRTY-NINE

An hour and a half after we leave the slammer, we finally make it back to Curated, which seems empty with Roux still in Jersey with Bump.

Scarlett took her time getting Flynn settled at her apartment, which I would have done too if she were my sister. To say the normally ballsy girl was shaken is probably an understatement. But Q had a point—what she does on a regular basis is dangerous, and if she didn't like being locked up, she probably should reconsider her stance on street racing.

I'm not sure whether that'll happen or not, but regardless, Scarlett and I will both be here to answer the call if she needs us again.

"You think they'll drop the charges?" Scarlett asks as she twists her hair into a messy bun.

"If she gets a lawyer on it. They'll be able to prove she's a student, no problem. And with her grades and her family's good name, hopefully it'll be an easy case."

"What if they ask about the money she's been using to pay her tuition?" Scarlett asks, concern creasing her features. "Wouldn't large cash deposits suggest she could've been engaging in illicit behavior?"

"Hire her a good lawyer. I doubt it'll even get that far. They'll take care of it. I promise, ladybug."

Scarlett bends her neck from side to side, and I move across the room to stand behind her and press my thumbs into her traps.

"Oh God, that feels so good."

"Makes my dick hard when you moan like that."

She twists to look over her shoulder. "Really?"

I lean forward to nip at her lips. "Of course. Damn near every fucking thing you do makes my dick hard. Taking your hair down. Putting your hair up. Watching you walk. The way you chew on your lip when you're working through a problem."

She turns in my arms, and I resettle my palms on her shoulders. "So . . . I know it's been a long day, but . . ." Her gaze dips to my mouth.

"You asking me if I'm up to making you scream my name when you come? Because the answer to that question is always a yes, ladybug."

A smile tugs at her lips as she leans in for a kiss. "Good. Because I could really go for a few orgasms right now."

"As you wish."

I take her mouth, deepening the kiss and tilting her head to the side. The first taste of her always sets me on fire and clears my mind of anything but Scarlett.

Dropping one hand to her ass and burying the other in her hair, I maneuver her toward the kitchen counter. My dick jerks against my zipper when she spears her fingers through my shaggy blond mane.

"I could kiss you forever," she whispers against my lips, and I pull back.

"Good, because that's the plan." I lift her up onto the countertop and get lost in her. Her scent. Her sounds. Her shallow breaths that turn into whimpers when she wants more.

She's greedy, reaching for the hem of my T-shirt and tugging it upward, scraping her nails across my abs, which are more pronounced now that I've been training like a madman and neurotic about my nutrition. Her moan of appreciation as she glides her fingertips across the planes of my muscles makes every fucking minute of work completely worth it.

As soon as my shirt clears my head, she stares at what she's uncovered. "I told myself I'd make this last. That we'd go slow. But . . ."

"You want it hard and fast," I say, my voice deepening, turning husky with the need she unleashes in me.

Scarlett catches her lower lip with her teeth and nods before releasing it. "At the gym . . . when you were all sweaty . . ." She squirms on the counter.

"You liked that."

Her needy gray eyes answer for her.

"You wet now, thinking about it?"

Another slow nod.

"Damn, baby, that is so fucking hot." I grip the edges of the countertop on either side of her legs and fit myself between her knees. "Don't know why I'm surprised. You're a five-alarm fire every damn time I get my hands on you. I'd let you burn me alive."

Her pupils dilate, and I have to clench my teeth not to rip her off the counter and take her on the kitchen floor.

"I'll fuck you like that anytime you want, ladybug. Including right now."

I tuck my fingers into the belt loops on her jeans and yank her to the edge before freeing the button and tugging down the zipper. As I peel the denim down her legs, I press my face into her pussy, breathing deep.

"Goddammit, but you smell so fucking sweet. I'm gonna eat this pretty little cunt of yours first before I fuck you."

Scarlett releases a shuddering breath, and her head rolls side to side.

I toss her jeans to the floor and scrape my teeth over the lace of her panties. Lavender. So fucking innocent and sweet. The exact opposite of what I'm going to do to her right now.

"You like to wrap that sweet pussy up pretty for me, don't you?"

"Just for you," she whispers.

"I fucking love it, but they've got to go." I tug her panties aside, revealing her plump, slick pussy lips. It's only been a few days since I've had my hands on her naked, but it feels like a lifetime.

I drag my tongue up one side of her slit and groan at her taste. "Like fucking whiskey. You go straight to my head."

I give the other side the same treatment before circling her clit as Scarlett tries to buck against my face. I reach out and snag a wrist in either hand before flattening her palms out on the counter.

"Keep them here unless you want me to lose it and fuck you on the floor on your hands and knees, ladybug. I ain't got much control tonight."

Her fingers flex under mine, where they're pinned, and I glance up at her face. Those gray eyes burn with hunger now.

"What if I want that? Should I do this?" She yanks her hands out from beneath my palms, and faster than I know what she's going to do, she grabs my head and presses my mouth straight against her clit while she rides my face.

Holy fucking hell. My dick almost hurts with how hard it throbs, begging to be free.

Instead of jerking back immediately, I give her what she wants. I eat her cunt like it's my last meal, grinding into her until her fingers tense and her scream breaks loose. I push a finger inside her just in time to feel her inner muscles flutter hard from her orgasm.

When I pull back, we're both gasping for breath, and I'm ready to *fuck*.

"You asked for it."

Her eyes widen as I pull her off the counter, stripping her of her shirt and pulling her messy bun into waves around her shoulders. She doesn't miss a beat, going for my zipper and tearing it down, like it's the one thing standing between her and salvation.

As soon as my dick is in her hand, she squeezes, and I grit my teeth against the massive wave of pleasure.

"I'm not coming in your hand, baby." She starts to speak, but I shake my head. "Not your mouth either. I want my pussy, and I want it *now*."

Standing naked in her kitchen, Scarlett's lips curl into a siren's smile. One that I'd follow all the way to hell, if that's where she wanted to lead me. "Then what are you waiting for?"

My control snaps, and I reach for her, spinning her around so that her back is to my front, before lowering her to her knees on the floor. I set new records with how fast I move, covering her with my body, nudging her knees apart, and sliding my cock between her legs.

The slickness practically drips onto my dick, and I've never been so fucking desperate to get inside her before.

This is primal.

Animal.

Raw.

And it feels so fucking right.

FORTY

Scarlett

I reach between my legs and guide Gabriel's cock to my opening. I don't know what's happening to me. I may be on my knees, but I've never felt this bold and powerful before. I wanted him inside me five minutes ago, but now I might die if I don't have him *right this second*.

"Please, I need . . ."

With a single thrust, he powers inside me, and I inhale sharply as my body stretches to accommodate him. Gabriel leans down and drags his teeth across the skin where my shoulder meets my neck, and growls.

Holy. Shit. I clamp down hard, because I think I might already be ready to come.

"Oh God," I whisper.

Gabriel's dark chuckle echoes in my ear before he pulls back and thrusts inside again and again, pausing only to find my clit with his fingers, and then I *lose it*. The orgasms come so hard and so fast that I can't separate one from another. I scream words that make no sense, because I couldn't think if I wanted to.

I lose my grip on time. Space. Reality. Everything. All that exists is the pleasure shattering me.

And when my arms go limp and I drop to brace myself on my forearms, Gabriel roars my name and his cock pulses inside me.

For the space of three heartbeats, neither of us move, speak, or even breathe.

My forehead drops to the floor, and I haul in a breath of air. With a shaky voice, I whisper, "I thought once we got used to each other . . . sex would start to feel the same."

Against my back, I can feel Gabriel's entire body shaking with what I assume is laughter. He shifts, pressing a kiss to my shoulder.

"Never with you. It's always a battle not to come. You're the best thing that has ever happened to me in my entire life, Scarlett. And just know, anytime you want it like this, all you gotta do is grab my head and shove it in your pussy. That can be our signal."

And that's how I found myself belly laughing, naked, on my kitchen floor, happier than I've ever been.

"That's how I unleash the beast? Very subtle," I say as Gabriel reaches for a kitchen towel hanging from the stove handle.

"Yeah. That's how you unleash the beast," he says to me with a massive smile on his face. "You planning on doing that again anytime soon?"

I school my features into what I hope is a serious expression. "Every chance I get."

He tackles me, and round two is just as good. Maybe even better.

When we finally get out of the shower, both wrapped in our robes—because I bought a big fluffy one for Gabriel with a *G* embroidered on the breast, and he seemed pretty appreciative from the breath-stealing kiss I received in exchange—we walk back into the kitchen.

I stare at the spot on the floor, in front of the stove where we just went at it like sex-crazed animals. "I don't know if I'll ever be able to think about my kitchen the same way again."

Gabriel laughs when he sees where I'm looking. "I'll probably never be able to eat in here without a hard-on, but I ain't complaining. You hungry? I'm cooking."

"We can order takeout if you want."

He shakes his head. "Can't until after the fight. I need to get some protein down, especially after that cardio. You want me to finally teach you how to make those fluffy scrambled eggs you liked so much from Gabe's Diner?"

His mention of the menu from when I was healing after my surgery fills me with warmth. "I would *love* to learn how to make those fluffy scrambled eggs from Gabe's Diner."

FORTY-ONE

When I wake up Tuesday morning of what I've dubbed *fight week* in my brain, Gabe is already gone. I reach out to touch the sheets, but I know they'll be cold. He's been training like a man possessed, and I suppose that's exactly what he is.

I've never seen a man more determined to win at anything in my life. I'm in awe of Gabriel's dedication, especially because he's still made as much time for me as he can, even though I've told him repeatedly that when this is over, we'll have plenty of time for each other again.

I smile, remembering that Christine is flying in today from LA to spend time with Ryan, his family, and all the friends she left behind in the city when she headed west with her father upon his retirement. Plus, both Ryan and Christine are coming to the fight.

They shocked the hell out of me when they told me they'd secured tickets. *"Did you think we wouldn't do whatever it took to be there? We know how important this is for you both."*

Warmth filled me at their support. I may not have family who will do anything for me, but my friends are the best a girl could ask for. Harlow, Monroe, and their husbands will be coming, and so will Kelsey and her brother Jon. Flynn is the only one who won't be there, because all eyes will be on the club, and it's too well known that she's underage. Additionally, with the bit of trouble she found for herself, she's laying kind of low for good reason until it's all settled.

Legend will be closing after tomorrow night, and the club will remain closed until the doors open on Saturday to let in all the eager fight-goers.

I'm excited about the fight, because Gabriel has worked his ass off, but I'm also terrified. I've never had to see the man I love get punched in the face with no pads to block the blows. There's a good chance I'm going to be watching the whole thing through my fingers, like a little kid sitting through her first horror movie.

Hopefully not, though. I can be strong for Gabriel.

But Bodhi Black is out for blood, especially since it sounds like he doesn't believe Gabriel wasn't behind the failed attack to take out his knee. No one has heard from Rolo either, which makes him look even more guilty than the vague suspicions Gabriel had before.

Even more than Bodhi Black, I'm worried about Moses Buford Gaspard. Gabriel said the mob is covering him and not to worry, but that's easier said than done.

Why can't he just disappear and never come back? I think as I roll out of bed and slip on the robe I tossed on the chair last night. *That would make life so much easier and less stressful.*

A knock comes on my interior front door, and I glance at the clock. Amy shouldn't be here for another forty minutes, so I pad toward it and peek through the peephole.

"Christine!" I unlock the door and yank it open before flinging myself at her in a hug.

"Oh God. Really? It's too fucking early for this bullshit, Scar. Get it together," she says, all the while laughing.

I pull back to stare at the freckles dotting her creamy

complexion. "I swear to God, you're the only person I know who hates being hugged this much. And how the hell have you managed not to get *any* sun at all living in LA? You still look like a New Yorker in the dead of winter."

Christine rolls her eyes as I shut the door behind her. "Yeah, you look great too. Like you've been getting laid on the regular. It makes you glow and shit. Wait, are you pregnant?"

"No," I say with a shake of my head. "Definitely not. But, hopefully, that won't be too far off in the distant future."

Her expression morphs into shock laced with horror. "Not you too. Really? You're gonna do the rug-rat thing *already*? God, I'm going to have to buy baby presents and shit, and you know how much I hate that. Ryan's already put me through that special kind of hell twice, and I really hoped that was all the torture I'd have to go through in this life."

"I've missed you, Chris. It's really good to see you. And hug you, even though you hate it."

She shivers, as if the human contact has truly grossed her out, sending her brown curls bouncing. I know better and ignore her, leading the way into the kitchen—careful to avoid those spots Gabriel and I have christened—and she follows.

"You know I love you, Scar. I've missed you too. And damn, I've missed this city. Why did I move to LA again? I must've been crazy."

"You know you'd never let your dad that far out of your sight to move back, so you'd better learn to love the concrete jungle."

"The things we do for family," she grumbles. "Speaking of which, how is Daddy Dearest? Have you talked to him lately?"

I shake my head. "Don't know. Don't care. Don't have any plans to speak to him anytime soon either."

She lifts her chin. "I don't blame you. If he called me, I wouldn't even bother to listen to the voice mail, after I hit the fuck-you button on him."

"I thought you weren't getting in until later?" I ask, changing the subject.

"I took a red-eye. I wanted to see how you're really doing. I know you told Ryan and me to stay the hell out of your personal business, but I needed to know that you're good. Clearly, I had nothing to worry about, because you look better than ever."

A wide smile stretches my lips. "Thank you. I'm happy. I mean, nervous as hell about this fight, but that's to be expected. You want a double espresso?"

"Please. My blood-caffeine level is dangerously low."

I grab two demitasse cups and set up the espresso machine to begin brewing. As the scent of coffee fills the air, Christine sits at my kitchen table.

"Is Legend going to win the fight?"

I lean back against the countertop and nod. "Yeah. He will. There's no other choice."

One of her reddish-brown eyebrows rises. "And if he doesn't? You two going to be okay?"

"Of course. We'll be fine, no matter what."

"And the club?"

My gaze drops to the floor, and I bite my lip. "It should be fine."

"Should be?"

I make an executive decision, swear her to secrecy, and then fill her in on Moses. By the time I'm finished, her mouth is wide open like a manhole without a cover.

"Jesus, Scarlett. You've kept this all from us this whole damn time? We could've found ways to get him money that he wouldn't know had come from you. We could've had Legend make a windfall on some business deal. This could've all been taken care of the day after that asshole showed up."

In my heart of hearts, I know she's wrong. Moses won't take money the easy way. He wants Gabe to suffer for it, and that makes me hate the monster even more.

"It doesn't matter now. He's under control by the mob, apparently, and he won't be making an appearance."

"This is some real *Godfather* shit, you know?" she says.

"Tell me about it."

When our espressos are ready, I slide one cup and saucer in front of her and take the opposite chair. She lifts her cup to her lips with a murmur of appreciation.

"This is amazing. So much better than that shit on the plane." After she sips, she sets it down in front of her. "So, tell me what I can do to help. I'm here for you, even if Ryan thinks I'm here to see his kids. We both know the truth."

Her distinct dislike for children makes me chuckle, but I don't have any answers for her. "Go see your niece and nephew. Everything is under control here, and there's really not much to do."

"Are you sure?"

"I mean . . . you could go take a walk through the store and buy a few things. You know, just to help a client and friend out."

Her eyebrow lifts as her head tilts to the side. "Are you forgetting I spent a grand on shipping last time I was here? I think about it every time I walk through my house, because it's full of your stuff."

"Perfect. Time for an update," I say with a smile.

FORTY-TWO

The soles of my shoes hit the pavement one rhythmic stride at a time. I turn the corner leading back to the gym, where my training is slowing down so my body is rested but prepared for Saturday night.

Jeb drives behind me slowly in his silent fucking Prius that always makes me laugh, and I almost miss a step when I see a tall man in a dark suit getting out of a Rolls Royce SUV in front of the gym.

I'd recognize him anywhere.

Creighton Karas.

"Everything good?" Jeb calls from the open window.

That's how attuned he is to me physically. I swear, my heart couldn't have an irregular beat without Jeb picking up on it. His coaching has been so different from Johnson's that there's no way in hell I ever could have had a chance at winning if I'd been training the way I used to. I'm a whole new fighter now, and I'm more confident than ever.

"A friend is waiting out front of the gym."

Jeb looks ahead. "Looks rich. Those are the best friends to have."

Karas turns to face me as I slip between two parked cars to take my last few steps on the sidewalk. When I reach him, I bend over, resting my hands on my thighs, and drag in some deep breaths.

"You're really giving it your all, aren't you?"

I glance up from under the sweaty hair falling over my forehead. "You expected me to just be fucking around with this?" I stand up straight and scrape the damp strands back.

His gaze zeroes in on my face. "If I thought you were just fucking around, I wouldn't have a briefcase of cash sitting in my back seat." Karas glances up and down the street. "You want it here? Because if you get jumped and someone takes it, I'll own you for the rest of your life."

My head swivels toward the back seat instinctually. "How much fucking money did you bring?"

The low chuckle steals my attention back. "Enough so that if you win, you'll be able to pay me back, pay off all the investors, and then some. Enough to set you free."

I blink, replaying what I think I just heard through my brain. "Why?" It comes out quieter than I planned.

Karas studies me. "I see something in you that reminds me of me. Given the right opportunities, you could become a player in this town, Legend."

I blink slowly and shake off the sweat running down my face, pretending I'm not shocked by Karas's words. He's a fucking billionaire, for Christ's sake. I'm a kid from a shit-ass trailer park in Biloxi, Mississippi.

That thought fades as he continues.

"Saturday could be the first day of your new life. If you don't lose, that is."

I reply instantly. "I'm not going to lose. I got too much on the line, regardless of what's in the bag. You want insurance I'm going to win, know that I'm faster, smarter, and a hell of a lot more determined than Bodhi Black ever was, is, or will be."

I motion to Jeb. "And thanks to Bohannon, I've had the best fucking coaching staff in the city. I'm ready. I've lived this moment of victory a thousand times in the last month. Saturday, I make it a reality."

Karas's face smooths out, and one corner of his mouth rises. Approval glints in his eyes. "I believe you. I suppose Bohannon does too." He turns to Jeb. "We'll bring Legend back in thirty minutes. Keep up the good work, Coach."

Then he gestures to the open back door of the Rolls. "Get in."

Normally, I'd sputter about being told what to do, but let's be honest. *I'm about to ride in a fucking Rolls Royce for the first time in my life, and this dude is practically handing me a new lease on life.*

I guess faith does just show up sometimes.

"Appreciate the lift," I say with all the nonchalance I can muster and slide inside.

Jesus, even the leather feels like it's too expensive to touch my sweat-soaked pants. The aroma in the air is better than anything I've smelled—except for Scarlett. And, *holy fuck*, there's a *big-ass* silver hard-sided briefcase in the center that I have to lift myself over to settle in the seat.

Karas gets in and straightens his suit coat before looking at me. "I'm not an idiot, and I'm not risking you fighting for your life on the sidewalk over some cash."

Some cash. I almost laugh at how casually he talks about what is definitely the most money someone's ever given me at one time.

Once Karas's driver climbs inside and shuts the door, virtually every noise from the city is muted.

"Damn," I whisper, and Karas's expression halfway approaches a grin.

"First time in a Rolls?" he asks as we pull away from the curb.

"Yeah. That obvious?"

He gives a small jerk of his chin. "Nah. You should've seen Holly." Only when he mentions his wife does his expression soften to easygoing. "She didn't know what to think about the money. I grew up surrounded by it, so I barely noticed anything like that anymore. Watching her experience things I took for granted was like getting a second chance to appreciate life. She changed everything for me."

My mind goes straight to Scarlett, and I realize Karas might be one person who would understand what it was like for her to grow up surrounded by luxury.

"I always thought growing up with money would make everything easy," I tell him as I wipe my hands on my pants before I dare touch the leather. "Never worrying about where your next meal was coming from. No hearing gunshots outside your door at night. Never having to fight for your life to make a buck." I give my head a small shake. "But meeting Scarlett has taught me a lot that I didn't get before."

"I can imagine. I grew up with a completely different mindset; it was unavoidable. Privilege can also blind a person, and it rots plenty of them."

"Yeah, and then you get someone like Scarlett who is as fucking true as they come. She's genuine and honest, and I don't think she could tell a good lie if she practiced in front of a mirror for a week. She wouldn't realize if she was being scammed, because she thinks everyone has a good heart, just like her. She's a fucking miracle."

Karas chuckles quietly. "She and Holly would get along well then. Holly grew up with more than you, but much less than Scarlett. She personifies grit and grace. She's smart and stubborn, and will outwork me if I'm not careful. I get what you mean by a miracle."

He turns toward me as we approach the club. "You'd better take good care of Ms. Priest. A woman like that will make the rest of your life worth living, in a way nothing else can."

I think of every time Scarlett has made me smile, laugh, or just stare at her in wonder. "That's the plan."

"Which is why you won't lose Saturday."

"Damn right. Which means the mob better be real fucking sure that they got Moses under control, because I'm not taking a chance that bastard is going to touch a fucking hair on her head. You understand me?"

"Don't question the mob or me. You're covered. Moses won't hurt her. Now, get that shit out of your head and focus on the fight." He grabs the handle of the briefcase and offers it to me. "Put this in your safe. I'll see you Saturday. Good luck, Legend."

"I don't need luck. But thanks anyway."

Q stares at the stacks of cash I take out of the case and stow in the top shelf of the safe. "You just rode in a Rolls Royce with Creighton Karas, and he gave you two million dollars—*in cash* —for the hell of it?"

I reach back to grab another stack and put it inside. "Yep."

Q wipes his hand across his mouth and shakes his head. "That's some way to start the day, brother."

A small smile comes over my face when I think of what Karas said to me. *"You'd better take good care of Ms. Priest. A woman like that will make the rest of your life worth living, in a way nothing else can."*

It's the goddamned truth too, which is why the first thing I'm buying after I win is a ring. One that she deserves. Because I'm going to be the man she's always needed, even if she didn't know it.

I still remember what I said to her at the hospital when she came out of surgery. *"I'm not what you need, but I'll learn, ladybug."*

The money I'll make Saturday night won't put me on par with what Scarlett's got in the bank, but it doesn't matter. *I'll* be enough for her without it, and I finally fucking get that. She doesn't care about what I've got. She cares about who I am and how I treat her. *And if a cool mil of my own helps me treat her even better . . .* no harm, no foul.

"It's not just gonna be a great fucking day," I tell Q with a smile. "This is the start of a great new fucking life for all of us, buddy. Just wait."

"I believe you, Gabe. You haven't let me down yet."

FORTY-THREE

I head back to the gym, more in the zone than ever before. My focus is turned up to the max, and determination fuels every punch.

I bob and weave, throwing combination after combination.

Chadwick—*smack.*

Lawrence Priest—*slap, slap.*

Rolo—*bam.*

Johnson—feint.

Moses—*whack.*

Lucy—bob.

The list repeats in my head ad nauseam, and by the time we finish, the grin on Jeb's face is as wide as the cage I'm going to dominate on Saturday.

"You're fucking ready, kid. I wouldn't believe you were the same fighter as when you walked in the door if I hadn't trained you myself."

I hold my gloves together and give him a small bow. "I appreciate every minute of the extra time and coaching. Johnson agreeing to jump teams might've been one of the best damn things that ever happened to my fighting career."

"No shit. They're going to be expecting a totally different fighter than the one who shows up. You've gone over Saturday's schedule?"

I nod. "Yeah. And my office is ready. It looks like a locker room with the mats and equipment. It'll work."

"Good. Then let's wrap it up here." We head toward the cage where my sparring partners wait, and I shake out my muscles, ready to rock.

On my way out of the gym, my phone buzzes with a text.

I make two stops, and then I head home. It's not until after I park in front of Curated that I realize *home* is now wherever Scarlett is.

FORTY-FOUR

Scarlett

Gunter delivers my dress on Thursday morning.

I'm practically giddy about Sunday because it means I'll stop waking up in bed alone. Those brushes of Gabe's lips on my forehead in the dark as he leaves make me want to pull him back in bed and find some other way to do his cardio. I promise myself that will come *after* this is all over.

The garment bag's zipper hisses, dragging me back to Gunter and the dress.

"Oh my goodness." I gasp. The dress shimmers like liquid gold.

"You like?"

I turn to Gunter, my mouth open. "You've outdone yourself. This is *stunning.*"

"I hoped you'd think that. It's elegant and sophisticated without being overdone, and yet daring enough to make every woman in the place jealous."

The confidence Gunter has in his designs has always awed me. "You're not wrong."

"I never am, darling. And you're going to look radiant in it.

Here." He unhooks the hanger and holds it out for me. "Run along. Try it on."

I take it from him, marveling at the weight of the dress on the hanger. I expected it to be heavy, but it's unbelievably light.

"What is this material?" I ask the talented man standing in my apartment.

Gunter winks. "Magic."

I slip into my bedroom and carefully step into the dress. "Holy shit," I whisper as the silky fabric glides over my skin, leaving a shiver in its wake.

"I'll zip you up, darling," Gunter calls.

I come out of the bedroom, and the only way to describe his expression is *beaming*.

"Yes. *Absolutely, yes. Divine.*"

My cheeks hurt from how big I'm smiling. "I know, right?"

"Come, come. Let me do you up."

I give him my back, and he manages the zipper.

When I turn around to face him again, he shakes his head with a lopsided frown. "If only your mother could see you like this. She would have loved what you've done, Scarlett. She'd be so proud of the woman you've become."

"You think so?"

"Without a doubt. If she'd known it was possible to be as happy as you look, she would have wanted exactly that for you."

My face shifts and my smile fades. "What do you mean, if she knew it was possible to be this happy?"

Gunter turns around, busying himself with the second garment bag he brought with him. The one I haven't bothered to ask about yet. "You know what I mean. Your mother had her demons."

After hearing that, I'd rather know more about the bag. "What's in the bag, Gunter?"

He glances over his shoulder. "A surprise, darling."

Goose bumps rise on my skin, and I'm not sure why. I've

known Gunter most of my life, and he was one of my mother's best friends for all that time.

"My mom was happy, though. I mean, after she left my dad."

"Yes, thank God. Lawrence was a terrible choice for her. I tried to talk her out of marrying him, but she wouldn't hear of it."

Metal clanks against metal, and I brace. Paranoia swims through me because suddenly I'm wondering if Gunter could be . . . if it's possible he could be the one who has been . . . *No. Gunter can't be the troll.*

Still, I hold my breath, waiting to see what he pulls out.

When he turns around, he's holding a suit on a hanger, and I exhale.

"What is that?" I stare in confusion, slowly relaxing my hands, which had balled into fists.

"I made Gabriel a new suit from the measurements I took for the tux. I thought he deserved to be the most dapperly dressed man in the club, even if it's not for long. You, of course, would overshadow any man in that dress, so I had to help him out as well."

I swear, my heart squeezes. *How could I ever have suspected my dear old family friend? I need to chill out about this troll business before I start assuming the worst about everyone.*

"Gunter, I don't know what to say. This is incredible. Thank you."

"Of course, my dear. It's my pleasure. I have to say, I approve of your choice of man, even if I didn't expect to."

"I didn't know I needed your approval," I say, raising one brow.

"You don't, but you have it all the same. I hope you use it in place of your father's, since he's a miserable jackass who doesn't know how lucky he is to have you as a daughter. I wish it had been my privilege instead, darling. Except, you know, your mother didn't play for my preferred team."

I step forward, and he lifts the suit to the side with a flourish so I can throw my arms around him. "Thank you, Gunter. You have no idea how much I needed to hear that."

He pats my back with his free hand. "Of course, darling. Whenever you need fatherly reassurance, you know where to find me."

I loosen the hug and step back. "You know what? I'll take you up on that." Tears burn behind my eyes. "I think . . . *I know* I've got to let it go. Let him go. Lawrence Priest will never be the father I need him to be." I shake my head as I blink back tears. "But I don't need him. I've got way too many other people who care about me. And besides, him not needing me as a daughter made me into who I am, and since I like me . . . I'm okay with that. It's his loss."

"I've never been prouder of you than I am, right at this moment," Gunter says with a soft smile. "And your mother would be too."

I nod, and the conversation I had with Meryl a few weeks ago flashes through my brain. "I've realized she wasn't a saint either. She was a woman with her own issues who was trying to figure things out for herself too."

One of Gunter's dimples flashes. "How enlightened. Yes, I would agree with that, but I also know your mother did her best. What more can you ask from someone than that?"

"That's true. She did."

"So, why not remember her that way? After all, the best parts of her live on through you. Her beauty. Her drive. Her kindness."

My mouth forms a small smile once more. "Thank you." I meet Gunter's eyes. "When did you become so wise?"

"I got old, my dear. My body may no longer be young, but I'll take the perspective I've gained throughout the years any day." Something else flashes in his eyes, and he smirks. "Well, most days."

"Are you going to tell me what that's about?" I instantly wonder if Gunter's got a younger guy on the radar.

"No," he replies with a secret smile. "Enjoy yourself Saturday. I've placed a bet on Legend. I'm confident he won't let me down. I could use a vacation with my winnings."

"I'm confident he won't either," I tell him. "Gabriel is the most determined person I've ever met in my entire life. I believe in him."

"Then he's a very lucky man, indeed." Gunter leans in to unzip the dress and pats me on the shoulder. "Good-bye, my dear."

FORTY-FIVE

Metal grates against metal as a crew assembles the cage in the middle of the club on Thursday. I finished my morning training and came in to check on the setup before I go back for my afternoon session. We've slowed the pace to let my body rest, but continuing to go through all the moves keeps me sharp.

Q comes down the stairs and stops beside me. His suit and tie are a definite contrast to my sweats and T-shirt. And yet, this is my club. Something about that makes me smile.

"You get any more info from the mob on Moses?" he asks. "Why didn't they just take him out?"

I look at Q. "The last words from Creighton Karas were that you don't question the mob. I gotta believe they have it handled, or it'll fuck with my head thinking Scarlett's not safe. Karas said he's adding guys to our security team too."

"Yeah, that's why I'm asking. I got word from our security firm earlier. They said they're being invaded, and Karas's guys are going to be calling the shots."

My head pulls back. "No shit?"

"I'm not sure if it makes me feel better or worse, Gabe. Why the extra measures if they're sure they've got Moses contained?"

I glare at him. "Are you trying to fuck with my head?"

"No. I'm trying to decide if Scarlett should even come tonight."

"What if that's what Moses wants?" I ask, my voice hushed as I remind myself that Moses is even more calculating and devious than he used to be. "What if he knows I'm going to win the fight, and he thinks we'll keep her locked up somewhere else? What if the safest place for her is here, especially with Karas's security team running things?"

Q's gaze drops to the floor for a few beats before he looks at me again. "Hell, you might be right. I don't know the guy, but if he's that Machiavellian, maybe it is." He jams a hand in his hair. "I'll be glad when this fucking week is over. If I get gray hair from this, I'm blaming you, asshole, and you're paying for my dye jobs for life."

"Good to see it's your vanity calling the shots, brother."

"Shut the fuck up, Gabe." He leans over and gives me a rough hug. "Just don't fuck this up. We're all counting on you."

With the weight of the world already on my shoulders, Q's statement lands heavy. "I know. And I've got this."

Thankfully, I'm not lying.

FORTY-SIX

When I wake up Saturday morning, I already know Gabriel is gone. He told me what time he had to be at the gym to go over the game plan with Jeb one more time. I won't see him until later, when he comes home from checking last-minute preparations at the club to shower. Then we'll ride to the club together.

I told him about the suit from Gunter, and his whole face lit up. "No shit?"

I giggled. "You must've made quite the impression when you went to be measured. He likes you. He told me you've got his approval."

The moment his face softened and quiet happiness settled over it, I snapped a mental image entitled *Gabriel Feeling Loved*. It's an expression I'm determined to see even more often.

Today is just the beginning. What we have is going to grow and change, and become old and wise like Gunter. All we have to do is get through tonight.

When I sit up in bed, I spot a box and a note on my nightstand.

"What is that?" I say to the empty room.

I pick up the note. In Gabriel's bold handwriting, it reads:

Ladybug,
We're sleeping in tomorrow. I love you.
—G

My heart melts as my smile stretches wide across my cheeks.

I lift the package off the nightstand and carefully open the shiny black paper to find a white box. I open it and pull out something round, wrapped in tissue paper. When I peel back the layers, I release an audible sigh.

"Oh my *God*."

It's a ladybug salt shaker. I reach into the box and unwrap the matching ladybug for pepper. *Goddammit, that's it. I'm going to marry this man.*

But, first, I'm going to watch him win this fight, and hopefully see him realize exactly how incredible he is too.

Gabriel Legend, you are a special man. I won't stop until you see yourself like I do.

FORTY-SEVEN

I step out of the shower and scrub the towel across my skin. We didn't do much training at all today, given that I need to save my energy for tonight. But Jeb had me go through his fight-day protocol, which included an hour of film pointing out Bodhi's weaknesses for the last time, and then visualization exercises.

I'm prepared. More prepared than I've been for *anything* in my life. Once I step inside that cage, anything can happen, but I'm ready. Beyond fucking ready.

When I got home, I checked on Scarlett, who was with Kelsey in the master bath, working on her makeup. I gave her a kiss on her lips, which were still bare, and then headed to shower in the guest room.

I wrap the towel around my waist, brace my palms on the counter, and meet my gaze in the mirror.

"Tonight, we win. Tomorrow, we take out Moses." I make the promise and then head for the guest room, where my suit from Gunter hangs.

I was surprised the old man made it, but what he said to Scarlett gave me something I didn't know I needed. Approval from her people. It feels pretty fucking great that they don't think I'm reaching above my station. Apparently, I've been the only one hung up on that this whole time. And now, I don't give a damn what anyone thinks.

I slip on the silk-lined black suit pants and button up the tailored black shirt. The black vest is next. Black on black on black. The old man's taste is impeccable, not that I should be surprised. With the jacket still on its hanger, I head out into the living room and hang it on a hook near the door that leads into the rest of the building.

I check my phone to see if I've missed a notification while I was showering, and there's only one. It brings a smile to my face, and I reply immediately.

FLYNN: *Kick some ass tonight, bro. I'm proud of you, win or lose.*
LEGEND: *Consider it done, lil sis.*

Kelsey's voice carries from the bathroom and out through the bedroom so that I can hear some of what she's saying.

"I swear to God, love is the best highlighter there is. I don't think you've ever looked this radiant, Scar. All my clients need a Gabriel Legend, if they want to glow like you."

Scarlett's response isn't loud enough for me to overhear, but I don't need to. She loves me. I see it every time she looks at me. It took a little while for me to be able to recognize the emotion, since I didn't have a hell of a lot of experience with it, but now I can't mistake it for anything else.

"Let's get your dress on and then do your lips," Kelsey says in a singsong voice. "I'm *dying* to see this look come together."

I settle into one of the chairs in the living room and cross an ankle over my knee. Kelsey isn't the only one who wants to see Scarlett, but I'm in no rush. We've got an hour before we need to leave for the club, and then roughly another three hours before Bodhi and I are up, depending on whether the undercard fights go the distance.

Because my fights have never been sanctioned, tonight is technically the start and end of my professional career. Bodhi had a run in one of the pro organizations a few years back, before he realized the money was better underground. So, the odds are firmly in his favor, which is ironic, because I beat him last time. Either way, that only helps me. Betting on an underdog who pulls out the victory is the most profitable way to go.

My head jerks up at the squeals of excitement coming from the bedroom.

"Oh. My. Gawd. This is . . . Jesus Christ. Gunter is a wizard. You look *amazing.*"

Well, hell. I guess it's time to put on my jacket so I look the part too.

I move to where I hung it and slide it over my shoulders . . . just in time to see Kelsey poke her head out of the doorway.

"Oh, good. You're here. Damn. You two are going to set records tonight for the hottest couple in history. But don't take my word for it . . ." She trails off and steps to the side.

A moment later, Scarlett comes into view.

Holy. Fucking. Shit.

She's a goddess. There's no other word for it.

"Wow." The word slips from my lips, but in no way does her justice.

Molten gold hugs her every curve, set off by her shimmering blond hair and creamy skin. She barely looks real . . . at least, not until her lips curve up into a dazzling smile.

"Wow, yourself. You look incredible."

I shake my head, coming toward her. "Jesus Christ. You . . .

fuck, ladybug . . . you're stunning." I reach out to take her hand and slowly lift it to my lips.

"Oh shit, that's too fucking cute. Hold on," Kelsey says, but I can barely hear her over the blood rushing through my ears.

Scarlett stares into my eyes. "I wanted to make you proud tonight."

"You could wear sweats and a ripped T-shirt, and you'd still do that."

Her grin widens. "I'm glad you think that."

A light flashes from Kelsey's direction, and Scarlett and I turn.

"Oh shit, yes. That picture is epic." She looks up from her phone and sees us watching her, and her shoulders lift up to her ears. "Shit, sorry. Carry on."

We both laugh, and Scarlett holds out her hand. "You might as well show me, since you got the shot you wanted."

"Here, look. Isn't that amazing?"

Scarlett gasps. "Oh my God. Okay, I'm really glad you did that."

I glance down at the screen and see what she's excited about. We look like something out of a movie. A blond goddess and a slightly scandalous mortal. But we look damn good together.

"Will you send me that?" I ask Kelsey.

"Of course. And, Scar, you gotta post it. The interwebs will go *crazy* when you post a picture of the two of you together. I mean, *shit*. How could they not?"

Scarlett's attention cuts to my face as her lips press together. "Do you care if I post it? I know it's a big step, but . . ."

There's no way she can know the smile tugging the corners of my mouth comes from the fact that I plan on a much bigger step a hell of a lot sooner than she expects. "Do whatever you want, ladybug. I got nothing to hide about the fact that I'm in love with you. I don't care who knows it."

"Oh my *God*," Kelsey says with a long sigh. "I think my heart is officially melting now."

Scarlett shoots a look at her friend. "Kels . . . you have no idea."

Kelsey breaks into a giggle. "Let me get my kit, and I'll get out of your hair. I'll see you at Legend. Good luck, Gabe. Knock him out. Or whatever you're planning to do."

She sneaks behind Scarlett, and I lead my golden girl into the middle of the living room.

"All I want to do is kiss you, but I'm not messing up that lipstick. Not yet, anyway."

"As long as you plan on kissing me later, that's all that matters."

Kelsey rolls her suitcase out of the bedroom and nods at us both. "Beautiful. Handsome. I'll see you later. Off to get myself ready!" With a wave, she's gone.

"I think Kelsey has a crush on you now," Scarlett says to me.

"I'm all yours, so that's too bad."

Scarlett reaches out to straighten the lapels of my suit jacket. "You're damn right, you're all mine. I'm so proud of you, Gabe. No matter what happens tonight, you're it for me. I love you."

Hearing her say that it doesn't matter whether I win or lose means more to me than any victory ever has. But, even so, it doesn't cause my confidence to waver in the slightest.

"I'm going to win. The rest of our life starts tonight. I've got big plans for us both, ladybug."

Her smile is shimmering in its brilliance. "Good, because I have big plans of my own too." She leans her head toward me and ghosts her lips across mine, and I savor the faint taste of her.

When she pulls back, our eyes lock.

"I love you, Scarlett. Thank you for being you. Thank you for believing in me. Thank you for showing me that life was about more than I realized. You have no idea how much you've changed me for the better."

"It goes both ways. You taught me about living. How not to

just stand on the sidelines. I can't wait to see where we go next, *after* you win."

She smooths her delicate fingers across my hair, the gentle movement slowing my heartbeat. It's the peace I need. The calm before the storm.

FORTY-EIGHT

The ride to Legend has never felt quite like this before. Hal's driving us in a snazzy Range Rover, but we're not alone. We've got security in front of us and behind us in black SUVs.

Scarlett hasn't said anything about it, but I assume it's not her first time arriving somewhere with an entourage. When we pull up to the club, there's a red carpet rolled out, and even though I didn't expect to see many cameras, given the relatively early hour, there's plenty.

She must read my thoughts from my expression.

"And . . . that's probably because I posted our picture and said we were on our way." She turns to me with a hesitant expression on her face. "I hope you don't mind."

I rake my gaze over her in that dress and rub my fingers over my mouth. "The more pictures of you in that dress, the better. You're gorgeous, ladybug."

Her smile lights up her entire face, which is already glowing, like Kelsey said. "Bump, Zoe, and Q are already here, right?"

I nod. "Zoe and Q have been here all day. Bump is coming with Big Mike and Joanie."

"Are they bringing Roux?"

"Of course," I tell her with a grin. "My girl wouldn't miss it for the world. Bump's been taking good care of her, though. It's going to break his heart when I tell him that she's coming home with us because I'm done training."

"Maybe we need to get Bump his own puppy so he won't feel the sting quite so much."

"Maybe we will," I say as Hal glances back at me.

"You two ready? You want me to get the door?"

"We're ready," I reply, and Scarlett nods. "Let's do this."

As soon as Hal opens the door, the paps lean into the barriers, craning their necks to see who's in the SUV. As I step out, they start calling my name.

"Legend!"

"Gabriel!"

"Do you really think you can beat Black?"

I hold out my hand for Scarlett and help her out of the vehicle. As soon as her feet touch the carpet, she turns an incredible smile on the paps, and together, we walk toward the lineup as they shout questions at both of us. About Bodhi. Our last fight. Whether Scarlett and I are engaged. Getting married. Whether she's pregnant.

The questions go on and on, but Scarlett doesn't respond to them as we walk and pause and pose, then keep moving. As she takes my arm to carefully climb the steps in front of the club, I have to marvel at her poise.

"You're really fucking good at that, you know?"

"Don't worry, it'll be second nature before you know it. You never need to answer their questions. It just adds to the mystery."

Once we're inside, the paps' questions are replaced by the bustle of the club coming to life for the event. The cage is in the center of the expansive dance floor, surrounded by rows and rows of seating. With the columns rising up to the ceiling, it looks pretty damn impressive, if I do say so myself.

Zoe rushes up to us. "You're here! And *wow*." She blinks at Scarlett's dress. "You look unbelievable. Not too shabby yourself, boss," she says with a grin after inspecting my one-of-a-kind suit.

"Bump and your folks here yet?" I ask her.

"Not yet, but they should be on their way. Your coaches are up in your office, though, so after you've checked everything down here one last time, I assume you'll head up there."

"Good work, Zoe. Couldn't have done this without you and Q."

"It's our pleasure. And just so you know, we both put money on you. No pressure, though."

I laugh, like I don't already feel it. "Thanks. Come on, ladybug."

FORTY-NINE

Scarlett

Other than those fights I watched on YouTube and the time I spent at the gym with Gabe, I don't know anything about mixed martial arts. I certainly have no idea how things work before a fight, but my education is happening quickly and firsthand.

Gabriel did one last sweep of the club, talked to Q, and then we went up to his office. It's been turned into a locker room for him to warm up with sparring partners and all three of his coaches, who will be in his corner for the fight.

Thankfully, Gunter's suit was photographed about a thousand times before we came inside, because Gabriel stripped it off first thing to change into his warm-up gear.

Before they start with whatever comes next, there's a knock at the door, and Bump pokes his head inside.

"Gabe! You're here!"

"Come on in, bud."

The door opens farther and Roux streaks inside, bounding right to Gabriel. Used to her enthusiasm, he's ready for the dog's excitement.

"I knew she'd be so happy to see you!"

The man and his dog bond on the mat as Bump, Joanie, and Big Mike enter the office and shut the door.

"We don't want to bother you. You've got warming up to do, but we wanted to say good luck before we take our seats," Big Mike says. That's when I notice he and Bump are wearing matching suits, and both look as dapper as can be.

"Bump, I love the suit," I say, rising from my seat in the corner and coming toward him.

His eyes light up when he sees me. He holds out his arms like he's going to rush forward to hug me, but then he stops in his tracks. "Am I even allowed to touch you right now? I don't wanna mess you up. Not like that time with the rug, but you know what I mean."

"I will accept nothing less than a hug."

His head bounces as he practically skips toward me. "You're so pretty."

"And you are as handsome as can be."

Head in the air, he's as proud as a peacock. "Big Mike says if Gabe wins, he'll take me to the titty bar and let me celebrate. He said the girls love a man in a suit."

Joanie's gasp follows Bump's comment, and she slaps her husband's arm. "Michael . . ."

"Getting me in trouble was not what we discussed, kid."

Bump scrunches his shoulders and giggles. "Oops. I wasn't supposed to tell."

Gabriel comes toward us and throws an arm around Bump. "Q will take you another night. You can still wear the suit."

"Does that mean you're not going to win?" Bump asks as his face falls.

The entire room goes silent, and the air vibrates. Gabriel is the only one who doesn't hold his breath.

"I'm gonna win, bud. Don't worry."

"Okay, good. That's what I thought." Bump shrugs like it's no big deal. "I mean, you beat him before. How hard can it really be to do it again?"

Gabriel's booming laughter fills the office turned locker room, and everyone else follows suit.

"Damn right, he's gonna beat him again," Jeb says from across the floor. "I don't train losers. Now, whoever's staying, take a seat. Time to get our boy ready."

Gabriel crushes Bump to him with a hard hug. "Stay out of trouble tonight. Okay?"

"Ten-four, good buddy."

Roux curls up in the corner in the dog bed that's a few feet from my chair, and Mike and Joanie both wave as they lead Bump out of the office.

Q comes in a bit later to let us know the undercard is starting, and that the club is damn near at full capacity but everything's covered. Gabriel nods at him and thanks him, but goes right back to the pre-fight sequence that I'm guessing Jeb has down to a science.

I stare at Gabriel's body as he moves in ways I didn't know were possible for a man to do with such grace. It's captivating and fluid, and I could watch him for hours, especially since no one is trying to punch him in the face for real right now.

The next knock on the door is Hal, and he's here for me. "Scarlett, if you'd like to come down with me, I'll show you to your seat. They'll be up for Gabe in five to ten minutes."

Gabriel rises off the mat and comes toward me. "You good, ladybug?"

I nod, suddenly nervous as hell. Terrified that I'm going to do or say the wrong thing. Terrified that everything could go wrong, even though I believe it's going to go right.

"You sure?" he asks a little quieter.

"I love you, Gabe. So damned much. More than I knew was possible. Give 'em hell and then tomorrow, we're definitely sleeping in, and I'm going to use those ladybug salt and pepper shakers to make you fluffy eggs from Scarlett's Diner."

A grin takes over his face, which is shiny with sweat. "That sounds like a hell of a plan, and I can't fucking wait. I love you too. Relax. Everything's going to be fine."

I lean in to kiss him, inhaling the masculine scent wafting off his skin. "I'll see you soon."

As I walk out of the room, I wave at Jeb and the guys, keeping my head held high. As soon as Hal shuts the door behind me, I pause and release a huge breath.

"You okay, Ms. Priest?"

I turn and meet the older man's green eyes. "I don't know, Hal. I really don't know."

He pats me on the back. "Pre-fight jitters. I've seen it a thousand times. You're gonna be fine, sweetheart, and so is he. This is what he's been training for. You gotta believe he can do it."

"I believe he can . . . I really do. But how am I supposed to be okay with watching someone try to hurt him?"

Hal shrugs. "It's all part of the game. You'll feel better in a bit. All your friends are waiting for you."

With another shaky breath, I let him lead me down to the main level and out onto the floor. People call my name as I walk by, and I smile blindly at them but I don't stop. I can't possibly make conversation right now with someone who needs me to be "on." I don't have it in me.

As soon as I spot Harlow and Jimmy, Monroe and Nate, Ryan and Christine, and Kelsey and her brother Jon, a layer of nerves fades away. They're my people, and if I'm freaking out, they'll understand.

"I'm so glad you're here," I whisper as I scoot down the row past Harlow and Monroe.

"Girl, you look . . . *insane*. Good God."

I've long since forgotten about what I'm wearing and have to glance down at the dress to remember. "Oh, yeah. Thank you."

Harlow catches on first. "Shit, you look like you're going to puke."

I inhale a slow, calming breath and release it. "I'm really glad you're next to me, because I'm gonna need to hold your hand. I swear I'll try not to break it."

"You got it, girl. Whatever you need."

I give a wide smile to the entire audience as I scan it before turning to sit down. One face almost makes it falter.

See. You. Next. Tuesday. Herself. *Lucy Byers.* She's at the end of the row, near the door to the cage.

I turn and drop into my seat before my smile turns into a jealous-for-no-reason glare. "What is she doing here?" I whisper to Harlow through clenched teeth.

"Who?"

"Lucy."

Harlow turns to look before I can tell her not to. "That fucking bitch. I didn't see her earlier. You want me to have security tell her to get the fuck out of here?"

I shake my head. "No. Because then she'll cause a scene and I'll have to kill her, and I don't want to be stuck with only seeing Gabriel naked during conjugal visits for the rest of my life."

"Wait, are you getting married?" Harlow asks loudly enough for Monroe's head to turn on a swivel.

"Whoa. What did I miss? Did you get a ring?" she asks, reaching for my hand.

"No. No, I was just saying—"

"Lucy Byers is here," Harlow says, explaining to Monroe before squeezing my hand. "If she bothers you, I'll handle her. Okay?"

"Me too." Monroe lifts her chin. "I hate that bitch."

"Everything good?" Kelsey asks from the row behind us.

"We're perfect," Harlow replies with another squeeze.

The lights dim in the club, and everyone goes quiet before the music starts playing.

I don't recognize the song, but then Jon Pak says from behind us, "Whoa. 'Sweet Revenge' by Motorhead. That's one hell of a message."

Those nerves I felt earlier? They're rising strong as Bodhi walks out down the aisle toward the cage, looking like a giant in all black.

Jesus Christ. I forgot how big he is. Gabriel's not small, but Bodhi is massive.

"They'd never be able to fight if it wasn't catchweight," Jon Pak says.

Part of me wants to turn around and tell him to shut the hell up before I freak out . . . and the fight hasn't even started.

Bodhi strips down to his shorts and waits while a man smears what appears to be Vaseline on his face. A second man, a ref, steps up and checks his nails and mouthpiece, then makes Bodhi tap his cup. When they're finished with the ritual, he climbs the short set of stairs leading into the cage. It's the shape of an octagon, with eight black-coated chain-link sides and padded rails at the top.

My former self-defense instructor jogs around the center before the music goes silent for a beat, then changes to a Tom Petty song that I've heard many times before. But it's never given me chills like it does tonight.

The entire club is on its feet as the lyrics of "Won't Back Down" blare through the speakers, and we all wait for Gabriel to make his entrance.

As soon as I catch sight of movement in the aisle, my heart skips a beat. I squeeze Harlow's hand tightly.

"Here he comes!" She squeals, bouncing beside me. "Gah. This is happening!"

FIFTY

I waited until the last minute to decide on my walk-out song, but I think "Won't Back Down" sends exactly the right message as I jog down the aisle, slapping the hands of people in the crowd.

This may not be the biggest fight in the biggest venue, but it feels that fucking way to me because I've never had more on the line. My coaches are behind me, and my confidence is at an all-time high.

Bodhi has come for his revenge, but he won't be finding it here tonight. Not a fucking chance.

Everyone is on their feet, and the energy inside this club, the club that *I built*, is electric. I feed off it, letting it flow through my body as I approach the cage. I stop in front of the ref to strip off my shirt, kick off my shoes and socks, and peel my pants off. The cheers grow louder, and the crowd starts to chant.

"Legend. Legend. Legend."

I may be an underdog in the odds, but clearly I'm the favorite with the people in this club tonight, and that works for me.

There's more pomp and showmanship tonight than for any of

the fights I've been in before, but it feels right. I'm here, in front of the city I've adopted as my home, to win.

After the cutman greases me up and the ref checks me out, I head into the cage and send up a prayer.

Don't let me forget who I am and what I came here for.

I jog a lap around the inside of the cage, my gaze trained on Bodhi. He's just as big, if not bigger, than he was before. Fighting at catchweight puts me at a disadvantage, another reason for the odds, but he doesn't intimidate me in the least. Not ever before and certainly not tonight, in my house.

He may be bigger, but I've got knockout power too, and I'm younger, faster, and smarter. That's all going to play in my favor.

As the announcer tells the crowd what they're in for, I find Scarlett in the front row. Her face is pale, and I know this isn't easy for her. I've never had a woman I gave a damn about, or who gave a damn about me, watch me fight before. That's new and different, and I have a feeling she's going to feel every punch the same way I do.

But she's strong. Stronger than even she knows. I shoot her a wink to help put some color on her cheeks.

Just once, ladybug. Just hang with me through this once, and I promise you don't ever have to see it happen again.

I toyed with the idea of continuing to fight after tonight, but I don't need to. I've got nothing to prove after this. I'll put Bodhi down, collect my fat stack of cash, and call it good.

The ref steps into the middle of the cage, and Bodhi and I approach from either side. He gives us the final instructions and tells us we can touch gloves.

We don't.

He backs off, and the bell rings.

It's time.

We both come in hard and fast, both wanting to make the first move and draw first blood. Bodhi throws a right jab, but telegraphs it like crazy. I swing with a hook, catching him on the chin. Spit flies from his mouth as I sneer at him.

That's right, old man. This dog's learned new tricks.

FIFTY-ONE

I don't watch through my fingers, but I might have broken a few of Harlow's in the first round.

Five minutes has never seemed so long in my life. Gabriel and Bodhi go at each other, punch for punch. People behind me scream and yell things like, "Stand and bang, boys!" and "Hit him!"

I've never felt this kind of raw energy before. The crowd wants blood, and by the time they retreat to their corners, both men have it on their faces.

Gabriel has a cut on his cheekbone that his team goes to work on right away, pressing something against it.

"Oh God. He's hurt," I say to Harlow. "I don't like this."

Behind me, Jon Pak squeezes my shoulders. "He's fine. It's nothing. Barely bleeding. Black looks way worse with that gash over his eye. The blood will impair his vision, and he won't be able to see as well in the second round."

I turn around to look at him. "Really?"

Jon nods, and Kelsey smiles at me.

"He knows what he's talking about. He's seen your man fight

before. MMA is pretty much his most favorite thing ever." She turns to her brother. "Do you think Legend won that round?"

Jon's gaze cuts from Kelsey to me. I'm not sure I want him to respond to the question, but I tell myself I need to know anyway.

I nod at Jon, giving him the go-ahead to answer.

Choosing his words carefully, he starts slowly. "It was close. Legend definitely needs to make some decisive moves in the next round if he wants to win it and keep the judges' scorecards even, if not in his favor."

I swallow the lump that's been growing in my throat ever since Gabriel gave me a wink from inside that cage. "Okay. Well, close is better than losing. And hopefully he'll make some good moves in the second round."

The words sound foreign coming out of my mouth, and I feel like the total novice I am at this.

Why didn't I watch more fights? Learn the lingo? Know what to expect? Clearly, I wasn't thinking right.

Oh yeah, because I was running a business and worrying about the cyber stalker who has been trolling me, and Moses coming to get us, all while falling head over heels in love with an incredible man who I want *not* to get punched in the face anymore, although that last part is a long shot.

Only two more rounds to go. I can do this. I take a deep breath and release it as the men surrounding both Bodhi and Gabe pack up their buckets and walk out.

The ref moves back to the middle of the cage when Bodhi and Gabriel are on their feet again. The bell sounds, and Bodhi *charges.* He flat-out *runs* at Gabriel across the cage, grabs him around the waist, and throws him to the canvas.

"Oh my God!" Monroe screeches from a few seats down, but I stay silent.

Oh God. No. No. No.

They grapple on the canvas, each man fighting for position

with fists and elbows flying. Somehow, Gabe wraps him up in a hold and stops the blows Bodhi is raining down on his face.

Oh God, Gabe. Come on, stud. You can do this.

They roll around, shifting positions over and over, and Jon keeps a running commentary behind me.

"Good, Legend. Keep him in your guard. You got this."

A few moments later, Bodhi breaks free and scrambles to a standing position. Gabe bounces up to his feet before Bodhi can come back at him on the canvas.

"All right, all right. Let's see who's got the better technical skills here," Jon says, but I don't really know what that means.

They start to box like Gabriel did with the pads. Each moves quickly, darting in and out. Bodhi lands a hard shot and Gabriel stumbles back a few steps, shaking his head.

"Fuck, he hurt him," Jon whispers just loudly enough for me to hear.

Part of me wants to tell him to keep that kind of comment to himself, but the other part of me needs to know what's going on through an expert's eyes.

"Come on, Legend!" Harlow screams from beside me. "Hit him!"

Gabriel moves forward, ducking under one of Bodhi's flying hands that looks like it would feel like getting hit with an anvil if it connected. When Bodhi's jaw is exposed, Gabriel's fist flashes out with lightning speed, and Bodhi's head snaps back.

"Fuck yeah! That's a fight!" someone in the crowd screams from behind me.

The roar of the crowd grows as the men trade punches and the clock ticks down. A wooden clapping sound echoes in the club.

"Ten seconds!"

Bodhi charges forward, his elbow slicing through the air. Gabriel loses his balance and lands on his ass, and more than anything, I want to scream, "*No!*" But I'm too terrified that I'll distract him. Bodhi pounces, landing on him and going after his face with those bricks he calls hands.

"Five seconds!" someone yells as Gabriel covers up and kicks out a leg, catching Bodhi in the thigh.

"You can make it, man!" Jon yells.

Finally, the bell dings and the ref jumps in between the men, pulling Bodhi away from Gabriel. As Gabriel rises, blood drips down his face from a cut above his eyebrow and his nose.

I want to murder Bodhi Black. I can't help it. *No one makes my man bleed without consequences.*

My bloodthirstiness doesn't surprise me. There is nothing I wouldn't do for Gabriel, and seeing him hurt is enough to fuel me to do things I've never considered before.

"Fuck. That didn't look good," Harlow whispers, whipping around to look at Kelsey and Jon. "Am I right? It's bad to end the round on the bottom getting beat up, isn't it?"

I turn just in time to catch Jon's grim expression. *He thinks Gabriel's losing this fight.*

Instead of fear wrapping around me like vines, determination fills my veins. I find my faith.

"It doesn't matter. He's going to win. He's going to end this fight just like he did the last time he fought Bodhi. Don't you dare count him out," I say, leaving absolutely no room for argument.

Kelsey's lips curve into a smile. "I believe you, babe. He can do it." She elbows Jon. "Right?"

Jon shrugs and nods. "Yeah. I mean, anything can happen in the cage. But he's down at least one round, maybe two. He's gotta end him in this round or . . ."

He doesn't need to finish his sentence for all of us to know exactly what's on the line. Gabe has to either get Bodhi in a submission hold or knock him out before the next bell rings in order to win this fight.

Come on, stud. You've got this. Five more minutes to make it count.

FIFTY-TWO

"Slow and steady. That's right. Breathe," Jeb says as he shoves a bag of ice behind my back.

I anchor my elbows on my knees as they work on my face, trying to stop the bleeding.

Bodhi is strong as fuck, and his hands feel like they've been dipped in cement.

I knew his power coming into this. I expected it. It's just been a long fucking time since I've been hit that hard.

He caught me. There's no fucking doubt about it. That right cross rocked me and put me right on my ass.

"Everyone's got a plan until they get punched in the mouth." Mike Tyson's quote has never been truer than it is right now.

"There's a good fucking chance you're down two rounds, Gabe. This is it. You gotta finish him before the bell."

"I know. I know." I say the words between long, slow breaths, pausing as Jeb squirts water in my mouth.

"He's not gassing out like I thought. He must've known you were going to try to tire him out, so he got his cardio up. That's not like him, but it means we gotta readjust. You got plenty of gas in the tank. You take him down and you submit him."

Jeb has never steered me wrong before, and I can't blame him for misjudging Bodhi's cardio. The man looks too big to be able to sustain a fast pace for all three rounds, or at least he always has been. But Bodhi's clearly got a fuck of a lot on the line here tonight too, or he's fueled with the power of hate.

I can't let that stop me. Whatever he has on the line, I have more. My whole fucking life. Everything I've ever wanted. And I have five minutes to go out there and fucking claim it.

"I won't fuck this up. I'm ending it. The ref is gonna stop the fight when he's either knocked out or tapping out."

Jeb slaps my shoulder. "That's right. Go in there and get to fucking work. You've got the skills. You've got the drive. You deserve this. Take what's yours. Get out there and show me that you fucking want this!"

I slap my hands on my thighs and rise to my feet, letting the ice fall to the cage floor. "This is my house. My fight. My win. And I'm gonna fucking take it."

Jeb slaps both my shoulders. "That's fucking right. Now, go get this win!"

The ref signals to us that it's time, and Jeb and the guys load up the bucket and leave me to get to work.

My house. My fight. My win.

Across the cage, Bodhi smiles at me with his bloody mouthpiece.

You think you've got this in the bag, Black? You don't fucking know me at all. Underestimate me. I dare you.

The ref lets us loose and backs out of the center. I stride forward, ready to knock this motherfucker out.

But as Black reaches me, his fists fly. Clearly, he has the same plan.

His glove wings at my jaw where he clipped me at the end of the second round, but I move my head fast enough that it doesn't catch me again.

"I'm not making this fucking easy for you," I grunt at him, and he glares.

"I'm gonna take your fucking head off." As soon as he bites out the last word, he telegraphs a jab, and I bob and strike with an uppercut.

Bodhi's head snaps back. I charge forward, following it up with a jab and an elbow.

He recovers, throwing a kick to my thigh. *Fuck, that stings.*

My hands move without thought, throwing a combination that pummels his body.

He flinches, and I know he fucking felt that.

I glance up to check the time, and Bodhi surges forward, totally catching me off guard. I have one thought as I hit the floor of the cage.

Fuck.

FIFTY-THREE

Oh God. Oh God. No.

Bodhi took Gabriel down with the force of a freight train, and now Gabriel's on his back again.

"Shit!" Jon yells. "Come on, Legend! You can turn this around!"

Gabriel moves his hips, and my jaw drops as he uses what appears to be pure magic to flip their positions.

"Go, baby, go!" I scream as Gabriel rolls on top of Bodhi's head. His limbs move so fast, I can barely tell what's happening.

"Legend's got a body triangle. Not sure he can submit him with that. Maybe he'll go for the arm bar," Jon says, leaning forward so I can hear him over the wild cheering surrounding us.

"Come on, Legend!" Harlow screams, and I jump to my feet with the rest of the crowd.

The cheers of *"Legend, Legend, Legend"* echo through the club, nearly deafening me.

But Gabriel loses the advantage, and they roll across the floor so fast, I can barely keep track of who is in the better position.

Then they change position again, and Gabriel bounds to his feet.

For a moment, Bodhi lies on the canvas, his arms and legs in the air, like he's expecting Gabriel to come back at him. When he doesn't, Bodhi jumps up and charges at Gabriel. Gabriel is ready this time, though, because he pushes off the cage floor to leap into the air. His right knee rams directly into Bodhi's bowed head.

Bodhi's entire body goes slack and drops, and chaos erupts in the club.

"Knockout!" someone roars as Gabriel pounces, ready to finish Bodhi off. But the ref waves his arms, shoving Gabriel away as everyone rushes toward the cage.

"It's all over!" Jon says as he slaps my shoulder from behind.

"Go, go, go!" Harlow yells at me, pushing me in the direction of the cage door. "He's going to want you in there when they raise his hand."

People are crushed together, surging out of their seats, and I can barely move. I try to maneuver through them, not thinking about anything but getting to Gabriel inside the cage.

Thank God, it's over. He won. He really won. Thank God.

I make it almost to the stairs leading up to the cage, and something jabs me in the side. *Hard.*

I jerk my head around and down to see what the hell I ran into, but all I see is Lucy Byers's malevolent gaze.

"That's a gun, and if I pull the trigger, you'll bleed out right here."

"What—" I start to sputter a question, but Lucy's claw-tipped fingers wrap around my arm and squeeze.

"Don't say a word. You're coming with me. Right now."

The riotous cheering of the crowd fades away as static fills my head. I look for Hal, but I was too fast out of my seat, and there's no way he'll be able to find me quickly in this madhouse of a crowd.

I jerk at my arm, but Lucy smiles, and I swear, her expression embodies pure evil.

"You'll be dead before you hit the floor if you try that again. Come on." She starts moving, and I glance down at the black barrel of a small handgun driving into the gold fabric of my dress.

This isn't happening. Not right here. Not with all these people.

That's when I realize what's really at stake. *I can't let her shoot me in this club. It'll never recover.*

I have a split second to make the decision. Fight right here and risk her shooting me—or someone else—sending the club into a stampeding frenzy . . . or follow her out of the club and subdue her where she can't hurt anyone else.

I've taken self-defense. I know how to do this.

Maybe it's not the smartest decision I've ever made, but I know what I have to do. *Protect Gabriel and the club.*

I walk with Lucy, a smile on my face belying the fact that I have a gun jabbing into my kidney. The crowd blocks anyone from seeing what she's holding as Lucy shoves me toward a door that nearly blends into the wall at the back of the club.

As soon as the door closes behind us, I make my move, jabbing my elbow into her stomach as I spin around to grab hold of her wrist and twist *hard.*

"You bitch!" she screams as she loses her grip on the gun and it clatters to the floor, sliding toward the wall.

We both dive for it, but Lucy must realize that I'm going to beat her, because she latches onto something else instead—the necklace I'm wearing. It jerks me back like a dog on a choke chain, cutting into my skin for an instant before the delicate links snap.

Doesn't matter, get the gun.

I crawl toward it, but a man's battered leather boot lands on top of the pistol before my fingers can wrap around it.

"Well, well, well. How about this shit?"

I look up and my gaze zeroes in on a new gun, this one with a really long, thick tube attached to the barrel . . . pointed at Lucy.

Oh my God. I've seen those in movies. That's a silencer.

I stare at the hand before my gaze tracks up his arm to his shoulder, and then finally to the face of the man holding it.

Recognition hits me first. He was the one who talked to Gabriel that first night I met him and Roux at the gym. He knew Bodhi. He wanted Gabriel to fight him. *What is his name? It's like the candy . . .*

"Who the fuck are you?" Lucy snaps out the question.

"Rolo?" I whisper, hesitantly trying it out.

"You got that right," he replies to me, looking down at the gun beneath his boot. "Now, what the fuck is going on here?"

"Give me my gun," Lucy demands.

Rolo squats down to pick it up, keeping the silencer trained on her. "I don't take orders from cunts like you." At least he's right about her being a cunt. When he rises, he's got a gun pointed at each of us. "Get up."

I slowly rise to my feet, and Lucy does the same, my necklace dangling from her fingers.

I sneer at her. "I hope whatever you had planned was worth this."

"He's not going to shoot me, but I don't give a damn if he shoots you," Lucy says, venom dripping from her words. "He'll be doing me a favor."

I glance at Rolo, wondering what the hell his plan is. Because you don't just show up in a club with a gun that has a *silencer on it* unless you plan to use it.

"You want Legend's bitch dead?" Rolo asks her, sounding genuinely curious. "That's what you were doing here?"

"The world would be a better place without that fake princess sitting in her ivory tower. So, why don't you do me a favor and pull that trigger?"

Rolo chuckles. "Damn, you're an ice-cold bitch. What the fuck did she do to you?"

"Good question," I whisper.

Lucy turns and glares at me. "Twenty years. For *twenty fucking years* I've had to watch you live your perfect fucking life and get everything I want. I'm done, which means *you're done.*"

I blink twice, trying to understand what she's saying, because she sounds like a deranged lunatic. "You've hated me for twenty years? And now you want me dead? What the hell, Lucy? Are you off your meds or something?"

When Rolo huffs out a laugh, Lucy turns her malice on him. "You don't get it. She had everything. Since the day her perfect fucking mom walked her into class, and everyone wanted to be her. *I was the one everyone wanted to be before you. You took that from me.*"

She's fucking nuts.

Clearly, I'm not the only one thinking that, because Rolo glances at me. "Bitch be crazy."

"Fuck you, asshole. Give me my gun, and I'll get her out of your way."

"Fucking crazy," he says with a shake of his head. "How were you getting away with this?"

Lucy flips her hair like she doesn't have a gun trained on her, making me even more certain she's gone off the deep end. "Oh, that part's easy. Everyone's going to be *so sad* when Scarlett's stalker finally kills her."

My mouth drops open. "You were going to frame the troll for this? Jesus Christ, Lucy."

Maniacal laughter breaks free from her lips. "Fucking Scarlett. Always the last to know. Bitch, I *am* the troll." She turns back to Rolo and holds out her hand. "Now, give me the gun. I've got shit to do."

I'm frozen. Shell-shocked. *It was her all this time?*

I don't know if it's the entitlement in her tone or what, but Rolo just shakes his head.

"Bitch, shut the fuck up."

Lucy charges him, and I see it before she does—Rolo's finger squeezing the trigger.

"Lucy! No!"

But the *pop* of the muffled gunshot comes next, and I throw myself toward the wall and away from her and Rolo. My body hits the floor at the same time Lucy's does.

Oh my God. He shot her. I want to look, but I'm terrified. *Jesus Christ. He* shot *her.*

His boots stop in front of me, and Rolo holds out a hand—except there's no gun in it now. *Where did he put Lucy's?*

"Get up. She ain't bothering you again."

I know I can't trust him. *He fucking shot her.*

"Come on, get up. You're lucky I shot that bitch. Couldn't have her killing you before I get the shit that belongs to *me*. Legend shoulda thought twice before cutting me out. Making me go through all this shit—shooting up the club, trying to fuck up Black. It's not fucking right. But she just made it hell of a lot easier to get to you, at least. Now, let's go."

Rolo shot up the club and went after Bodhi? Oh my God. I'm struggling to process Rolo's words when he grabs my arm and yanks me to my feet, shoving me down the hallway toward another door.

I jerk my head around to look behind us, and there Lucy is . . . with a dark pool growing around her prone body.

"Oh my God." I stumble, tripping over the hem of my dress, but he yanks me upright.

The gunshot. People had to hear the gunshot. Right? But my ears are barely ringing . . . which means . . . there's no way anyone could hear it over the crowd because of the silencer.

"Go, bitch. Unless you want me to shoot you right here too?"

I stumble forward, even more terrified of Rolo than Lucy, because I just watched him end her life without a shred of remorse.

Rolo shoves me toward the door with an EXIT sign glowing

red above it, and waves at it with the gun. "Open the door, rich bitch, or I will shoot you in the fucking head. You hear me?"

My hand trembles as I reach for the door, my self-defense skills no longer appearing as useful as I once hoped they'd be.

What do I do? Leave the club and go with him? Or stand my ground and die fighting?

Gabriel, what do I do?

FIFTY-FOUR

"**W**here the fuck is she?" I shout at Hal, who's near the cage but still out in the crowd, while the announcer comes out to declare me the winner of the fight by knockout.

"I don't know. She was coming up there. I can't find her in all these people!" he shouts from just feet outside the cage.

The ref grabs my hand and raises it in the air, but I don't give a shit about anything right now, including winning. Only one thing matters, and that's Scarlett.

As soon as they announce me as the winner, Jeb comes over. "Let's get a picture—"

"My woman's missing. Gotta go."

His expression morphs into one of seriousness. "What? How?"

"I don't fucking know."

I run for the cage door, pushing through the crowd at the stairs, and catch sight of Monroe and Harlow. "Where is she?"

Harlow shakes her head. "I don't know! She ran up there to get to you. She's *gone.*"

"Fuck!" I roar the word and plow through the crowd, ignoring everyone who is trying to congratulate me. Clap me on the back. Tell me *job well done.*

None of it matters. If Moses has Scarlett, my world is gone. No one knows the hell I'm living right now. Not a single person in this place.

Someone tugs my arm, and I'm tempted to throw an elbow until I see his face. Q.

"What's wrong?"

"Scarlett's gone. I don't know where she went right after the knockout. No one does."

His face pales. "Fuck. Fuck. Fuck." He reaches for a com controller I didn't notice earlier, attached to his suit. "Scarlett is missing. Lock the place down. No one goes in or out. Find her. Keep her fucking safe."

Security. He's talking to security. The extra security we have on duty to prevent this from happening to begin with.

"They have to find her," I tell him, charging toward the back of the club, not sure where the hell I'm going, but I know she isn't *here.*

Q follows me, and when we hit a pocket of empty space near the bar, he slaps a hand over my shoulder. "Someone thought they saw Rolo right before the fight. I didn't want to take a chance of telling you and fucking with your head. No one's seen him again. I'm sorry, Gabe. I didn't think he'd try to come. I didn't think he'd go after her either."

"Fuck!" I roar, and adrenaline dumps into my system. "Find her! Now!"

People in the crowd are staring, but I don't give a fuck. Nothing matters but Scarlett.

Not this club.

Not this fight.

Not the money.

Nothing.

I can't lose her.

FIFTY-FIVE

The door I'm standing in front of opens without me turning the handle, but Rolo doesn't realize that. He shoves me through the opening . . . straight into the arms of the very last man on this earth I want to see right now. The man who I last saw with a gun to Bump's head.

Moses.

"Whoa, darlin'. Damn, sometimes life just works out perfectly, doesn't it?" His accented words cut through the static in my head.

"Who the fuck are you? Let her go!" Rolo barks as Moses shoves me behind him.

My knees give out as I stumble and land on my ass.

"No problem, man," Moses says easily, like Rolo isn't training his weapon on him. "I let her go. What the fuck you gonna do now?"

"Shoot you in the fuckin'—"

But Rolo doesn't get a chance to finish his sentence. Moses's hand moves faster than Rolo's mouth. This time I cover my ears and turn away as Moses pulls the trigger. There's a deafening gunshot, followed by a thud.

Jesus Christ. No. No. No.

"I don't think so, motherfucker," Moses says to Rolo's body as my ears ring.

Desperate to get away from him, I scramble, crawling toward another damn door, the one I'm praying leads outside of this rabbit warren of hallways.

Gabriel. I need Gabriel. I have to warn him.

Footsteps slap on the concrete behind me.

"You're gonna ruin your dress like that, princess," Moses says over the gurgling sound coming from behind us. "Why don't you get on up now. You're too pretty to be shaking on your knees."

He says it so melodically. His deep timbre would almost be soothing, but *he has a gun and he's threatened to kill me before.*

But he's right. I'm not going to die on my knees. I turn my head toward him, tamping down the bone-deep fear coursing through my body.

"How? How did you get in here? Everyone is looking for you. *Everyone.*"

Moses's smirk lights up those eerie eyes of his. The light greenish-gold color belongs to a predator. His gun hangs by his side in a loose grip, pointed at the floor as I press my palms against the concrete.

"I'd venture to guess everyone's looking for you too by now, Ms. Priest. I did *not* expect that bitch to grab you. She threw off all my plans, and then Rolo offing her . . ." He shakes his head like he's annoyed. "Now shit's gonna get complicated."

"What . . . what do you want?"

"First, for you to get up. I don't like seeing women on the ground. Bothers me."

It bothers him to see women on the ground? I blink twice as I process what he said, but I make no move to stand.

He releases a sigh and shakes his head. "Lord, save me from women who don't know how to do what they're told. Get up, girl. I'm losing my patience."

I don't do it for him. I do it for myself and my self-respect.

"If you're going to kill me, why does it matter if I'm standing?" I ask as I regain my balance on my heels and straighten my shoulders.

One of his eyebrows goes up. "You think you know how this is gonna go? Because I suspect you don't."

FIFTY-SIX

"**G**unshot in the back hallway," Q says to me, and we both change directions and run.

I dodge people, shoving them out of the way. Men in black suits move through the crowd, heading in the same direction.

Q goes for his keys, but I yank the handle of the service door, and it flies open.

Fuck. So much for security having shit locked down.

We both bolt down the hallway, and then slide to a halt when we see a body on the floor. Black hair.

Not Scarlett. Thank fuck.

"Who is that?" one of the security guys asks as I step toward her.

"*Fuck,*" I whisper. "Lucy Byers. Some bitch who was hassling Scarlett."

"Jesus Christ, Gabe. What the fuck?" Q demands, his eyes wide.

"I got no answers," I say and keep going.

As much as I don't want to deal with a dead body in my club, only one thing matters—that body doesn't belong to Scarlett, and I need to find her as soon as fucking possible.

There's another body up ahead, before the door that leads to the service corridor that lets out into the alley. A man's. I slide to a halt, thinking it's Moses. But it's not.

Rolo.

Blood stains his lips as he coughs, pressing a hand against his chest. "Call me an ambulance." He hacks up more blood. "Fucking hurry."

Q stops beside me as security swarms us. "Jesus fucking Christ. What the fuck is going on here tonight?"

"Where is she?" I drop to my knees beside Rolo and grip him by the collar. "Where the fuck is she!"

"Same guy who shot me took her. Through there." He nods at the door.

"Fuck!" My voice echoing in the hallway, I release my hold on him and run for the door. Right now, I don't give a fuck about Rolo. I don't know how all this fits together, but the only piece that matters is Scarlett.

Where is she?

One of the security guys jumps in front of me. "Let us go first, Mr. Legend. We're armed. You're not."

"Find her!" I yell as he shoves the door open, but as soon as he steps through it, he freezes.

"Well, fuck. See? I told you this was going to get complicated."

The voice makes my blood run cold.

Moses.

I walk through the doorway, prepared to see my worst nightmare.

And there Scarlett is, standing in front of Moses like a human shield, with his gun to her head.

"Jesus Christ, Moses. She's got nothing to do with this. Nothing to do with what I owe you."

"Congrats on winning the fight, Gabe," he says with a lift of his chin. "But you seem to have disobeyed your orders, boy."

My stomach drops to my feet as I realize what I've done. The same fucking thing I did to the first woman I loved—put her in grave danger.

But I'm not letting Scarlett take a bullet like Jorie.

"I have your money. All of it. Just let her go."

He taps the barrel against Scarlett's temple. "Tempting. But, no. You see . . . I suspected you'd never take that dive, no matter what was on the line. Turns out, I was right."

"Moses—"

He interrupts me before I can say another word. "Tell all your little friends to put their guns down, or you're not gonna like what happens next."

Running on instinct here, I make the call. "Guns down."

Moses tilts his head to the right like he's waiting.

I glance around and see that they're all still trained on him. "Everyone, put your fucking guns down. He will shoot her."

Moses smiles, and every muscle in my body tenses when I see her shiver and a tear roll down her cheek.

Don't cry, ladybug. He'll have to kill me first.

"You're learning, Gabe."

A few seconds later, metal scrapes against the concrete as guns touch the floor behind me.

"They're down. Let her go, Moses. For fuck's sake, don't you dare fucking hurt her."

He studies me. "How much you win tonight?"

"I don't know. A lot more than I owe you."

"And you'll give it all to me if I let her walk away right now?" he asks.

"Every fucking cent. I don't give a shit about the money, Moses. All I want is her."

His smile widens. "You really do love her, don't you?"

"Yes, I fucking love her, and I will beg you on my goddamned knees if I have to. Don't fucking hurt her."

"I saved her, Gabe. Why the fuck would I kill her now? I could've just let Rolo do that, but instead I capped his ass. Of course, it was self-defense. Wasn't it, princess? You can thank me anytime for doing you a favor."

My gaze cuts to Scarlett's pale face and back to Moses's disturbing smile. "What the fuck kind of game are you playing here?"

"As far as I'm concerned, the game's long over. Now, I'm gonna walk out of here, untouched. That's the only way nothing happens to her. You hear me? I came to watch the fight. I wanted to see just how right I was about you, in person. It's just not the same if you don't see it yourself." He jostles my whole world in his arms. "One hell of a fight, boy. You really delivered."

"What?" Confusion ricochets through my brain like a stray bullet. "What the hell are you talking about?"

"You won me a lot of money tonight, Gabe. Seems we're finally even. That is, if you back the fuck off and let me open that door to the alley. I'll be gone in under a minute. You'll never see me again."

Nothing he's saying makes sense. "You *won* tonight? I thought you wanted me to lose. You were betting on Bodhi to win. You told me—"

"Exactly what you needed to hear to decide you didn't give a fuck about what I wanted. How much more determined were you to win, Gabe? You think I don't remember you? Think we don't share the same Mississippi mud in our veins? You think I didn't listen when Jorie talked about you? By the way, not to speak ill of the dead, but you've really upgraded here. This one's a prize. Besides, I ain't into killin' women anymore either. Haven't been in fifteen years. Only reason I ordered Jorie taken out was because I thought she told you about the truck. I thought that bitch played me so you could rob me. I was wrong about that, obviously. And I do have regrets."

My jaw drops. There's too much information coming at once.

Moses bet on me.

He wanted me to win.

He killed Jorie because he thought she told me about the truck.

He lied to me and manipulated me.

Holy fuck.

"You motherfucker!" I roar, but he jerks the gun to Scarlett's head again.

"Don't fuck up now, Gabe. That Jorie shit is old and cold. Dead and buried. You got a lot to live for now, and so does your little princess here."

Scarlett's lips move. She finds her voice, and surprisingly, it's steady. "Please let him go, Gabe. I believe he won't come back. He saved me from Rolo."

Moses shifts the gun away from her temple an inch. "See, she's a smart one. I don't need to come back. I got what I came for. You just bankrolled me a new life, *Legend.* Now it's time for me to go claim the woman I've been wanting all these years. She's gonna be expensive, which is why I needed you to win this fight."

My gaze moves from Moses to Scarlett and back again.

He played me. Jesus Christ. What in the actual fuck is going on right now?

I take a breath, staring at Moses's face for any hint of a lie. I can't trust him, but I can't let him take Scarlett out of the building either.

"Scarlett's not leaving with you. You open that door, you're not taking her with you."

Moses's chest shakes as he laughs. "I don't need your woman. Boy, didn't you just hear me? I'm going to get my own. And just so you know, before you decide you're gonna hunt me down and kill me dead for this, know something else. Without me, you wouldn't have even gotten this opportunity."

My head jerks back. "What the fuck are you talking about?"

"That other club that was supposed to host the fights. Who do you think made sure it got raided?" There's pride in his hellish eyes.

"Holy shit." This comes from Q, who stands to my right. "No fucking way."

"Y'all been playing checkers while I've been playing chess," Moses says, his Creole accent growing thicker. "Long game, Gabe. It's all about the long game."

And suddenly, he shoves Scarlett toward me. I move before I even have a chance to think about it, catching her in my arms.

There's a whoosh of air behind us as Moses slips out the door. Security is yelling around us, running toward the exit, but I sink to my knees with Scarlett in my arms.

Someone bangs on the door. "He's locked it from the outside. Fuck."

I block out their voices as I cup the sides of Scarlett's head in my hands. Physical pain shreds my lungs as I stare into her eyes.

"I'm so sorry. So fucking sorry. I promised you that he'd never touch you. That none of this would ever touch you. I failed you."

She reaches up with a trembling hand to stroke my cheek as she shakes her head. "It wasn't your fault. Lucy grabbed me. She's the one who started it all. That didn't have a damn thing to do with you, Gabe. You can't take the blame for that."

"She hated you because of me," I say, ready to take every bit of guilt and bury myself with it.

"No," Scarlett says with force in her voice. "Apparently, Lucy hated me for years. She was the troll. My stalker. Rolo killed her."

I stare into Scarlett's soft gray eyes while I try to make sense of what she's saying. "Wait. Lucy grabbed you, Rolo shot her . . . Rolo tried to take you . . ."

She nods. "And Moses saved me from Rolo. So, basically . . .

he's the reason I'm here right now, instead of God knows where with either of them."

I press my sweaty forehead against hers. Tremors rip through me as I realize how fucking badly this night could have gone. "I don't even know what the fuck to think right now."

"That I love you, and I'm so glad that we never have to go through this again," Scarlett whispers against my lips.

I release a long breath and squeeze her as hard as I dare. "Never. Never fucking again."

"Um . . . Gabe," Q says from above us. "Not to break this up, but we gotta get Rolo to a hospital, or he's not gonna make it."

FIFTY-SEVEN

As soon as we enter Gabriel's office, after giving statements to the police in the conference room, Bump tackle-hugs us both.

"I'm so glad you're okay! Nothing can happen to you, Gabe. You either, Scarlett."

Gabriel pats him on the back as Bump trembles in our arms. "We're okay, bud. Totally okay. Nothing happened to Scarlett. She's fine."

Bump loosens his grip to look at us. "You got hit in the face a lot tonight. I thought you weren't gonna let him hit you this time?"

Gabriel gives him that half grin I love so much, even with his battered face. "I tried not to, but at least I won, right?"

Bump nods soberly. "But Moses came back. He wasn't supposed to come back."

"He's gone now, honey," I tell Bump, running a hand over his short-cropped hair. "He's never coming back. *I promise.*"

"You promise? Are you *sure?*" His question carries all of the fear he's no doubt been storing up, and I know what promises mean to him.

"We promise, bud. Totally sure." Gabriel's reply must quiet some of his concerns, because the lines on Bump's face smooth out, and his whole body seems to deflate.

"Okay. Good. Because I don't think I can handle that again. No one hurts my family."

The word *family* sends warmth unfurling through my chest. That's what I have now. *A family.*

There's a knock at the door, and Q pokes his head inside. "Before you leave, there are some people who want to talk to you."

"Who?" Gabriel asks, and it's clear from his tone that he doesn't want to talk to anyone.

"My folks, Scarlett's friends, and Creighton Karas and his wife. What do you want me to tell them?"

Gabriel looks at me. "You up for this? Because if you want, Q can tell all of them we'll talk to them later."

I think of what Bump just said—*family.* That's what my friends have become too. That's what Q's parents are for Gabe. In the end, family is all we have, and all we really ever need.

"They can come in," I reply.

Q nods and opens the door.

Harlow, Kelsey, and Monroe burst through first, all with their arms outstretched as they rush toward me.

"Oh God. I can't believe Lucy! And she's dead? Oh my God!" Tears stream down Monroe's face as she yanks me into a hug first.

Harlow and Kelsey wrap their arms around me from either side. "We're so glad you're okay," Harlow says.

"I would kill her myself, if she weren't already dead," Kelsey adds.

"I love you guys."

"Flynn has been calling and texting you, and she freaked out when you didn't answer," Harlow tells me. "She called me, and I kind of had to tell her what happened."

I freeze. "Oh shit. Is she flipping out?"

"I talked her down. You have to call her, though. She's demanding proof of life."

"I will," I whisper as I squeeze them all close. "Thank you. Thank you for being here and worrying about me."

Harlow cups my cheeks. "We love you right back, and this is what we do for the people we love."

Kelsey presses a kiss to the top of my head.

"Did you know you have two seriously famous people standing six feet away from you right now?" Monroe tries to whisper, but it comes out much louder.

I twist my head out of Harlow's hands to stare at Monroe. I *actually* whisper, "What did you just say?"

She turns my head in the other direction, and I catch a glimpse of Silas Bohannon as he steps over to give Jeb a backslapping hug. And then my gaze locks on an imposing man in a dark suit and the petite brunette standing next to Big Mike, Joanie, Ryan, and Christine.

Creighton Karas lifts his chin at Gabriel, and then moves toward me as the girls shift to stand beside me. "Ms. Priest, it's a pleasure to meet you. We're very happy to hear that you came to no harm after your ordeal. I promise we won't stay long. I just wanted to offer my sincerest apology to both you and Legend for what happened tonight."

The girls step back, and Gabriel comes to my side, curling his arm around my waist. "It wasn't on you. No apology necessary."

"I told you not to worry about Gaspard because there was nothing to worry about. The fact that he was here and my security team didn't prevent him from causing Ms. Priest distress proves that I was wrong."

"Moses saved me from Rolo," I tell the billionaire. "So . . . maybe it's a good thing you were wrong?"

Beside him, his country superstar wife smiles at me, proving that tonight can't get any more surreal.

"No harm, no foul," Gabe adds.

"Still, I feel responsible for that, and to make amends, I'm forgiving the debt you owe me. Congratulations on winning tonight, Legend."

Beside me, Gabriel goes still. "But . . ."

"Please," Holly says with an apologetic smile. "It's the least Crey can do."

I had almost forgotten Creighton Karas loaned Gabriel money, but I remember vividly now. *Whoa. He doesn't want it back?*

Gabriel steps forward, offering his hand. "Thank you," he says, his voice hoarse, as Creighton shakes it.

"Great fight. Have a good night. We'll get out of your way, Legend. Ms. Priest."

Creighton inclines his head as he presses a hand to his wife's back. As they turn toward the door, Holly meets my gaze.

"I know this isn't really the right time . . . but I'd love to see your store before we head back to Nashville next week. I've heard amazing things. But only if you're up to it. I'll be back again."

I can only imagine that my eyes are as wide as dinner plates. "Of course. I would love to have you come to Curated."

Kelsey springs toward them, holding out a piece of paper. "Here's her card. Scarlett's cell is on the back."

My friends are amazing, I think as Holly takes it.

"Thanks. Talk soon, Scarlett. We're both so glad you're okay."

As soon as the billionaire and his wife leave the office, everyone seems to release a breath.

"Well, shit," Q says with a wry grin. "Maybe we should have fights more often."

Gabriel hugs me close to his side. "Let's table that discussion for another night. Right now, all I want is my woman, a shower, and an ice bath."

"You killed it in the cage, man," Silas says, coming forward to shake Gabriel's hand. "I won't take up much of your time.

Just wanted to tell you I was impressed as hell, and congratulations."

Gabriel gives him a nod. "Thanks to you. I couldn't have done this without Jeb. He's a mastermind."

"Damn right I am," Jeb says from the corner of the room with a laugh. "But you made it easy. Worked your ass off. This one is all you, Legend. It was a pleasure to be in your corner. Now, go get that ice bath, or you'll be useless tomorrow."

The corner of Gabriel's mouth tugs upward as he meets Silas's gaze again. "I'd stay and chat but . . ."

Silas shakes his head. "No worries, man. I'll be around. You haven't seen the last of me."

Gabriel gives him a nod, and then he looks down at me with his battered face, which is swelling as we speak. "You ready?"

"Absolutely. Let's get you home, champ."

He leans down to kiss my nose. "I like that one, ladybug."

FIFTY-EIGHT

"**R**olo didn't make it," Q says when he calls the next morning after Scarlett and I devoured all the fluffy scrambled eggs she made, and the pancakes I added to our spread. "But they got his confession about killing Lucy, at least."

"Damn," I whisper with a shake of my head. "Does that mean they're looking for Moses?"

"The detective didn't seem too concerned about justice for him, if you want to know the truth. He said Lucy Byers's family was practically cheering when he called them to let them know."

"That's morbid."

"They don't believe she would pull a gun on Scarlett, and they want the whole thing swept under the rug. The detective made it clear that he has been ordered to consider the investigation closed."

I stare at Scarlett, standing at the sink, washing dishes. While I was in my ice bath last night, she and I had a long discussion about all the possible ways we could handle this.

Her request was that we keep it as quiet as possible so as not to embarrass Lucy's family or hurt the club. It was hard for me to swallow, but I can't say no to her.

"And the cops are going to go along with that?"

"Unless Scarlett pushes for a full investigation."

I scratch the back of my neck, not believing it's all finally over. "She won't."

"Then, yeah. It'll all be tidied up, and Moses will walk. You sure that's what you want?"

I think of how I felt with Moses holding Scarlett with a gun to her head. I wanted to kill him, but more than that, I just wanted Scarlett safe. Her well-being trumps everything.

"If Moses had wanted all of us dead, we'd be dead," I say quietly, but Scarlett hears me anyway, dries her hands, and comes to me. She slides her arms around me and presses a kiss to my cheek. "But that's not what he wanted. You heard him. He was playing chess while we played checkers. Wherever the fuck he's headed, good riddance."

"Fair enough," Q replies. "I hope that woman he's after is smart enough to turn his ass down. I'm thinking we should call in some favors and keep tabs on him, just to be safe. I've been doing some digging. Did you know he's from New Orleans, not Biloxi?"

I think of the few conversations I had with Moses back in the day. "No. But it doesn't surprise me, given that Creole blood of his. Call in the favors. Keep tabs. It's time for us to learn to play chess."

"On it, Gabe. Have a good morning. Tell Scarlett I said hi."

I hang up the phone. "You hear the rest of that?"

She nods. "Yeah, and sadly, New Orleans *was* on my bucket list."

"As soon as Moses gets shut down by that woman he's after, we'll go visit. Get you some Cajun food and beignets."

"You think she'll shoot him down?"

I stare at Scarlett, loving how her gray eyes get even softer when she's close to me. "You don't?"

She shrugs, and the oversize sweatshirt she's wearing slips off her shoulder. "I don't know." She wraps her other arm around me. "But as long as he's far away from us, I'm happy."

I lean in to kiss her lips, carefully, because of the cut near the corner of my mouth. "As long as you're happy, ladybug, I'm happy. I fucking love you."

"I love you too. Now . . . are you ever going to tell me what your real last name was? I've been dying to ask, but there hasn't really been a good time."

I grin. "You really want to know?"

"Of course."

"It was Champion. Gabriel Champion."

Her mouth drops open, and she starts to giggle as she shakes her head. "Only you would want to upgrade to Legend."

I steal another kiss. "Just wait until I make you a Legend, ladybug."

SCARLETT

"**A**re you sure you're up to this? We don't have to haul the picnic basket all the way out here. We can sit by the sidewalk," I say to Gabriel as he leads me to a spot in Central Park on Monday morning.

He's black and blue, which pains me to see, but he doesn't seem to mind. Especially not after he told me how much money he'd bet on himself, and with the odds, what he'd won.

Legend will be his, free and clear, next week. Well, almost. He's making Q a full partner.

"Only so I don't have to feel guilty about him working all the damned time."

But I know it's more than that. Gabriel wants to share his good fortune with his best friend, and I'm fully in support of it.

Bump asked yesterday if he could go back to Meryl's center to see the kids, and that's where we're headed tomorrow.

I had a nightmare after the fight, mostly about Lucy. When a ghostly Rolo entered my dream, I woke up from a dead sleep. Gabriel held me and promised it would get better, adding if it didn't, he'd insist on taking me to see Kitty at the gentleman's club since it worked for Bump. His joke did make me feel better, but I passed on the titty bar all the same.

Instead, I made an appointment to go back to Dr. Grand's office, but this time to see someone specializing in trauma. In the meantime, I'm writing in my gratitude journal twice a day, because I have even more to be grateful for now. I won't take waking up in the morning for granted. A brush with death will do that for you.

"Are you saying that because you want to get back to the store so you can help rearrange everything because Crey's wife is coming?"

Holly Wix called me last night, and she's coming in on Wednesday for her first appointment at Curated. To say I'm nervous is an understatement.

I whip my head around to look at him. "Miss a breakfast picnic with you to rearrange things? Never."

He chuckles as he sets the basket on the ground. "I almost believe that."

I come toward him and slide my arms around him, gingerly, because of the bruising. "You know there's nothing I'd rather do than spend time with you. Always. Nothing will ever change that."

"Good, because this would be pretty awkward if you said otherwise." Gabriel peels my arms away from him as I stare in confusion.

"What do you mean?"

His answer is to walk another dozen steps away from me and take a knee . . . *on a rug?*

"Is that the rug from your office?" I stare at it in confusion, wondering how the hell I didn't see it as we walked up.

Gabriel's lips curve into that incredible half smile of his as I close the distance between us.

"How . . . what . . ." I can't put two words together in a coherent fashion, so I go silent and wait for him to explain.

"I was going to wait until we were done eating, but I can't. I can't wait another fucking second to ask you this question."

When he pulls a ring from his pocket, my jaw nearly hits the very carpet that Bump rolled me up in to kidnap me.

"Oh my God," I whisper.

"I know we were never supposed to meet, but fate intervened. You brought me back to life, Scarlett. You showed me what I have and what I've done isn't who I am. You've made me a better man in every respect."

"Oh my God, Gabriel." Tears stream down my face as he smiles up at me with two black eyes.

"I want to wake up beside you every morning. I want to leave you notes that you save and reread. I want to give you babies with golden hair and gray eyes, and live a messy life with you. Scarlett Lourdes Priest, will you do me the honor of becoming my wife?"

I drop to my knees in front of him, throwing my arms around his neck. "Yes. Absolutely, yes."

"Thank God," he whispers against my hair. "Because we've got a hell of a future ahead of us, ladybug. I know it."

I nod against him before wiping at the tears. He reaches for my hand, and I finally see the ring as he slides it on my finger. It's *stunning.*

"When did you . . . How did you . . ."

"I picked it out before the fight. Just needed the cash to buy it. I knew there was no way I could lose, because I couldn't wait any longer to do this. Q went to the store last night to pick it up." He glances down at the rug. "He and Bump helped me with this too, in case you're wondering."

I laugh and stare down at the delicate band with its massive stone, the oriental rug beneath us, and then back into his shimmering blue eyes. "Just so you know, I would've said yes, even if you'd proposed in the bathroom with a piece of dental floss."

Gabriel winces as the smile stretches his face wide. "You deserve to be treated like a queen, and that's exactly what you get."

I shake my head. "Not a queen. A Legend."

ACKNOWLEDGMENTS

I always say it takes a village to write a great story, and that's exactly what this one took. I'm blessed to have an incredible team that helps me every step of the way. Massive thanks go out to Mo Mabie, Pam Berehulke, Kim Bias, Julie Deaton, Erin Fisher, and Martha McLendon. I appreciate all of you so much. And to my husband, Jacob Wilson, who plays a bigger role in my writing and storytelling than anyone truly understands—I love you more than words can adequately describe, and I can't wait to see where our next adventure takes us. Our future is fucking bright, BDJ.

As always, thank you to all the bloggers who tirelessly promote my work solely for the love of books. You're rock stars.

To my readers—I am so fucking grateful for all of you. Thank you for coming along on this wild ride. I promise, we're just getting started.

Until the next one—dream big, my friends. You never know what could happen.

ABOUT THE AUTHOR

Making the jump from corporate lawyer to romance author was a leap of faith that *New York Times*, #1 *Wall Street Journal*, and *USA Today* bestselling author Meghan March will never regret. With over thirty titles published, she has sold millions of books in nearly a dozen languages to fellow romance-lovers around the world. A nomad at heart, she can currently be found in the woods of the Pacific Northwest, living her happily ever after with her real-life alpha hero.

She would love to hear from you.
Connect with her at:
Website: meghanmarch.com
Facebook: @MeghanMarchAuthor
Twitter: @meghan_march
Instagram: @meghanmarch

Made in the USA
Coppell, TX
12 January 2020

14402316R00173